TRUE LOVE

Diane E. Lock

ZEBRA BOOKS
KENSINGTON PUBLISHING CORP.

For Arthur,
who believes in me

ZEBRA BOOKS are published by

Kensington Publishing Corp.
475 Park Avenue South
New York, NY 10016

First Printing: February, 1994

Printed in the United States of America

One

For the thirtieth time since midnight I stole a glance at the clock. It glowed 12:57 a.m. in bright blue numerals. I hate digital clocks. It wasn't "almost one," it was exactly 12:57 a.m. Gone also, I mourned, were vague phrases like ten past, a quarter to, and nearly half past, relics from a time when hours were divided into sections by the hands on the clock, all replaced now by the brilliant blue gleam of precision. 12:59 a.m.

Kelley was late, as usual, and I flipped over to my stomach, punching the pillow in frustration. I always lay awake until she was safely in for the night. Mothers do that. Stuart, sound asleep in fatherly fashion, snored in rhythmic counterpoint to the chorus of tree frogs chirping in the woods behind the house. Otherwise the night was absolutely still.

It was August, a stifling hot Saturday night, and Kelley was out with her latest beau, a boy I hardly knew. Where were they at this time of night, I wondered, conquering the urge to peek at the clock again. She had just turned eighteen, and I should know where she was. Necking, I supposed, if kids still went in for that stuff. In this seaside town they probably went to the beach. If this were Oakville I'd know for sure, I thought, and chuckled. I used to know all the good spots there.

Everybody's favorite was a place called the Point. It had always been called that, though it didn't jut out into the water; it was just a wide strip of dirt that had built up beside the road over the years. There were a few boulders strewn around, probably from when they paved the road, and you had to be careful not to hit them in the dark, but it was hard as rock and safe for cars. It was about half a mile past Vinnie's Market at that bend in the river across from the Country Club. I grew up around the corner, and we used to go parking there all the

FANTASY IS NOT AGAINST THE LAW . . .

"Welcome to our little assignation!"

Que sera, sera, I thought with a sigh.

We drove wordlessly into the beauty of the autumn day, then parked at The Point. Our favorite place . . . back then. We found an inviting spot under the trees and sat close to each other on a carpet of moss. He reached for my hand, and at his touch my knees grew weak. Then, with a groan, he crushed me in his arms, buried his face in my hair, hungrily kissing my neck, my nose, my lips. I kissed him with undreamed of passion, pulling him closer.

Was this the end of an old love, or a new beginning?

"I knew we would find each other again," he whispered. "There are chapters still unwritten. I've always loved you, Andrea. I love you still."

My heart took wing, soaring with pure joy, and the hurt hidden deep inside me slowly melted away. His eyes glowed as he looked straight into mine, a look of such intense love that my eyes filled with tears. He loved me. A void had been filled, a circle completed.

I was whole.

time—to watch the submarine races, as we used to say.

These days I went there only when I dreamed of Richard.

The Point was a hangout, and on a summer day five or six cars would crowd in side by side, radios blaring out Elvis' "Blue Suede Shoes," or Buddy Holly's "Peggy Sue". The boys drank beer and smoked and polished up the chrome on the cars and told stupid jokes to get our attention. The girls sat on the rocks in the sun wearing short shorts and halters, bare feet dangling in the water, smoking and giggling and working on tans and pretending we didn't notice the boys.

That was during the day. Summer nights were for necking, sitting in one of those shiny cars listening to romantic music on the radio. If it was a Saturday there was probably a dance at the Country Club, and the sound of band music floated across the river, or you'd hear a lone piano playing something nice and slow, like Floyd Kramer's haunting "Last Date" . . .

I still remembered every second of my last date with Richard. We had gone downtown to the theater on Main Street to see James Bond in "Doctor No," crossed the river and stopped for a soda at Sal's, and got to the Point at about half past twelve. Richard parked the car and we sat quietly for a few minutes, just holding hands. I knew my mother expected me to be home by that hour but I was twenty-two years old, for heaven's sake, and she still treated me like a kid, worrying when I was out after midnight.

It was a humid July night and the air was heavy and still. All the windows were rolled down, in case a breeze came up, and we could hear the gentle splash of the water and the crickets chirping like crazy.

He put his arm around me and my stomach fluttered in response. He smelled of English Leather, my favorite aftershave. His dark eyes glistened as he gazed deeply into mine, then slowly closed as he held me tighter, the long, thick eyelashes drifting down like curtains. When he bent to kiss me, his breath felt warm on my face, and I saw a secret little smile playing over his lips before my own eyes closed.

Richard Osborne, my boyfriend. All the girls thought he was about the coolest guy in town. And the sexiest . . . he could charm the pants off me. And did, often. I pressed my body closer and kissed him back, breathy anticipation growing as he went smoothly to work. Go to sleep, Mom, I thought, it's going to be a late night.

His lips barely touched my skin as he trailed a trickle of kisses down my neck, into the hollow of my throat . . . The thrill shot right down to the pit of my stomach, and I pulled away, just a little . . .

He nibbled on my ear as he tantalizingly, slowly undid the buttons on my blouse with one hand, the other reaching behind to unhook my bra, and I tensed when he delicately cupped my bare breast, breathlessly waiting until his fingers lightly brushed the nipple before I pushed his hand away.

He was used to my feeble protests, and didn't even hesitate. Deftly slipping the lacy garment out of the way, he bent to kiss my breasts, one in each hand, his tongue teasing, sending shivers through me . . .

Don't stop . . . don't . . .

"**STOP!** Oh Richard, you have to stop!" I was an old hand at this game.

"Now?" It was too dark to see his face, but I felt his smile against my breast, his tongue teasing again, the nipples growing hard. His hand settled lightly between my thighs, burning the soft skin there, while his fingers delicately slipped inside the cuff of my shorts. "Ooh, Rich . . . stop . . ."

"Now? Right this second?"

"Mmmmm, now, yes . . ."

"Why?" I was almost prone on the leather seat, and his question came from far away, murmured against my bared midriff as he slowly drew down the zipper of my shorts.

"Because . . ."

"You don't like it?"

"No . . ." We both knew that was a lie.

He raised his head, his voice teasing. "But last night you loved it."

Mmmmm, I thought, last . . . ! Wait a second, we weren't here last night! Sluggishly dragging my mind from its sensuous vacuum I pushed him away, using both hands against his chest, and struggled to sit upright.

"What do you mean, last night?"

A look of surprise crossed his face, then he gave me a stupid sheepish grin, like a little boy caught stealing cookies.

"A little mistake. I meant the last time we were here."

"No you didn't, Rich, you meant last night. And I didn't see you last night."

He tried to come up with a plausible story to pacify me so he could get back to business, and I watched the wheels at work behind his face. A feeling I could only identify as loathing began to churn like sickness in the pit of my stomach, spreading and replacing the ecstasy of the moment before.

Last night, for God's sake, my mother had dragged me to the church basement to play bingo to raise money for The Ladies' Sodality. If he had been fooling around in his car, it wasn't with me. He was cheating on me, the creep.

"Who were you with last night, Rich?"

He could have lied, said nobody, insisted that he had mistakenly said last night. Fool that I was, I probably would have believed him. But he was so sure of me he didn't bother to lie.

"She isn't important to me, Andrea. It

doesn't matter who she is. You are the only one who counts with me." I was supposed to melt back into his arms at that.

"Was it one of my friends, Rich?" If it was someone I knew I would die of embarrassment.

"No, of course not . . . she doesn't live . . . it doesn't matter anyway. I'll never see her again, I swear."

I tried to pull away from him and suddenly became aware that I was practically naked. My body was hanging out in the most revolting way, and I held my shirt together, trying to hide my breasts while I fumbled around on the floor for my bra. My shorts were unzipped, my underwear . . . it was disgusting, and I felt dirty and used, where a moment before I had felt loved and desirable. He tried to put his arm around my shoulders, but I pushed him away, my body stiff and unyielding. I had to know.

"Who is she, Richard?"

"Someone I know from Bakerstown. She goes to college with me. But we didn't come here, Andrea, I wouldn't do that to you."

"Do you see her every time I'm busy?

Or are there other girls at school, Richard? Do you have someone from the North Shore? How many other girls are there?"

"They don't mean . . ."

He started to answer, but suddenly it didn't matter. What difference how many? He was playing around when he was supposed to be mine—we were practically engaged to be married, for heaven's sake. I loved him, he said he loved me, but he was cheating on me. A cavern opened wide and the hurt rushed in, filling all the spaces, spilling over into tears . . .

I opened my eyes, overwhelmed by a fresh sense of loss, then realized I had been dreaming. I hadn't seen Richard in over twenty years; these days I saw him only in my dreams, when my defenses were down. An old, old story, but it haunted me still.

Must have dozed off while waiting for Kelley, I thought, fuzzy with sleep, but something had woken me from my dreams . . . the froggy chorus had long since finished their entertainment for the night, and the peaceful serenity of our street had been shattered by a sound like an erupting volcano. Recognition dawned as my mind clawed its way back into the present. Not a volcano, not a bomb, but a truck, roaring and shrieking and screeching to a halt in front of our house.

Back in time and place, I sat up and focused my eyes on the clock. The glowing blue numbers showed 1:32 a.m. Kelley was home at last, and only an hour past her 12:30 curfew.

At times like these I felt very close to my mother. She thought she had it bad with me. "What you plant today will grow tomorrow"—her version, I think, of "you reap what you sow," but no matter what words she used, "what goes around comes around" was the implied threat.

In Oakville, the mill town where I grew up, a truck rumbling around at half past one in the morning wouldn't have raised an eyebrow, but this wasn't Oakville. In this sedate seaside town near Plymouth, Massachusetts, on a quiet residential street like ours, a truck at high noon would have caused a commotion. At this time of night, when the tiniest sound was magnified a hundred times, that damned truck sounded like a derailed freight train about to crash through the wall.

I sat up in bed, fiercely willing them to turn off the engine. But of course it was already too late! Moses, our sheepdog, with a bark that could wake the dead, was already going crazy in the back yard!

What an idiot! Sitting out there with his engine rumbling like rolling thunder, for crying out loud! The combination of barking dog and roaring truck had actually disturbed Stuart, I noticed, as he tossed in his sleep.

We had spoken to Kelley about the truck a few times before, in fact every time people complained. Damn it! This time someone would call the cops for sure! Please, please turn the stupid thing off, I begged silently. I could already hear Mrs. Swensen, our next door neighbor, who would make a point of coming over to talk to me in the morning.

"So, Mrs., your girl vas out again, very late, I tink? It voke me up, the car, ven she came home? My husband, Mr. Swensen, vas much disturbed."

Mr. Swensen disturbed, my foot! He was deaf as a doorpost! But even the pesky Mrs. S. had a right to a peaceful night's sleep.

She was a senior in high school, this daughter of mine, and I thought she was a handful. I remember my mother complaining about the burden of raising teenaged girls, but I couldn't possibly have been this much trouble for my parents! To begin with, I didn't have nearly as much freedom as she had.

Kelley wasn't a bad kid, but she often got into scrapes. I was never quite sure if these incidents were accidents, occurring because she was in the wrong place at the wrong time, or if she actually looked for trouble. She pushed every rule to the limit, wisely gauging my breaking point then backing off. She wasn't obstinate, she didn't sulk, she simply did what she wanted and waited to see what I would do about it. Clever strategy—never giving me any warning of what might come next, so I was always a step behind. A brilliant smile was her answer to every challenge, and she kept her thoughts hidden from me. We never fought, hardly ever argued, but I lost every round.

This guy, now. His name was Chris—no, it was Carl . . . he was her first boyfriend with his own wheels, which no doubt made him a hero in her eyes, and caused much envy among her friends. We'd seen him a few times, picking her up, or dropping her off—they never came in to wait, or say hello! Sounded old fashioned, maybe, but parents of seventeen-year-old girls get real old-fashioned real fast, I was learning! Stuart objected to the earring and the lightning bolts carved into his hair. I didn't care about that, lots of kids looked like that, but from the little I'd seen of him, I thought he looked older than the other boys she knew.

In any case, he wouldn't have been too bad if he didn't drive that noisy truck. It was a beautiful machine, really, jet black and shiny, sitting high and proud above its oversized tires, obviously his pride and joy, but it made me nervous. When Kelley was out my imagination worked overtime, and I envisioned them speeding along a highway and crashing into a wall or an overpass, bits and pieces of my daughter splattered all over the landscape.

Her father thought I worried too much, that I was overprotective, and he was probably right. She was usually at her friend Sue's, or they went into town to see a movie or grab a bite to eat at McDonald's, a round trip of five miles at most.

Nothing bothered Stuart, I thought, listening to him snore peacefully through the noise, probably the only person still asleep in the whole town!

I was rehearsing my tired old lecture about the hour and the racket, when, like the crack of a rifle, a door slammed and the truck roared off in a blast of sound that rattled the windows, probably leaving an inch of rubber behind on the pavement.

In the ringing silence that followed I heard Kelley running up the path, and the muffled sounds of crying as she passed under my bedroom windows. Muted sniffles changed to mournful sobs while she fumbled with her key, and then the door slammed shut with a resounding crash behind her. I sat up, waiting, straining to hear, but she didn't come up the stairs. Silence hummed loudly in my head.

A gentle breeze stirred the sheer curtains at the bedroom windows, carrying the scent of honeysuckle into my room. Now that the truck was gone and the serenade from the woods was over, it was just another peaceful summer night, and I wanted nothing more than to curl up next to Stuart and get back to sleep. Instead, sighing heavily, I sat on the edge of my bed, rubbed sleep out of my eyes, and felt around with my feet in the dark for my slippers. She needed help, and I was it.

I picked up my light summer robe from the chair and with an envious parting glance at Stuart, quietly left my room, stopping at the top of the stairs to prepare myself for whatever awaited.

Please, God, I prayed, don't give me a major crisis. A minor incident, like he smiled at some other girl, will suffice. It's late, and I'm tired.

She had thrown herself on the stairs in a messy heap, sobbing into the carpet, and I draped an arm across her shoulders as I sat down on the step beside her. She looked up, turned toward me, buried her head on my shoulder, and cried on, her heart breaking. I let her cry without interruption, and after a few endless minutes she calmed down.

"Kelley, honey, what is it? What happened?"

"Oohhh, Mom, it was awful. He's awful."

"Yes, sweetie, but what did he do?"

"Well, we were down by the lighthouse, where all the kids go, y'know, just, y'know, doing stuff, and first thing I knew he ripped my shirt open, he was grabbing at me, touching my . . . Ugh! It was awful! I just wish I could die!"

Bursting into fresh tears, she sniffled and fumbled for a tissue, which I supplied her from my pocket. I noticed the front of her blouse gaped open when she blew her nose. The jerk had torn some of the buttons off.

I wrapped my arms around her, hoping this was comfort enough for the moment. I figured there was more to this story, or else our daughter was far more innocent than her dad and I had dared to hope. I couldn't imagine, at her age, that no boy had ever touched her breasts before.

"Is this the first time he's tried anything like that?" Playing for time, wondering what was still to come.

"He's an animal. He's usually so quiet, but he got rough, and started yelling at me! Oh God, Mom, I was so scared, we were all alone, and he pushed me down on the seat, he h-had it out . . . he was trying to . . . to . . . ! How could he think I'd let him do that? It was disgusting!"

Oh my God. My body felt leaden, weighted down with fear. "He didn't hurt you, did he? He didn't actually do anything? He only scared you, right?" Mute, she nodded her head, her eyes filling again with tears, while my mind screamed *attempted rape.* This was far more serious than anything I had anticipated. I was ready to jump up and run for Stuart and the police! But then I thought, cool down, Andrea, they're only teenagers, just kids . . . maybe without realizing it she had acted like . . . maybe he thought she . . . ? I had never heard of date rape.

I tried again, more calmly. "You've been seeing him for a couple of months.

Has he ever tried anything like that before?"

"Nothing I couldn't handle, just, you know . . . Oh Mom, I can't tell you about this stuff!"

"Oh yes you can, and you will! Now, has he ever tried to force you before?"

"No, never, but tonight he got out of control."

"Were you drinking? Was he drunk?"

"No, we were talking, and just kind of like, touching . . . oh, you know . . . !"

I nodded, taking her off the hook. I really didn't want to know all the details. Just the facts, ma'am, I thought with wry amusement.

"So we were sitting there, with his hands all over me, and I'm trying to get out of his stupid truck, but I was kinda stuck, you know, and he goes 'I've had enough of this teasing missy, it's time.'

" 'Time for what?' I said. He laughed, real mean, and he pushed me down flat on the seat and got on me and . . . and . . ." She was crying again.

"J-just because I let him t-touch, it wasn't an invitation to rape me. Oh Mom, it was so scary."

"Yes, I can imagine," I murmured

against her hair, when a thought struck. "What made him stop?"

"He . . . another car came into the lot, and it turned out to be somebody he knew, probably some old girlfriend. I guess they recognized his truck, because they pulled up right next to us. He yelled at me to stay down, not to show my face, but when he leaned over to talk to them I managed to get the door open and I ran."

"But didn't he drive you home?"

"Yeah—he caught up to me on the highway, and begged me to get in. He said he was sorry, that it wouldn't happen again. I knew you'd get mad at me for being so late, and it's such a long walk . . ." She shuddered in my arms.

I recalled a few unhappy encounters in cars when I was her age. Once an over-eager pimplefaced kid broke a bra strap, and I repaired it myself when I got home, but was terrified that my mother would notice it and ask questions when she did the laundry. Another time I walked almost all the way home from the Point to escape this really nice kid who turned into a sex-crazed maniac as soon as he parked the car. I smiled a little, remembering how he drove beside me, begging me to get back in, which I eventually did, afraid my parents would find out. And, of course, Richard . . .

I hugged her tighter, wishing I could make it all go away with a kiss, like the bad dreams she had when she was a little girl. Kids of eighteen do this stuff, though, and it doesn't necessarily lead to rape. Which reminded me . . .

"How old is this jerk?"

"He's, um . . . twenty, I think. Well, maybe twenty-one. Or twenty-two." The last was whispered through stiff lips.

"Maybe twenty-two? Kelley, for God's sake, where did you meet him? I thought you knew him from school."

"No, no, he's a friend of Sue's brother Phil. I met him there. Just hanging out, you know, no big deal. He drove me home a couple of times, and we went to the movies, but he's not, like, my boyfriend or anything."

Phil Marsden was a few years older than Sue and Kelley, but I thought he was away at college.

"This Carl, does he go to school with Sue's brother?"

"No, they know each other from high

school, but he was a year ahead of Phil. Carl doesn't go to college—he works for Green Acres Landscaping. He makes real good money! That's how he got his wheels!"

Oh great! A real winner. Dropped out of school so he could make money and buy a car! The guys with the cars are the coolest, and the wheels invariably lead to trouble.

"Now, honey, I don't want to excuse his behavior in any way, and I certainly don't want to imply that you were leading him on, but boys do try . . ."

"But this never happened with anyone else, Mom! He's just a pig!"

"That may be true, but he's older than the other boys you know, and he's probably used to girls with more experience than you. I don't want to sound like I'm on his side, but maybe you were teasing him or leading him on!"

She squirmed, trying to push me away, and I stopped talking, holding her tighter. I was shocked at myself! This was definitely not the way to reach her. I took a deep breath. "Sorry, sweetie, that's the kind of crap I used to get from my mother. I can't believe I said that. I'm upset, I guess."

True, I was worried and upset that some idiot had tried to hurt my baby, but she was the one who had just experienced what might be attempted rape. I had to stay cool. She was home, she was safe, and it was my job to help her calm down.

"Let's assume it was all a mistake, that he wanted to have sex, but you didn't. He misunderstood your signals, got too aggressive, and scared you. Seems to me that if you find his advances repulsive, he's not for you. Do you agree so far?"

She nodded. She was listening, and I plunged on.

"We can assume that you are not in love with him. But someday you'll meet someone who makes you tingle, not cringe, and you'll want to have . . . um, you'll want to . . . you know what I mean . . ."

Now it was my turn to search for words, afraid to say what I wanted to say, as I was struck with the image of my daughter hot and sweaty with sex and desire.

It had been so much easier when she

was younger, asking interminable questions, when the answers were hypothetical, and motherly advice was easy to give. But she was growing up, and things had changed. Should I tell her some of my experiences? No, I decided, too personal, and anyway, what kid would believe her mother's escapades? I dove back into Anthropology 101!

"Sexual attraction is important in a relationship," I continued. "It takes much more than scintillating conversation to have a loving and happy marriage. So even though you're scared now," I said, finally reaching the point I was trying to make, "you will probably feel differently with someone else." The Westminster chimes on the mantel clock rang out quarter past two interrupting my lecture. I wasn't finished, but my thinking wasn't clear, and I welcomed the excuse to quit.

"Good Lord, it's late. Do you feel a little better now?"

She nodded, apparently sleepy herself. I delivered my parting shot. "If I were you I wouldn't see him any more, but I guess you're old enough to make that decision on your own."

She grinned at me, no more than a

tearful grimace, but I felt forgiven for my earlier remark when she said, "You can assume, Mom, that I will never see him again!"

I kissed the top of her head. Her shampoo smelled of apples, and I breathed in the clean sweet scent and hugged her, a rare pleasure these days. We went up the stairs together, and I waited as she closed her bedroom door tightly behind her. Please God, I prayed, keep her safe.

I disturbed Stuart a little when I crawled back into bed, but he adjusted his position without waking. I was very tired, but I had too much on my mind to sleep. Kelley normally discussed intimate secrets with Sue, her best friend, but if I hadn't disappointed her, she might begin to trust me. A major breakthrough. Unlike myself and my mother, I thought; we had never been able to communicate.

I lay beside my husband and mulled over my lecture. Did I get my point across? What point was I trying to make? Maybe I should have ranted and raved about his behavior, but I wanted to play it down, not to panic. Did she feel any better after talking to me? This mother business was a pain—it had been so easy when a kiss made everything better! But she was growing up—she was grown up, and had to learn to handle boys—God, they were men now!—who were too aggressive. She had to know when to say "when". Even when I was young, the limits changed from one guy to the next, and things had changed drastically since I was eighteen.

Kids thought they were immortal, but with life-threatening diseases like AIDS overshadowing the moral issues, and free sex rampant in the dating world, how could parents hope to keep their children safe? What approach was right? Supplying condoms, threatening hell and damnation, force-feeding the Pill, or buying a good old-fashioned chastity belt?

I wondered again if he had been drinking. Kelley and Brian were invited to drink wine when we did, with dinner, although they seldom did. Stuart wasn't keen on it, but I felt it was an important part of their education. Just like Dad, I thought, smiling in the darkness. In his house, wine was served with every meal, and he had encouraged a drink now and then when I was a teenager, much to my mother's horror.

"You'll turn her into a drunk!" she'd argue.

"She has to learn about alcohol sometime," he would answer, defending his position. "I want her to learn from our example that drinking in moderation can be a sociable part of her life. Drinking with the old fogies takes away some of the thrill, and might keep Andrea and her friends from sneaking into the liquor cabinet when we aren't around."

Perhaps drinking could be learned with Mom and Dad, but the issue here was sex in the back seat of a car, or, in Kelley's case, the front seat of a 4x4.

Hoping for inspiration, I tried to remember my mother's lectures, dripping with morals and proverbs that she made up as the occasion demanded. But I found no help there; with mother everything was black or white, and all sins were treated equally. She was rabid on the subject of sex, which I assume she indulged in from time to time, but she was equally violent about smoking, which she didn't. "Smoke at one end, fool at the other!" was the mildest invective she threw at Dad when he lit up.

She had never smoked, and long before the Surgeon General or anyone else began to warn of the dangers of smoking, she insisted that filling your lungs up with smoke was dumb.

But smoking was chic, not dangerous, an entry to the adult world. Virtually every romantic scene in every movie included the lovers gazing into each others' eyes over glasses of liquor while a silvery wisp of smoke rose between them. Romantic leads always offered their ladies a cigarette which they had lit in the most chivalrous manner! By the age of fifteen I was puffing with my friends, and we thought ourselves very elegant indeed. So I tried to shut out her rules, and her stupid, boring moralizing. Mother didn't want me to smoke, and I knew that was great, so she was probably wrong about sex, too!

Having sex, or "going all the way," in my world, was definitely sinful! Richard and I never went all the way, no doubt thanks to mother's endless moralizing, and certainly not thanks to him, but we contented ourselves by committing lesser sins . . . the memory gave me goose-bumps even now, but I wasn't taking any more trips down memory lane tonight.

Stuart shifted in his sleep, oblivious both to my soul-searching and our daughter's woes. My thoughts drifted, and gradually my concerns about Kelley gave way to musings about myself, and Stuart, and since it seemed to be one of those nights, Richard too.

When I met him, Stuart was a mature, even-tempered man of twenty-eight, very different from Richard, who had been sensual and irresponsible. But real life wasn't like the movies, a thrill a minute. I had been married to Stuart for almost twenty-two years, and I had nothing to complain about.

So why did I feel I had missed something? And why did I have recurring dreams of Richard? Remembering how my insides melted when he touched me, I felt a rush of longing, a sudden yearning to have him make love to me. I blushed in the dark. Stuart never aroused me like that. Our lovemaking was no tumultuous coupling of man and woman, but a subdued union, suitable for a married couple, followed by peace and tranquility. Disappointing, I guess, but I had found security with Stuart, longer lasting and far less dangerous than passion.

I pressed closer to him for comfort and the reassurance that I was not alone in the dark, but all I got was a grunt. I pulled the sheet tightly around my shoulders and curled into a ball, staring into the darkness, watching it lighten and turn to the rose of dawn before I finally fell into a troubled sleep.

Two

I met Stuart when I moved to Boston. We worked together. Well, not really together, but in the same building. Actually, I don't like to advertise this, but he picked me up in an elevator. Literally.

Romance was the furthest thing from my mind at the time. It had been only a year since I'd broken up with Richard, and my wounds were still fresh. I had sworn that never again would anyone have me in the palm of his hand, and I wasn't looking for a relationship of any kind. I didn't even want to date, which was fortunate, because no one in town would ask me out. I had gone with Richard for so long I was still his property, and all the guys I knew stayed away.

Which was just fine with me; I wouldn't have gone if asked.

I was twenty-two and free for the first time in my life. My girlfriends were getting married one after the other, and my calendar was filled with showers and weddings, but I wasn't the least bit envious. My best friend Janice fixed me up with the best man at her wedding, a terrific dancer, but although we had a good time together at the reception, when he called me afterwards, I was simply not interested.

I guess my parents worried about me. In fact, my dad was chiefly responsible for my move to the big city.

One rainy night, a few months after I broke up with Richard, as I sat staring aimlessly out at the empty street in front of our house, Dad came into the darkened living room and sat beside me. We stared out together quietly for a few minutes, then he gently made the point he had come to make.

"Andrea, knights in shining armor do not customarily ride up and down our street, searching for damsels in distress. You have to start over again, meet new people, and find someone else."

"Dad, I'm fine," I protested. "I'm happy with things just as they are, and I don't want to get involved with anyone right now. Anyway, if I were interested—which I'm not—just where in this town do you think I would meet someone new?"

"This sitting around in the dark—this is not a life for a lively young girl," he went on. "All your friends are married now, and many have left town, like Janice. Your mother and I worry that you could end up alone, like her cousin Carmella."

"Oh God, Dad, Carmella! She was an old maid when she was twenty!" I remembered her well, though we hadn't seen her in a few years. She must have been fortyish, and she always sat against the wall at big family weddings with all the old women, gossiping in Italian, thin and brittle looking, her mouth an unfriendly red line. She wore dark brown dresses with beige lace collars and cuffs. She smelled like medicine. She had hairs on her chin.

"Well, bella, I'm sure Carmella didn't plan to spend her life alone, and your mother's greatest fear is that you will get left, too. We think you need to go out and have fun."

Fun! Really, Dad, fun is for children, not for grown women with broken hearts.

"It's true, this is a small town. Maybe you should spend some time in Boston, get a taste of big city life."

"I'm fine, Dad. Don't worry about me."

He kissed me and went up to bed, and I sat and stared outside some more, while shadowy images of Boston waved at me from the back of my mind. Without knowing it, Dad had sown the seed of an idea, and over the next week or so I gave it some serious thought.

I realized that I couldn't stick around that dusty little town twiddling my thumbs, providing gossip for all the old biddies sitting on their stoops . . . Ai, poor Antoinetta, her girl Andrea, still at home, drying up without a man! Not like my (Maria or Laura or whoever, married to handsome young Rocco or Tony or Sal), two bambini and another on the way . . . I shuddered. Dad was absolutely right, I had to find myself a life, preferably somewhere else.

Once I made my decision it didn't take

me very long to leave. I found a job in town and moved into Boston, only about an hour and a half but a world away from home.

My move came as a surprise to my parents. This had not been part of their plan, and both Mom and Dad were upset when I announced my decision, but we talked it over, and eventually we all realized it had to be done. Mother had her pride, it could be said that her daughter had taken a big job in the city! They finally capitulated, even though my apartment was not in the North End (read Italian ghetto), where they had friends, but in a big old building in the Back Bay. With some of the treasures from their attic, and my bedroom suite, I furnished a studio apartment so that it was livable.

Over the next few months I discovered that I enjoyed living on my own. My days were filled with work, and I visited my family most weekends. When I didn't go home, I wandered for hours around flea markets and secondhand shops, picking up a lamp here and a print there, slowly filling the empty spaces in my apartment, ignoring the empty places in my heart. I liked to cook, and tried new recipes. I read voraciously, and spent most evenings alone in my apartment with a library book and a record on the beat-up hi-fi I had picked up for thirty-five dollars. Surrounded by the constant motion of city life, I wasn't aware of loneliness.

I had found a decent job with the venerable law firm of Markham, Markham and Doucette. There were no Markhams—both father and son had passed away before my time—but there was a Doucette hidden away somewhere in a walnut paneled inner sanctum, and seen only on the stateliest of occasions.

When I was in high school I had thought of a legal career, but that meant college, then law school, and there were a few obstacles in the way. One was the prohibitive cost of law school, but that was small potatoes compared to the opposition from my family. To be a female professional was to fly in the face of all that was holy.

"What? a lawyer? The law is a man's profession," said my mother, and that was that! Girls were not lawyers, doctors, or priests! Girls did girl stuff, like nursing, or teaching, or even, God forbid, hairdressing! My father argued for me, but his heart wasn't really in it either. My parents came to this country as children from Italy during the waves of immigration after the First World War, and some of their ideas were so Old World it was painful. I didn't have the courage to fight them both, nor the confidence that I could make it on my own. Someday, I promised myself, I would go to law school, but I was young, and free, and the future stretched out forever.

I rebelled by not going into one of their chosen fields, but took a secretarial course instead. They had reservations even there; they thought the office world was a little dangerous for single young girls! Good thing they never heard some of the stories the nursing students told!

As a legal secretary I worked on the fringe of a career that I considered fascinating, but I was content, settling for an adequate salary and token independence. In those days I lacked ambition and the determination to turn my dreams into reality.

That came later.

* * *

The offices of Markham, Markham, and Doucette faced west on the twentieth floor of a brand new forty-five story skyscraper downtown. They had been there almost a year when I joined the firm, a great improvement, I was told, over the dark, musty rooms on High Street, where they had been since forever, but I would have preferred the old ground floor location.

The suite was beautiful. Boston harbor and the waterfront were out of sight around the building, but we had a fine view of the Back Bay area, the Charles River far below no more than a silver ribbon winding through the landscape on its way to the ocean.

The company that rented the space advertised that all suites had an ocean view, and they were absolutely right. Standing on tiptoes behind the desk in the left-hand corner of Mr. Bronsky's office, with your head at just the right angle, a small crescent-shaped sliver of the Atlantic was definitely visible.

During the winter months, when the sun set early, there was an undeclared five minute break to watch the brilliant ball of fire drop below the distant horizon, leaving the sky brushed with streaks of red and orange, fading gradually through rose and mauve to gray as the sun disappeared. It was breathtaking.

Because my boss's office was in the corner, I had the envied spot next to the window, actually a wall of glass. Without the definition of walls, there was no sense of containment; just the world outside, as far as the eye could see, thousands of feet below! It scared me to death!

How could I know I was afraid of heights? I had never been more than three or four stories above the ground, never flown in a plane. Approaching my desk meant walking toward the wide open spaces beyond the glass, and I went slowly, head averted, my eyes clutching the pattern in the carpet.

The girls I worked with thought it was amusing. With my back to the window the creepy feeling would come over me that there was nothing between me and empty space. I'd feel a cold draft on my back; I'd get sweaty and nervous. For as long as I worked there I never lost the fear that I would get sucked through the glass and fall twenty stories to my death.

The first time I noticed Stuart, I was rushing across the lobby to catch the elevator, filled to capacity, whose doors were slowly closing. He held it open so I could squeeze in. Crushed up against him, out of breath, I smiled my thanks. I'd be late if I had to wait for another car, since the morning elevators stopped at nearly every floor, and all ten of them were somewhere in transit.

He nodded acknowledgment, then returned to watching the floor numbers flash by above the door.

He had big, gray eyes, the dark gray of clouds banked on the horizon when a storm is coming. Fascinating! I love gray eyes, and never fail to notice them. Gradually the elevator emptied, stopping at floor after floor, and he nodded again as he alighted at the eighteenth and stepped out of my life. I thought.

A couple of days later I arrived in the building with time to spare, dressed in a new gray glen plaid suit, set off with red shoes and handbag—very smartly turned out. He was there, also dressed in a gray glen plaid suit.

"We look very nice," he said, smiling. "I'll have to find some red shoes to complement my outfit, too." We laughed together, and his eyes, those wonderful gray eyes, crinkled at the edges and warmed when he smiled. Pleasant looking, I thought. Thirtyish, maybe. Didn't look anything like Richard, and certainly didn't set my heart a-thumping.

Left up to me, nothing would have developed. But apparently he had determined to make me part of his life. I met him several times in the lobby waiting for the elevator during the next couple of weeks, and we'd smile or exchange a few words while waiting. Much later he told me how he would arrive early in the morning, buy a coffee, and wait patiently near a pillar until I came through the revolving doors, casually placing himself nearby to ensure our trip up in the same car.

"Isn't it a beautiful day! Have you ever been to the top floor?" he asked me one morning.

"No, I didn't know you could get up there." It was forty-five stories up.

"You can see the whole city from up there," he said, coaxing.

Really! "I'd rather not, thanks."

"You get a bird's eye view of the city. It's beautiful. And it's still early."

"I'm kind of afraid of heights," I answered, embarrassed.

"But this isn't some windy tower with a flimsy railing," he said, making light of my fears. "This is a regular floor, just like the one you work on, with walls and windows. Come on, you'll love it."

By some fluke I had plenty of time, and I had conquered the twentieth floor, which must have gone to my head, because, like the birdbrain I was, I went along with him.

When the elevator reached the forty-fifth floor its doors opened onto the most breathtakingly beautiful panorama of dark blue ocean, the harbor filled with large and small boats, and the city, its tall and small buildings all spread out far, far beneath us. When the elevator doors closed again, I was still inside, passed out cold on the floor. I came to with my head on his lap, staring up into those incredibly dark velvety gray eyes, at this moment filled with concern.

"Jeez," he said profoundly. "What happened?"

"Vertigo, I guess. The doctor told me I had it. Now I know what it is!"

"I feel terrible about this. Look, let me make it up somehow. Let me take you out for dinner!"

"I couldn't possibly think about food right now," I said as I felt my stomach heave. "Just get me back downstairs to work, okay?"

"But I'm responsible for the way you feel. Please, let me do something! How about tomorrow night?"

By the time I was back in the lobby of our suite of offices, with a glass of water in my hand, beginning to feel human again, I knew from experience that I would want dinner again sometime. He seemed a decent type of guy, kind of a co-worker, and after all, I knew him already. The distress in his face was more than I could stand.

"Dinner tomorrow is good. Meet me here at five-thirty, okay?"

"I promise we'll eat at ground level, a basement if I can find one that serves decent food. By the way, in case you wondered," he added, "my name is Stuart.

Stuart Walsh." He smiled, showing slightly crooked teeth, but managing to look almost handsome.

"Oh, yeah, I'm Andrea. Corelli," I answered. Later, when I took the time to be surprised that I had made a date with a man whose name I didn't even know, I realized that he wasn't a stranger any more. In the past few weeks he had quietly become a fixture in my life. I looked for him in the morning in the lobby, and missed him if he wasn't there, and I loved his eyes, and his crooked smile. Learning his name was merely a formality.

Stuart was an accountant, and had a good job with a CPA firm. He worked hard, his future was secure, he was twenty-nine and ready to get married. A methodical man, with his life carefully planned.

There was absolutely no sense of adventure or romance in Stuart. At a time when virtually every man in America wore orange or pink shirts with psychedelic ties, Stuart's shirts were white button-down oxfords, and he wore dark ties with tiny dots on them. That should have told me something.

His idea of a date was dinner in a good restaurant, where the prime rib was rare and tender. For entertainment he liked symphony orchestra concerts, although he did have a spot in his heart for Arthur Fiedler and the Boston Pops. He didn't read novels. He always had his nose buried deep in something dry and technical, and his idea of a light read was the entire *Story of Civilization* by Will and Ariel Durant.

My taste was more eclectic. Musical theater, and Indian food, not yet popular and very hard to find in this city, and disco music. I was a really good dancer. Richard and I . . .

Stuart didn't dance very well, and he didn't drink much, so we didn't party, or go bar hopping with the gang. He didn't gang. I conformed.

But there was no pretense about him; honesty and integrity were printed on his face. He didn't lie, or embroider stories to make himself look good; what you saw was what you got. I saw someone who cared for me, and when he said he would love me all the days of his life, I had to believe him. Not the kind who would fool around behind my back, and I needed that kind of fidelity.

We never went "all the way" either, but this time it was Stuart who showed the greatest restraint. We necked, even petted a little, but before we got to the hot and sweaty stage, when we might perhaps forget ourselves, he would pull away, straightening his tie, apologizing for getting fresh. He was older, he was different, he respected me, he was too classy to be grabbing at my breasts.

He came close to losing it only once. A girl from my office invited us to a party at her apartment, and I dragged him with me, against what he called his better judgment. Turned out he was right; we didn't belong there, and we should never have gone. But I was glad we did, because two good things came of that party.

It was an early sixties type bash, typical of others I had gone to before this. Small underfurnished apartments stuffed to overflowing with people who barely knew each other, the scent of marijuana hanging heavily in the air, filling mouth and nostrils until those not smoking were just as high as those who were.

Couples stood against the walls making out, and a peek into the bedrooms convinced me that we had no business going into either one.

Stuart and I joined a stream of humanity oozing from one unfurnished room to the next. Slowly we slid past a counter where there was warm white wine, and we filled plastic tumblers, flowing on through the galley kitchen into what should have been a dining area, bare and empty of furniture like the rest of the apartment. Off this room was a sliding door to a balcony, and I grabbed the frame, hoping to catch a breath of fresh, undrugged air.

It was like stepping off a conveyor belt, and soon we were squashed into an airless corner, surrounded by people neither of us knew, jammed together so tightly I could feel the outline of the keys in his pocket pressed tightly against my thigh. Suddenly I was rudely shoved into him from behind, and I realized that the bulge was not his keys.

He stared at me for a few seconds, then gestured for me to hold his drink.

With both hands he tipped my face up ever so gently, and in that dark, smoke-filled room he bent and kissed me, a long, lingering kiss that left me breathless! There was more passion in that one kiss than he had demonstrated in all our months of courtship, and afterwards he crushed me close to him for several thudding heartbeats. His smoky gray eyes were filled with something like desperation as he looked down at me, then he awkwardly took back his drink, acting as though he didn't know what to do with his hands.

He seemed upset. "I'm sorry," I said, feeling the need to apologize for our predicament, and his discomfort. "I just wanted fresh air!" I shouted towards his ear.

"Fat chance in here!" he yelled back, bending close to my ear. "I want . . . out!"

Eventually we worked our way back into the stream and were carried on the swell of the mob to the open front door, finally making our escape.

We sat in his car, laughing and gulping fresh air like people who had escaped a near drowning. But the air around us was electrified. He recovered first, taking me into his arms and looking earnestly into my eyes. "I don't know if it was the pot in that place or your beautiful brown eyes, but I nearly went over the edge. All of a sudden I wanted to make love to you like never before. You're lucky it was so crowded, or I would have thrown you to the floor and had my way with you then and there!" His bantering tone, however, did not erase the pounding of his heart in my ear, crushed tightly against his chest.

He never lost his cool again, but that strange party accomplished two things. First, I realized that he was normal, that what appeared to be desperation in his eyes had actually been lust! And he asked me to marry him. "Andrea, I love you. I want to make love with you every night and wake up with you every morning for the rest of my life. Will you marry me?"

We were so different. I was noisy, loved to sing and dance, Italian, and Catholic. Stuart was none of these; he was the most adult person I knew, and with him

I thought myself mature. In my naiveté I supposed that I was now truly grown up, and I adjusted my idea of a good time from a noisy party with beer and a crowd to a quiet dinner for two and home by midnight.

Conformed. Adjusted. Interesting, my choice of words to describe the changes my personality underwent as I saw more and more of Stuart.

Breathless excitement, shivers and goosebumps of anticipation were adolescent fantasies from another time and place. Now I was a grown woman, loved in a subdued quiet way by a man I could rely on forever, who would always be there for me.

Was my head filled with the ringing of bells, the singing of birds? Did my heart soar when eventually he took me into his arms and kissed me? I wouldn't go that far, but I felt secure and content with him.

The folks thought he would have been perfect if Italian, or at least Catholic, but he was great even with these major flaws. At first they seemed overawed by his education, and were a little shy with him. But after their initial reticence, they took to him wholeheartedly. He discussed baseball and gardening with my dad, and he swore to Mom that our children would be raised little Catholics, and that he was willing to marry in the Church, which pleased her immensely. Of course, as she told me later, there was no question that I would marry in the Church; it just was so much more pleasant not having to fight about it.

"Knights," said my father, "come in a variety of disguises. They are not always handsome men on great chargers. Cherish this man, Andrea, he loves you very much. You will be happy with him."

"So calm, quiet, dependable," said my mother. "Bells?" she said when I asked. "What do you want with bells? You need someone to care for you, stand by you, a friend. You've got him. Be happy."

My sister Lorraine, almost five years younger than I, thought he was kind of stuffy.

"He's very mature—not like some of your friends!" I retorted, defending him.

"He's stuck up, he isn't fun. I liked Richard better."

Thanks a lot, kid.

And me? I thought I loved him. He was

kind, hardworking, not bad looking at all, and he cared for me an awful lot. Really, what more could a girl want? Love that wrenched and hurt and soared and thrilled all at the same time, so you never knew which end was up? Dependency so strong that a smile or frown dictated your outlook for a whole day? Pounding in your chest when you imagined the thrill of coming together, making love? I'd had it with that stuff! All I wanted was someone who would be there when I needed him, with maybe a little contentment thrown in for good measure.

Stuart gave me freedom and confidence, like a net under a tightrope walker, and a strong sense of myself as a person. It took many years for me to understand what he did for me, and it was almost too late for us by the time I found out.

Almost a year after we met, on a brilliantly clear and sunny April day, we were married, with no Mass because of the mixed marriage, but at the Church of San Giovanni in Oakville. My mother didn't have to hang her head in shame like Mrs. Sabatino down the street, whose daughter married in some Protestant church; her Andrea had received special permission to marry the Inglese in the Catholic Church.

The reception was held on the flagstone terrace at the Oakwood Country Club. It was a lifelong dream come true for me, and undoubtedly the single largest expense of my father's entire life.

Stuart's family, and most of his friends, of course, were not of Italian descent, and after many heated arguments with my mother, we settled on a wedding feast of chicken breast with creamy white sauce, and peas and carrots and mashed potatoes, with sherried consommé first and ice cream after. Nothing could be further from the nine course Italian dinner she wanted, but it was elegant, and a cut above the lousy buffet we had at my cousin Isabella's wedding, held the month before at the Knights of Columbus Hall.

The terrace at the country club was set with round tables and real cloth table covers, crystal and china, and the weather was almost balmy for New England in the Spring! After dinner, subdued dance music was provided by Ken Wright's Music of the Night Orchestra, alternating with the club pianist. Dancing with Stuart to the melody of "Fly Me to the Moon," I thought about the kids who were probably parked across the river at the Point, listening to the music and the tinkle of laughter, and prayed specifically that Richard was there to hear it.

I was a virgin of twenty-four, and Stuart, almost thirty, was too. Our honeymoon was a sweaty, painful nightmare, a contest of endurance. My adventures with Richard had been fun, and even though we had never actually had sex, I knew I would like to make love. But Stuart was too repressed. I didn't dare tell him what I wanted him to do—he was sure to wonder why I knew about such things. Making love was as serious a part of marriage as providing us with the best insurance coverage, as though we might jeopardize our marriage if we got silly and had some fun. Sex, especially at the beginning, was a ritual that had to be suffered through. Awkwardly, and with some discomfort, he made love like he was afraid to hurt me.

Where was the warmth of intimacy, the

joy of discovery, the rewarding satisfaction? What was the big deal? We never found any magic, but eventually we developed techniques that gave reasonable pleasure to both of us, and that was that.

Shortly after we married the dreams started. I'd relive the night Richard and I broke up, or wake up in a sweat, having fantasized a night of love with him. Years later I'd dream of meeting him, accidentally of course, the lovely poised young matron with a well-behaved child . . . my tinkling laughter proving how happy I was, how much better off I was without him.

I heard he had moved away from Oakville, some said to New York, others thought he was in Los Angeles. No one really knew where, but it didn't matter. He was gone from my life.

Three years after my wedding, Kelley was born, and Brian came along almost three years later. For me, the joys of motherhood replaced the disappointment of the marriage bed.

Three

Brian, three years younger than Kelley, didn't seem to have the rebellious streak inherent in his sister. He had his daddy's temperament, though he looked more like me, with brown eyes and darker coloring. He had also been blessed with a twisted sense of humor, and God only knows where he got that!

By the time he was eleven or twelve, he had taped dozens of "Doctor Dimento" shows, a weird radio program that aired late at night, playing only comedy and parody, songs by Tom Lehrer and "Weird" Al Yankovitch, to name only two. He had memorized most of Monty Python's old routines, quoting them at every opportunity, and his favorite movie was *The Holy Grail,* featuring the British comedy troupe.

Any aggression he did possess was saved for the hockey rink, and it was startling to watch him on the ice, combining the skills of graceful skating and excellent stick handling with the rough and tumble pugnacity of a hockey player. He was a starting defenseman for the Devils, our town's youth hockey team, and hoped to make the High School Varsity team as a freshman this coming year. He was protected with the best equipment money could buy, and I had long ago become accustomed to the shoves and sprawling falls, the bumps and bruises that went with the sport.

By the ripe old age of fifteen, he had been playing hockey for twelve years, and I couldn't even begin to count up the hours Stuart and I have spent in icy cold rinks, waiting out practices, living through dismal losses, celebrating joyful wins, lost in the crowd of parents filling the bleachers.

Stuart absolutely loved the game, and had coached Brian's team at one time. He attended all of Brian's games, arranging business trips so as not to interfere with the game schedule, and watched the team practice whenever he could, later making suggestions to Brian on how to improve his backward skating, lifting the puck when shooting it, stick handling, penalty killing, and on and on.

When I had to do a practice, I brought a book, or talked to someone to pass the time, and had no tips for Brian—I didn't watch! I liked the social stuff, the dances and the tournaments. A weekend spent in a motel on Cape Cod in February, when you can't swim, or April in Vermont, when you can't ski, appealed to my twisted sense of humor.

When the kids first started skating, their parents had little in common, each intent on watching and cheering their precious little hockey players, but warm friendships developed after years spent together in the damp cold atmosphere of the rink, or on a weekend in a motel at a tournament. That's how I met Ellen McGrath, my best friend. An odd phrase, perhaps, for an adult woman to use, but if I were forced to choose only one friend, it would be Ellen.

We met about seven years ago when our boys were trying out for the same team. I liked to chat with her while waiting through a practice. Her wry sense of humor made her a very entertaining bleachermate, and it didn't take long for me to recognize a kindred spirit.

Before long, we became great friends, swapping books and recipes, skiing together, or gossiping like two old crones on the phone. We confided our fears and dreams in each other, secure in the knowledge that the other would be interested, supportive, or would, at the very least, laugh in the right places.

Early in September, a few weeks after Kelley's frightening experience, Ellen and I went into town together. This was an annual event, originated when our children were young and we celebrated their return to school—and our return to freedom—after the long, hot summer.

We had two simple rules: the trip had to be during the month of September, and we ate no Indian food. That was Ellen's contribution.

"I hate curry, Andrea, I've told you that a million times."

"There are fifty-seven varieties of

curry, Ellen, and some Indian dishes don't even use it. You and Stuart make a great pair!" I would often say.

Nowadays there was no need to escape from our children, but we both worked part-time, so this provided an opportunity for unmotherly, single girl type fun. We perused the Sunday *Globe* for the very latest activities, and varied our pleasures, visiting art galleries, ethnic food fairs, chic new boutiques, avant garde theater, nouvelle cuisine restaurants, combed Filene's basement looking for bargains; absolutely anything that took our fancy—with the exception, of course, of Indian food.

When we stopped to eat, we talked a lot, frequently annoying the staff in a restaurant as we sat talking and laughing over a lunch that might last until 3:00 p.m. This time we ate at Cheers!, a Boston landmark, and I told her about Kelley's unhappy incident with Carl, who was now history.

"At least it ended okay. There's so much to worry about today. I'm sure this sounds weird, but I was surprised at her innocence. She reminded me somehow of myself, and I spent the rest of the night thinking about my high school sweetheart, and how we broke up."

"Not so surprising, really," said Ellen. "Kelley's problem was sex. I'll bet that's why you broke up with your boyfriend."

"Well, aren't you the perceptive one."

"Not really—that's just how it went. You didn't come across, they took off."

"We went together for a long time, almost five years, Ellen, and I thought he was serious." Remembering, feeling the pain. "Then I found out he was cheating on me."

"Were you sleeping with him?"

"No, Ellen, of course not!"

"For heaven's sake, don't sound so horrified. Lots of people do, you know."

"Well, we didn't!" I sounded prudish and self-righteous in my own ears, considering how close we had come to the ultimate act.

"He probably talked marriage just to see how far he could get with you." I digested that remark silently, finally admitting that she was probably right.

"Did you, um, sleep with anyone, back then?" I asked, hoping it didn't sound like prying.

"Yes, I did," she answered promptly.

"Of course, it wasn't just sex for us, it was true love." She rolled her eyes as she said this, underlining the sarcasm in her words. "We were special, you know, different from all the others who were just having sex!

"His name was Marvin . . . don't laugh, it was! My junior year in college, he sat next to me in one of my art classes. He asked to borrow a pen, we had lunch together that day, and he was into my underwear that night. We had found a love to last until the end of time. It lasted until the end of the semester." She laughed, a harsh, unhappy sound. "I thought we were going to get married when we finished school."

"What happened?"

"Other girls, nicer pens. Who the hell knows? We went to a semi-formal dance at the end of the semester, and he hung around an awful lot with another girl, a real nice-looking blonde. I was so stupid, too; I picked a fight with him about it—right there at the dance, because I thought he was making a play for her. But he already knew her . . . intimately! It was so humiliating. He left me standing there, and went to sit with her at her table for the rest of the night."

She stared down at her plate, pushing a shrimp around with her fork as though she had lost her appetite. Usually funny and sarcastic, but now lost in her memories, Ellen looked very sad.

"I never saw him again," she said quietly.

"And you thought he loved you?"

"Well, yes, of course. I had never been intimate with anyone else, so I thought this was true love. We spent all our free time together—at least I thought we did. He lied to me, of course, because he found time to spend with this bimbo, and no doubt countless others. In the end, it was just sex after all, and telling me he loved me was an easy way to get me to come across. A valuable lesson learned.

"He made a fool of me," she continued, after a long pause, "I trusted him, and after him I thought I'd never trust anyone again."

I knew that feeling.

"I guess this happens all the time," I said, "I wonder how Kelley will make out."

"She'll learn, Andrea, just like we did."

"I suppose you get wiser as you get older, and much less trusting. But you lucked out, meeting Kevin."

"Well, I was twenty-five when I met him, and a little smarter. Still, I had learned to hold something back, just to be safe. I didn't 'fall in love' with him, I 'liked' him, and later I liked him a lot. I guess you're right—it was luck. As time went by I stopped worrying about whether or not he'd stick around. Now there are times when I wish he wasn't there at all."

I laughed, but added "What does that mean?"

"Oh, nothing, I guess, it's just that we've been together for such a long time, we know each other so well, there are no surprises any more with Kevin. He's predictable . . . as I am, I suppose . . . just an old married couple. The thrill of the chase, Andrea . . . it's gone!

"Mmm, speaking of dull old couples, I ran into Marge Garelick a while ago, and you'll never guess what's going on there. Henry, that dull-as-ditchwater husband of hers, up and left her! For another woman! Can you believe it? He met someone he knew from years ago, back before he and Marge got married, and told Marge he was in love, for the first time in his life! I nearly died when she said that, Andrea—you know how proud she is. It must have been so humiliating for her."

We talked for a while about poor Marge in that smug way of women certain that nothing like that could ever spoil our own lives. "Imagine our husbands pulling something like that! Sounds preposterous, doesn't it? But it happens, and all you can do is trust each other, and hope it doesn't happen to you."

"Well, maybe Kevin, but not Stuart. He has no romance in his soul. Couldn't happen," I answered, knowing without needing proof that he was absolutely faithful to me.

"But can he trust you?"

"Of course he can, now that I'm old and fat!"

We had a good laugh, both of us seeing a kernel of truth in the statement.

"Tell me about your new job," said Ellen, ready to move on to something else.

"What's Bob Murphy like to work for?" Kevin's friend, our long-time neighbor, my new boss. I launched into a story about something that had happened the day I started working there, our previous discussion of marriage and trust and fidelity wiped from my mind.

We hadn't said anything of profound importance, and we joked about our marriages and our spouses quite often. There was no reason for it to stay with me. Too bad.

I don't think I'd ever given much thought to what makes marriage work, but if asked, I would have said it's built on a foundation of faith and trust. If that bond is broken, the structure collapses. If asked about my marriage, I would have answered that ours was as sound as the rock of Gibraltar.

I would have been wrong.

Four

"Suppose I went back to school," I said after dinner one night, half-seriously, but mostly to hear the idea out loud.

"Like what kind of school?" asked Brian from the floor, pausing in his game of "snatch the sock" with Moses.

At the same moment, Kelley, buried in *Seventeen* magazine, said, "You mean like cooking school? Adult Ed is starting in October at . . ."

"No, I don't mean cooking, or crafts, I mean school! Is that *so* damned weird?"

"Way to go, Ma!" came Brian's muffled voice from somewhere under the furry bulk sprawled on top of him.

"College, Mom, or high school, or what?"

"Kelley, for heaven's sake! High school! I mean law school. I always wanted to study law, and I've been thinking about it a lot lately."

Lately happened when I started my new job with Jackson & Waldstein, Attorneys, a law office in Plymouth. It had given me an urge to get deeper into the legal profession.

At last Stuart looked up from the *Boston Globe,* but his expression seemed less than encouraging.

"You remember, Stu, I always wanted to study law. This may be the perfect opportunity. No more babies, time on my hands . . ."

"It's expensive."

It wasn't the concept that got my back up, it was the tone of voice, dismissing the very notion of such a cockamamie scheme.

"Oh, well, I might as well crawl back into my hole. Be a waste of time to check it out, find out about the requirements, stuff like—"

"Check it out, Andrea. Look into it, then we can talk about it."

"I need your approval?"

"Of course not. You know I didn't

mean that. But it would be a major expense, especially with Kelley getting ready to go to college, and I'd hate to see you undertake a project so demanding—"

Wrong, Stuart. "Are you saying I'd drop out? Or am I too old?"

"Don't get all defensive. I just think you should think about it for a while. It's been a long time since you studied anything, and—"

"So I'm not too old? You don't think I can handle it? I've grown stagnant hanging around here raising your children, where the most difficult thing I do is make sure your socks match, but I still have a mind buried in here somewhere! Why don't you just say what you really mean! You think I'm too dumb!"

"Andrea, when you calm down you'll see for yourself—"

But I was beyond calming down. "Thanks for all the support, my dear," I threw back as I flounced out of the room.

Generally I'm a peace-loving person, a don't-rock-the-boat-er, but I hate to be told that I'm not capable of doing something. It's insulting, makes me angry, and unreasonable. At forty-six years old I'd be dead long before I finished law school, for God's sake, or I'd give up long before the end. But I was angry with Stuart for pointing it out, angry that he was right, and especially angry with myself for caving in and admitting defeat.

Fate intervened. I was wading through the mail one morning, separating the bills from the chaff, when a flyer caught my eye. I'd seen it before, triple folded glossy paper in sedate black and white, on the front a door flanked by Georgian pillars, implying an institute of higher learning. "BE A PARALEGAL, OPEN THE DOORS TO . . ."

Beginning October 7th, I read, classes would begin at campuses all around the state, including SMU, an easy drive from my home. Why, in less than two years I could be a practicing quasi-lawyer, carrying my own briefs in my own case, wearing pinstripe suits and sitting in court. It wasn't cheap, but it wasn't law school tuition, either. I was primed. I was hooked. I enrolled!

My romantic pinstripe vision did not include slogging through impossibly intricate legal texts half the night, nor was I prepared for the shock of sitting in a classroom full of people half my age, most of whom were not much older than my daughter! I've suffered through fat, ugly days before, but the blonde who sat on my left every Tuesday and Thursday threatened every smidgeon of self-esteem I had picked up during the eighties. But nothing would stop me, and, fueled by the huge chip on my shoulder, I plugged away month after month.

After his initial surprise, Stuart was quite supportive, great when I needed help memorizing and deciphering terminology, not so terrific when it came to making dinner. We compromised.

The kids were royal pains in the butt.

"Mom, how can I do my homework with your books all over my desk?" Brian complained.

When I tried to use the dining room, exposing Kelley scrunched up in a dark corner whispering into the telephone, I got *"Mo-o-m,* this is the only room in this whole house I can have a private conversation. If I had a phone in my room . . ." So we got her a phone, and the dining room table was mine.

* * *

Mom and Dad were not very encouraging. Though they didn't say it in so many words, it baffled them that living in this lovely home, caring for my lovely children and my wonderful husband wasn't satisfaction enough. What more could you ask of life!

I tried to explain once that my family was very important to me, that I wasn't being selfish. I was doing something for myself, a different concept entirely. "I'm growing, Dad, trying something new. Like they say, I want to be all that I can be!"

Impossible to explain to people whose entire lives had been lived within a five mile radius, who had never reached for the stars, but were content with what they had. Well, good for them. I needed more. "The children are practically grown up, Mom, you can't say I'm taking time from them." I'm sure I didn't get through, but their weird daughter was someone else's responsibility now, and they shrugged their shoulders over my foolish whims. I was lucky, apparently, that Stuart was such a patient man.

Mother did mention that "A woman's place is in the home," but if she was trying to bug me, for a change I didn't bite.

Stuart's father died when he was nineteen, and his mother remarried a couple of years later, a neighbor whose wife had passed away. She and her husband lived in Arizona, and we only saw them every four or five years, so in effect, we had only my parents.

They had a terrific marriage, glowing with that contented, deep-down kind of happiness that can't be faked. Leonardo and Antoinetta Corelli. She insisted on being addressed as Antoinetta, but Dad called her Toni, and though she professed to hate it, her smile was a complete contradiction.

She treated him like he was responsible for the sunrise, and though he didn't have much to say, when he looked at her his eyes shone with a special warmth.

Dad was her first love, and she loved to tell us how they met . . .

They lived in the same neighborhood, around Granite street, near where they live now. He went to school with her brother, Marco, and they hung out together at the local pool hall on Saturday nights. Of course, a guy didn't take a girl there, but he would talk to her, the baby sister, when he came by for her brother. They were handsome young guys, my dad and Uncle Marco. I never knew him, he was killed in Germany, but I've seen pictures. Lean, with mops of dark wavy hair, and mustaches. A pair of ladykillers!

Dad was older than Mom, seven or eight years, I think, but it seems he thought she was cute as a button. He took to walking past her house on Sunday afternoons, stopping to tie a shoelace or something at her front gate. If she was out in the front garden, where my grandfather had a swing, he would stop to talk, and before long she made sure she was in the garden when he came by. Pretty soon, instead of talking over the fence, he came in to sit with her on the swing. From there it was a small step to the ice cream parlor!

"And dancing, Andrea, your father was such a dancer! Saturdays, at the

Knights' Hall, with all of our friends after the war was over . . ."

She always paused there, remembering, I suppose, the friends who did not come home after the war.

"It was so thrilling to be young after the war, when the boys came home. Every week more of them, and on Saturday night of course they came to the Hall, to dance and laugh, to find the girls, to begin their lives again."

She loved to talk about when they were first married, young couples piling into cars to go to the beach, or picnics in the Berkshires. She has scads of pictures, black and white, with lacy edges, filled with smiling groups of family and friends.

"Were you ever alone, just the two of you, Mom?"

"Of course, you silly thing. We went for long walks, or to the movies after you and your cousin Isabella came along, Aunt Sylvia and Uncle Bert would bring her over here. They put you to bed while your dad and I went to the early show, and when we came home they rushed out to catch the late show. When they came back we would sit over coffee and talk about the movie." No babysitters; teenagers hadn't been invented yet.

"Most nights, after I made his lunch, we would sit and listen to the radio, or talk quietly after you fell asleep."

"I remember the big black lunch box he had. You made his lunch every night?"

"Of course! How else would the man eat! There was no cafeteria at the mill, you know."

He worked at the woolen mills, the reason for Oakville's existence, in dull red brick buildings that were over a hundred years old, with zillions of windows. And a steam whistle. I remember hearing it blow at seven in the morning, the beginning of the shift, noon and six o'clock at night, the end of a long day.

Dad walked home from the mill at night, along with many other men from the neighborhood. I don't know what happened in the other houses, but Mom watched for him between the curtains in the front room, and as soon as he came round the corner she ran to the kitchen to make sure supper was ready to put on the table under his nose as soon as he sat down.

"Wash up, Leo, I have your dinner ready." She said the same thing every night. He washed his hands at the kitchen sink, rubbed my head, sat down at the table and smiled at both of us.

"How was your day?" he'd ask. She would give him whatever neighborhood or family news there was, and then he would turn to me.

"Tell Daddy, bella, what did you do today?"

I was three or four, and it was such a thrill to report my day. Mom watched him eat. I had been fed earlier, and I don't remember her eating with me, but she watched and served until he was done. When he went into the front room to read the paper, she cleaned up in the kitchen.

They sat and talked after I had been put to bed. I couldn't hear the words, but I remember the sound of their voices rising and falling, with the radio playing softly in the background. Years later, when I first heard the ocean slapping against the beach in the night it reminded me of their voices in the front room. She would knit socks—argyle—I remember, with all these crisscrossing diamonds and little clippy things hanging with yarn looped around them, waving around her hands as the needles clicked their rhythmic song.

I'm sure they had problems—money, naughty kids, whatever—but I remember it all in a gauzy haze of happiness.

In all my years in their house they never had a real fight. I never saw them kiss or fondle each other, and if they ever made love I wasn't aware of it. But they were the most loving couple I have ever known. It had to do with glances, and gestures. His expression when he put her sweater over her shoulders, patting her back gently afterwards. The pride that beamed from her face when she walked to church on a Sunday morning, strutting proudly beside her man. They didn't have much time to spend together, only evenings and Sundays, since he worked at the mill on Saturday mornings, but time moved slowly, and they enjoyed each other to the fullest.

They never changed, always treated each other with love and appreciation. I wish I had learned something from them.

* * *

"Where's Dad! He promised me the car tonight! I'm going to be late for rehearsal, and I still have to get Sue!" Kelley wailed.

"Take mine–Dad's still at work and I won't be needing it with all the studying I've got to do."

"Thanks, Mom, you're a doll." She grabbed the keys from my hand, paused long enough for a quick peck on the cheek, and ran. "Sing like a bird, honey, and drive carefully," I called, watching her from the door. I'd better remember to tell Stuart the date of the Chorus Recital; he had to be there. Another night out–something I didn't need before my midterm exams, and the holidays coming soon. As I waved goodbye to Kelley, Ellen's car turned into our street, her turn for the rink run. We hadn't talked in weeks, and I missed our coffees. Maybe by the end of the week things would quiet down. I walked up to the car.

"Thanks, El, I'll pick up tomorrow." I shut the door, shivering as I went back into the dining room, my study, for a couple of hours more at the law books.

Seconds later the loud thumping caterwauling of some rapper or other filled the house; Brian in his room with the stereo cranked. He was doing homework.

"Turn that damn thing down!" I shouted from the bottom of the stairs. "I'm trying to work down here!"

His door crashed against the wall and he appeared at the top of the stairs. "Gee, Ma, I'm studying too, and you know I can't work when it's quiet."

Though I thought of our place as a madhouse, we were rarely all home at the same time any more. People came and went at all hours, and we didn't even eat meals together. Kelley was around only long enough to shower between school and dates, chorus and Graduation Committee meetings. Brian had school and hockey, and I had this damned course I had got myself into! We never saw Stuart at this time of year, he was so busy at work, getting things in order for the year end.

Five

Wednesday morning, the day before Thanksgiving, I nearly went nuts. Traditionally, dinner had always been at Mom and Dad's, and our plans had been made accordingly for the following day, but she was beside herself when she called me at 6:28 a.m. (those blue numbers again), waking me out of the first sound sleep I'd had in two weeks.

"Andrea, I'm so glad you're up. We can't have dinner here tomorrow," she declared.

"Mom? It's the middle of the night. Of course I'm not up yet. What's wrong?"

"Dinner, Thanksgiving dinner. We have to cancel it." She spoke slowly, patiently, to her idiot child. "The boiler blew up or something. Dad says it can't be fixed until Monday. The house is freezing and we have to cancel dinner."

I was waking up fast. "You'll have to get out of the house, Mom. Go to Lorraine's."

"I can't phone her yet; it's too early." I spluttered into the phone, a sound she misunderstood for sympathy. "No, don't worry, we'll be all right for a while. But Thanksgiving dinner, Andrea—I have the turkey here, and I always bake the pies . . ."

"No problem, Mom, we'll go to Lorraine's. Cook your turkey over there, I'll make the pies here and bring them with me." I had to go to the bathroom. "I'll call you there later, okay?" I was ready to drop the receiver back into its cradle. I might even be able to get back to sleep.

"That won't work, and you know it. Her dining room is too small for the whole family to sit together."

You had to know my mother. That was a dig at George, Lorraine's husband, who wasn't keeping her daughter in the style Mother thought proper.

"How about—"

"Here? Fine, Mom, that's terrific." Anything to get her off the phone, fast. "I'll call you later this morning."

I dropped the phone, ran to the bathroom, and then crawled slowly back into my bed, any possibility of sleep totally blown away. Although a visit from the Pope would be slightly more traumatic, having the family here tomorrow ran a close second. This place was a pit!

My parents still lived in the house they bought forty-eight years ago as newlyweds, where the only changes had been those made to accommodate their two children. And while my living room drapes became shabby and tired after ten years or so, and had to be replaced, Mother's curtains had been proudly hanging for almost thirty years, still fresh and bright.

"It's all in how you care for your things," she would say, on her hands and knees as she washed, with a small, soft brush, the upholstery on a couch that had been reupholstered long before I was married.

I had no patience for that stuff; I hired people to clean rugs or windows, and sent drapes out to be cleaned.

"The chemicals they use are too harsh,"

said my mother, in her wisest voice, "and fabrics wear out quickly. If you cleaned these yourself . . ."

Well maybe, just maybe, I preferred to change the look of my home every ten years or so! And so what if I was not a great housekeeper like my mother! I was lots of things she wasn't, and that suited me just fine! We were products of different eras, and I didn't get orgasmic satisfaction from a shiny kitchen floor like she did. As long as it came clean with my trusty sponge mop, I was quite happy. I had better things to occupy my time!

These thoughts chased each other around in my head as I scrubbed the kitchen floor on my hands and knees. The bedrooms had been done to perfection, particularly the guest room, where Mom and Dad would spend a few nights.

"We can't impose ourselves on George and Lorraine," she said when I called around noon, "when you have that big, empty house. "Better we stay with you until Monday." Down the tube went four days of studying, or relaxing over the long holiday. Tempers would be worn to a frazzle by Saturday—particularly mine, which was the one I was most concerned with. I always went through a frenzy of cleaning when they came, polishing and scrubbing until the house was spotless.

"But our bedroom closet is private," objected Stuart, when I cornered him at nine that night, insisting he clean up his tennis things strewn about our walk-in closet. "She has no business in here, and she doesn't come in here. You're doing that guilt thing again!"

"I don't do guilt. I just like to have things tidy when she comes, so she'll have nothing to pick at."

"No guilt, though," he laughed, "I'm glad to hear that. Maybe someday you'll explain why our house doesn't look like this all the time!"

"Lay off, Stuart, and get out of my way!" I snapped.

He was remarkably calm about the whole visit, but then Mother thought he was perfect, and he didn't have the problems I had with her. I liked to pretend my mother's opinions didn't matter a damn, but I couldn't stand the little shake of the head, the slight pursing of the lips that signified her displeasure when I had done something she didn't like, and I went overboard trying to avoid it.

Exhausting, but worth all the effort, I thought the next day, presiding with a gracious smile over a table laden with roast turkey and all the trimmings, which in our family included Italian roast potatoes, Dad's favorite garlicky spinach and mushroom dish, and warm homemade apple pie, à la mode! I sensed her satisfaction, and I was pleased.

"This was a lovely meal, dear, I can see that I trained you well," she said with pride.

I had a caustic answer ready on my lips, but I caught Stuart's eye telegraphing a warning not to rise to the remark, so I took a deep breath and accepted the back-handed compliment.

Kelley and Brian, with Lorraine's two kids, left the table right after dinner, having no desire to linger over coffee and liqueurs with the old folks, and went into the den to watch television. Lorraine had been very quiet during the meal. I guessed that twenty-four hours with Mom had done her in, so I wasn't surprised when she and George rose to leave shortly after we'd had our coffee.

I was clearing the dessert plates when Kelley breezed through the kitchen. "Mom, I'm going over to Sue's. I'll call you later. Bye, Gram." And she was gone. Plates in hand, I stood with my back to the dining room and waited, knowing what was coming.

It came, of course, from my mother. "You know, it's not my place to say, but a girl Kelley's age should be helping her mother in the kitchen after dinner."

"Mom, a girl's place is not necessarily in the kitchen any more . . . Brian is here to help clear up—I'll call him in a minute. Kelley had plans for tonight before we knew you coming."

"Well, you know I don't like to butt in," she said, proceeding to do just that, "but I think Kelley has too much freedom. It's a dangerous world out there, and you don't even know who she's with. She's so young. You need more control over her. Boys . . ."

She continued, and I gritted my teeth, trying not to listen, scraping plates so hard you'd think I was trying to remove the pattern along with the leftovers.

". . . at that age . . . one thing on their minds . . ." she droned on.

Wisely I had not told her about Kelley's near-rape in the summer; she would have kept her in a cage if I had.

I was trapped, a child again, as my mother went on about "dirty minds" and "opportunities for sin" behind me, and the familiar swell of frustration threatened to burst inside me. Good God, I had to get away from the sound of her voice, away from the same old stuff that I had heard when I was seventeen.

". . . And her boyfriends! What do you know about them?"

"I'll be right back, Mom. Go sit in the living room with Stuart and Dad. We can finish up later," I ground out, making my escape as I spoke.

Behind me the clatter of dishes being loaded into the dishwasher began. Of course she wouldn't wait, she'd have it done faster and better than I could before I returned. I stomped up the stairs to my room, deriving childish satisfaction in slamming the door behind me, and sat on the bed, staring sightlessly at the mirror. I'd done that when I was seventeen, too.

Kelley did *not* have too much freedom, I fumed. She knew the rules, she wasn't afraid to talk to me, and she tried to do the right thing when she was on her own. Above all, I trusted my daughter—something you never did, Mother!

By fifteen, though, I had worked out ways to get away from her. One of the boys usually had a car, and after school, or on weekends, I got out as often as possible. With her it was guilty until proven innocent! When I started going around with Richard, it was easier to lie to her, because everything I did was scrutinized and questioned. She was so afraid that something bad would happen to me, she drove me nuts! I didn't know anything about getting pregnant, or how not to, and she answered questions with "Why do you want to know? You have no business knowing these things." When, I wondered, was I supposed to find out? But we didn't discuss intimate things.

What a contrast between myself and Kelley at fifteen, when I told her that if she planned to have sex, I would get her on the Pill. Until now it had been easy to be a liberated Mom, but the Carl business scared me, filled me with the same fears, probably, that my mother had for me. And so, in the end, what went around came around . . .

I realized I had been sulking in my room a long time when I heard my mother's voice calling me as she came up the stairs. Opening my bedroom door, she asked, "Are you okay? I finished up in the kitchen and you weren't back . . ."

"I was feeling a bit lightheaded, Mom, so I came up to lie down for a few minutes. I'm fine now. Let's go down and chat for a while."

Kelley didn't come home that night. I needed that with my mother around!

I noted the time when I was getting changed for bed, thinking there'd be another lecture in store when she came home. But I wasn't worried. When she left for Sue's she said she'd call if they went anywhere else. So I assumed she had tried to call and the phone was busy, or she had forgotten to call, which she had done on occasion. Annoying, but not the end of the world.

My mother, however, couldn't settle down for the night unless all the little chickies were safely in the nest. I was saying goodnight to her in the spare room, when she glanced at the clock.

"12:11," she observed out loud. "Isn't it kind of late for Kelley to be out?"

"Her curfew is 12:30, Mom—don't worry about her. I'm going downstairs to close up. She'll be here in a few minutes."

I wandered around turning out lights and tidying the few crumbs that my mother had missed on the kitchen counter, and sprawled for a few minutes in the recliner in the den, savoring the silence. Just in case Kelley came home in something noisy, I brought Moses in for the night, and turned out every light but one.

At 12:35 I hit the bed next to Stuart, who was already sleeping peacefully. I was exhausted, too tired to read, and was just settling under the covers when I heard Mother at the door.

"She's not home yet," she whispered. Lord knows why she was whispering; Dad's snores were rattling the walls and Stuart was playing his own theme.

"I know," I whispered back hoarsely. "She'll be here soon. Sometimes she takes a few minutes extra, just to test me. She's okay, Mom. Goodnight."

"As you like," she conceded, disapproval heavy in the air. I was not doing my job right, but she was the last person in the world to question my authority over my children, hung unspoken in her parting sniff. She slipped back along the hallway and softly closed the door to her room. Peace at last. When the woman shut her door she was planning to sleep, to stay out of my business. From now on it was my responsibility to stay awake waiting for my daughter. She must be really tired too, I chuckled. My vigil lasted about three minutes, and I was out like a light.

At 4:21 a.m. Mother was beside my bed. "Andrea . . . And-ray-a, wake up!"

"Yeah, what is it?" I mumbled.

"I went to the bathroom, and thought I'd look in on the kids"—something she always did—"and Kelley is not in her bed."

Her whispered voice rose a few decibels, actually rousing Stuart to the verge of coming back to life! "Let's go into her room," I stage-whispered back.

I followed her across the hall, more or

less awake, my mind working on the possibilities, and sat next to her on the edge of Kelley's bed.

"Well, I'm really not concerned, Mom. She probably tried to call. Maybe Brian was on the phone, or maybe she just forgot to call—she's still a kid, after all. I'm sure she slept over at Sue's."

"Call them," she suggested.

"Right, Mom. Phoning people at 4:30 in the morning is not quite my style. I'll call first thing in the morning."

Of course, what we did was return to our own beds and lie awake for the remainder of the night. I tried reading, but my mind conjured up the various horrible accidents she might have had, the mugging she had been subjected to, or even the possibility that she was partying all night and would be hanged, drawn and quartered by her mother in the morning!

At seven I judged it safe to phone the Marsdens', and dialed from my bedroom, hoping it was late enough for them to be merely annoyed with me.

She wasn't there, said Greg Marsden, the father, when he returned from checking Sue's room. His daughter was alone, sound asleep, but Kelley wasn't around. He didn't know what happened. He had gone to bed before the girls the night before.

Could he please check with his wife, I asked, risking his anger. I waited, less than patiently, while he woke her up. She came on the line to tell me sleepily that she was getting ready for bed when she heard the front door shut around half past twelve, and assumed Kelley was going home, but hadn't checked, and really didn't know where she had gone.

"To be honest with you," she yawned, "I thought the girls had a disagreement; I heard what sounded like an argument before she left."

I heard Mr. Marsden's voice in the background, saying that he had prodded Sue awake, but she didn't have the faintest idea where Kelley went.

"Please keep us informed, and if we hear anything we'll let you know immediately," she said, awake now, her voice showing concern. "I'm sure there's a good explanation, and you'll laugh when she shows up."

Easy for you to say, I thought, thanking the mother whose daughter was safe in her bed, and turned to see my mother's face, a mask of worry.

"Oh my God . . . *Dio mio!*" She does that when she's very upset, switches to Italian. Her expression was frantic, and before she went in to disturb my father I dragged her downstairs with me to make a pot of coffee, where she paced back and forth in the kitchen, wringing her hands.

"Mom, there must be some reasonable explanation. She'll be here soon, or she'll phone, or something. Please stop worrying. You're making me crazy!"

Kelley strolled in just before nine, by which time her father, grandfather, and even her brother had joined Mom and me, helping us to worry and consume three pots of coffee. We were debating whether the police would consider her missing yet if we called them.

I looked her over quickly. Pale, no makeup, but wearing all of her clothes, no bruises or scratches that were visible, and not, apparently, suffering from amnesia!

"Where the hell have you been!" We shouted in unison.

She raised frightened eyes, and took a

deep breath. "You're not going to believe any of this," she began. "I can hardly believe it myself. Sue and I were supposed to meet these guys last night about ten o'clock, but they never showed up, so we went back to her place and just, y'know, sat around, listening to tapes and stuff. They called around midnight, to apologize, and asked us to go out then. Sue said she was too tired, she wanted to go to bed. I hadn't called you about sleeping over, and I had to get home sometime, so they said they'd pick me up and drive me home." A long pause, while she traced the vines in the tablecloth with long, blood red nails.

"So? We were all here at midnight. What happened?" Looked like Stuart was going to be the bad guy today.

"Well, it was so early—not even midnight—we drove around for a while. And, well, it got really late, and . . ." Another grinding halt.

"Kelley," I demanded. "What did you do? Where were you all night!"

Five tense, strained, tired faces stared at her, waiting for the answer.

"I won't go out with those guys anymore, I promise you that!" Emphatically.

"You won't ever leave this house again if you don't . . ."

"One of them had a bottle, okay! I didn't want to tell you this part, but you asked for it! Something white, tequila, maybe. And we drank it, shared it, like, and well, Todd—he was driving—said he had to stop, he could barely see. His pal was passed out, and I didn't have my license, and I knew you wouldn't want me to drink an' drive. . . . I had no idea where we were, somewhere down the coast, and I was really tired, so I fell asleep in the car. They had sleeping bags and stuff with them. When I woke up this morning, with the sun in my eyes and everything, well, I got really scared. I knew you'd be mad!"

"Mad doesn't begin to describe it! Your mother and father have been sick with worry! You could have been dead out there! You could have phoned . . ." Mother yelled, and I was grateful when Dad dragged her out of the room, mumbling about getting dressed.

"That little girl is lucky to be alive, Leo!" Her voice drifted back down until the bedroom door shut behind them.

"The sun has been up since six! What

did you and your friends do this morning for an encore?" Stuart wanted to know.

"I was afraid to come home. I knew you'd have a fit, so I made them bring me back to Sue's. I wanted to pretend I had slept there, but I couldn't get back into the house. I was afraid to wake everybody up, so I sat outside on the steps until her brother came out for the paper. He promised he wouldn't tell anyone what had happened, and I snuck up to Sue's room and crawled in bed with her."

"What time was that?"

"Well, I don't know . . . God, how do you expect me to know? Somewhere around seven, I guess."

"That's a lie! Your mother phoned over there at seven this morning, and you were *NOT* there!" Mother had returned.

"Yeah, Mom, but I called from the bedroom, and that clock is fast." It was probably 6:50 when I called over there, he went in to check on the girls, finding only his own angel sleeping soundly; moments later Kelley arrived and slid in beside her.

"Did you talk to Sue's parents this morning?"

"Yah, and were they . . . really upset with me. You should have seen Mr. Marsden's face when he saw me! They said you called and I wasn't there . . . I just got through explaining this whole story to *them..*"

"Boy, that's one for the books," said Dad.

"We thought *you* were good with the stories," added Mom, with a knowing smile, for the first time acknowledging that she knew I used to lie to her.

"But Mom, nobody in their right mind would make up something like that. I think she's telling the truth!"

It was a totally implausible story, but I had to confess I could see myself in that kind of predicament using the same lamebrained reasoning.

"Thank God she's here and apparently in one piece," said Stuart. "Anyone for scrambled eggs? I'm starving."

The atmosphere slowly returned to normal, but Kelley worried me sick. She would go to college in the fall, free to dream up harebrained schemes, far away from prying eyes. Ah well, out of sight, out of mind, I shrugged, then gasped in surprise. I sounded just like my mother! And then I wondered if she believed it any more than I did.

Six

Winter comes to New England with crisp, cold air and clear blue skies. Leafy patterns, like ferns, grow all over the windows, painted by the frost. The little creek that runs through the back yard, the main attraction of this empty lot early one March, and hidden from view most of the year, is finally visible again through naked trees, a narrow black ribbon bordered with snow covered rocks. It never freezes, but gurgles and bubbles merrily all year long on its way to wherever.

When I was a child, winter filled me with delight. I loved the squeak the snow made when it scrunched underfoot, and imagined that the world was covered with diamonds when it sparkled like myriad tiny mirrors in the sunshine. I still get a thrill when snowflakes fall thick and slowly, like something magic is about to happen. When Kelley and Brian were small I'd dress them in their warmest clothes, wrapped around in mufflers and mittens, and go out to play with them. Other mothers seemed content to stand around and watch their kids, but it wasn't enough for me. When they went sledding, we all went sledding, shrieking and giggling down an icy hill, each in a shiny aluminum dish, or all three on the old wooden toboggan. We'd follow rabbit tracks into the brush, hoping for a bunny at the end of every tiny trail, or find clear flat places where nothing had disturbed the fresh snow and make snow angels, mine ludicrously large compared to theirs, but childishly pleased that it was the best.

My birthday is in the winter, though I don't celebrate birthdays any more, which means, roughly translated, that I don't bake a cake. These days I simply enjoy the beauty of the season, and hope Stuart will remind the kids that though Mom hates birthdays, she never refuses a gift.

When schedules permit, we go skiing. Expensive, but terrific family entertainment, exhilarating and tranquil at the same time. Sliding along a winding trail covered in snow as soft as velvet, surrounded by the silence of stately pines, the squeaky swish of skis the only sound. Well, that's skiing at its best. Usually there are too many people on every trail, and after picking your way through the mob, you wait in an everlasting lift line to do it again!

Winter, however, can become tedious, with its short days and long hours of darkness, but just when things get dreary, Christmas arrives.

Christmas for me is a mixture of memories—special food, joyous music and—tangerines! When I was young they were available only in December, and to this day, whenever I smell a tangerine, it's Christmas!

Memories are made of little things, like a house filled to bursting with noisy relatives, the smell of pine, the way tree lights make giftwrap gleam and sparkle, attracting a circle of wide-eyed children. When Kelley and Brian were children, we read Charles Dickens' *Christmas Carol* every night from Thanksgiving to January! Ours was a pop-up book, fascinating us all with three dimensional scenes which brought the story to life before our eyes.

I still have that book somewhere.

As Christmas approached, the house filled with warm smells of baking. Fruitcake and mince tarts for Stuart, strufoli and other Italian goodies for me, and cut-out cookies by the dozen for Kelley and Brian. The kids and I had a ball, all of us covered in flour and sugar, while Moses stood by ready to catch any stray sprinkles that might hit the floor. From the stereo Christmas carols blasted their message of peace and love, driving Stuart crazy.

"Can't you kids listen to music without breaking the sound barrier?" he'd yell. We'd giggle behind his back. It was my fault, not theirs.

Every year we had an open house, a tradition we started about ten years ago. We invited half of the Western Hemisphere, it seemed. Preparations began weeks in advance, tension ran high, and almost always at some time I lost my cool.

Stuart always asked people from work, many who moved in circles more rarified than ours. I thought I had overcome Mom's social class hangups, but a few of these acquaintances made me feel uncomfortable, like the hired help at my own party. I tried not to let Stuart see how I felt, but he once pointed out that they came back every year, obviously enjoying the hospitality and my wonderful food. Maybe, but they still managed to make me feel inferior, and I worked like hell to achieve near perfection.

Frantically brandishing lists of food and supplies to buy, lists of delicacies to prepare, lists of guests invited or forgotten, lists compounded of lists—I was a basket case!

"Brian, turn off that TV—you promised to stack the wood today! It's your turn to clean and polish the silver! And lights! More lights on the tree! We're falling behind my schedule!"

"Kelley, get those bones out of bed! I know it's Saturday, but you promised to help me bake these cookies and breads—and I haven't even thought about appetizers yet! Oh God, I just know we'll run out of time!"

Stuart tried to stay out of my way, but no one was exempt. He was put to work replenishing the liquor supply, hanging decorations, moving furniture, vacuuming rugs.

"Did you get more lights? . . . What do you mean, you're finished vacuuming! There's still dog hair behind this chair! . . . Well, move the damned thing!"

They just didn't understand! Before making yet another run for groceries, I paused for a bolstering jolt of caffeine, and flipped through the mail. I like holiday mail—the cards and letters outweigh the bills for a change. Envelopes stuffed with scribbled notes or neatly typed manuscripts are fun to read, and precious links with old friends. Over the miles and the years we stay in touch, hoping to keep the glow of friendship and memory alive.

One of my oldest friends was Janice Churny, now Janice Burns. We grew up together, went to the same high school, but we had both moved away from home. She and Michael had moved around quite a bit since they got married, but had been in Chicago for the past ten years. We exchanged cards and letters, and met for an evening of nostalgia when they came East to visit her parents, still in Oakville. Spotting an envelope covered with Janice's scrawl, I sat down to read her card.

Along with Christmas greetings, she included, as always, a page of chatty family news. Hers was typed and run off on a copy machine, I observed, not as personal as my own handwritten notes. Along with news of Sarah's choice of college, the cost of Jason's orthodontic work, and Mike's glorious successes as a corporate wheel, was a paragraph that flipped me right out!

"Plans are underway," she wrote, "for our first reunion! It's been thirty years since graduation, in case it had slipped your mind. I'm on the planning committee, though I can't imagine why, I live so far away, but I'll send information and stuff after the holidays. It will be sometime in July. Of course you will be there!"

"Well, I guess so!" Excitement bubbled

as I absorbed this delightful piece of news.

"Listen to this!" I shouted, rushing back into the family room with my news. "We're going to have a reunion! Our first high school reunion! After all these years! We talked about a twenty-fifth, but didn't get things rolling in time! Imagine! Our thirtieth high school reunion!"

Names and faces tumbled over each other in my memory. "I hope Sharon will be there—we used to pool lunch money to buy cigarettes! I wonder if Anne will come from Switzerland—I wonder if Anne still lives in Switzerland!"

I was back in time, suddenly remembering people who hadn't crossed my mind in years. "Sal, who wanted to be a priest. And Bob, uh . . . Schwartz! Tanya, the brightest girl in our class . . ."

"Mom, you haven't seen these people in ages. I bet you haven't thought of them in a hundred years, so why would you care about seeing them all now?" This from my daughter.

"Spoken like the child you are. When I knew them our lives were unwritten, like yours, but after all this time we are the people we grew up to be. I want to know how they turned out, if they followed through with their hopes and plans, if their dreams came true."

She rolled her eyes. "If you really cared about any of them you would have stayed in touch."

"Now that thirty years have whizzed by, it's hard to believe I didn't. I'm sure you can't imagine this happening to you, but it probably will. First you'll go away to college and lose contact with many friends at home. Then along comes the love of your life, and before you know it you have a home and family to care for. Eventually you lose track of bunches of people! One day something reminds you of Jeff or Marilyn, from high school, and you realize you haven't thought of them in years. What became of good old so-and-so, you'll say!

"Now I have the chance to find out all about them, see how much they've changed." I rose to leave the room, then turned back.

"Did I ever mention Angela to you guys?" I squealed. "Ooh, she was classy! Definitely not an Angie! She was a blonde, rare for an Italian girl, with never a hair out of place. Her uniform always looked fresh, while ours got progressively rumpled throughout the day. She wore nylons that never got runs, and flats, while the rest of us wore thick white bobby sox and loafers. Think I don't want to know what she looks like now? Her nails were long, and perfectly frosted, and she used to scrape her nylons absently while she read. It made this swishy sound and acted like a mating call on all the boys!"

Laughing, I added "and on a few of the teachers, too!" particularly remembering Mr. Martinelli, who invariably lost track of the dull, boring poetry he was teaching, and the class snickered as he fumbled around trying to find the thread of his lesson.

"Then there was Doug Rhinehart, whose father was bald as a bowling ball. He used more grease on his thick black hair than anyone, and he worried that he'd go bald too. I wonder if he has any hair left!"

I giggled in anticipation, anxious to see them all again. Kelley was right—I had lost touch with most of my graduating class, even though we had been a small group. Moving away from home, marrying, changing names and lifestyles put an end to many friendships.

And still they crowded in, my thoughts leaping from one to another, cunningly managing to ignore the face that hung like a scrim in front of my mind. "Denise, um . . . oh, I can't remember her name! She was tall, and elegant, looked like a model. She went out with this guy Louie . . . DiSarro, that's it! The motorcycle jock of all time! What a pair they made, and I think they got married! Oh, Kelley, so many people, so many burning questions!

"I see the whole class together just as we were then. I bet I can lay my hands on the picture of our graduating class in a minute!"

Followed by the sound of my daughter's laughter, I went down the hallway to the room we used as an office, or Stuart's den. Somewhere in there was a box of treasures and mementos of my high school days, and the picture I wanted to find was taken when we donned caps and gowns, just before we filed into the hall to receive our coveted diplomas and awards. And still I refused to acknowledge the intensity of emotion boiling just below the surface.

After shoving a few things around in the closet, I found the box and started rummaging through it. Stubs of tickets from dances and football games, a papery brown thing that might once have been a corsage, a pink plastic autograph book filled with names I no longer remembered, belonging to faces I couldn't recall, snapshots taken at parties, on ski trips . . . My fingers had discarded the photograph before my mind became aware of it. I groped around in the box and picked it up, a chilly silence falling around me as I stared at the young couple, arms around each other, sitting in the snow against a dark background of pines . . . Richard and I, bundled up in ski jackets . . . and the memories I had been fighting burst to the surface.

Our school had a ski club of sorts, which we called "The Olympic Team," and every Saturday there was a trip to a nearby ski area. We were novice skiers, just out for fun. No one took lessons in those days, at least in our circles, and we learned the hard way. The day this photo was taken I'd been skiing on a trail that was too narrow and steep for my limited capability. I crossed the tips of my skis and took a flying leap, apparently crying out as I landed in a tangled mess of poles and goggles, wet snow packed into my hair and inside my jacket. One of my runaway straps had broken, and a ski took itself off down the hill.

I had a crush on Richard Osborne, one of the boys from across the river. He was skiing ahead of me—in fact, the reason I had taken this trail was to follow him. Richard heard me scream, and watched me tumble and slide. Stepping out of his bindings, he rapidly climbed back up the hill, collecting my belongings as he came. When he found me, I was sprawled on my back, covered in snow and embarrassment, weak with laughter. He bent to help me up, my hat and poles in his hand, and when I grabbed his arm he lost his balance and toppled down with me. We were laughing, and he took off his mitten to wipe the snow from my face. Laughter faded as he leaned close; his eyes softened, and he kissed me for the first time, the sweetest, the most tender kiss. I remember the stars bursting in my head . . . it was the best moment of my life.

We had gone to school together, so of course reunion plans would trigger inevitable memories of him. But I was badly shaken as it dawned on me that he had filled my mind from the first mention of a reunion. My dreams of him were lacy wisps of memory shrouded in the mists of nostalgia, and almost always focused on the night we broke up. But here he was, vividly alive, bringing with him uncontrollable stirrings of . . . something. And yet it would have been strange for me to feel nothing; he had once been the most important person in my life.

"Mom, haven't you got that picture yet?" Kelley broke into my reverie. She came into the room, saw me surrounded with mementos, and whooped with laughter. "Mom's been hit with nostalgia," she shouted back to Brian, and he laughed too.

I couldn't laugh, I felt stifled and crowded. I needed air, had to get out somewhere, alone, to clear these memories from my mind. I followed her back into the kitchen. "I think I'll take Moses out for a walk. Anyone interested in coming along?"

"Now?"

"Yeah, now. He hasn't been out yet today, since no one here would dream of walking him, and he really needs the exercise." As I hoped, I got a chorus of refusals. Thank God, I breathed, and escaped quickly before anyone had a change of heart.

Seven

"Settle down, you stupid mutt!" Moses' excited whining filled my tiny car, annoying me today, though I usually found it amusing. Somehow he knew that when we turned left at the bottom of our hill we were going to his favorite spot, and he could barely contain himself.

Finally, however, we arrived at the park, and I unhooked his leash, watching him as he celebrated his freedom, running tight little circles around me, grinning and yipping, soon flying off through the woods. It would be a long while before he missed me and came back to play.

Discovering that photograph had churned up many long forgotten emotions—love, anger, hurt—and I had to sort them out. When I reached the lake I sat on an upturned rowboat, shivering, and wrapped my jacket tightly around me to keep out the wind, glad that I'd taken Stuart's old sheepskin off the hook. Taking the picture from my pocket, I studied this young couple as though they were strangers.

Her dark eyes were filled with impish fun while somehow conveying shyness at the same time, the snap of the camera freezing forever her demure expression. A softly rounded face, which in youthful ignorance I had considered fat and unappealing. Not so unattractive, I decided now; she was radiant with hope and happiness.

Beside her was a very handsome young man, slender and tall, his long hair combed back, with sharp planes of cheekbones in a thin, serious face. He was looking at her, not the camera, with a faintly sardonic expression on his face. He must have just made some sarcastic remark, and I chuckled fondly . . . he was always doing that. But clearly there was love in those dark eyes.

I searched the photograph for a hint or a reason for all the heartache he caused later, but love was still new, and I saw none. I had loved him so much, and foolishly believed he loved me too. Huddled deep in my jacket, oblivious to the cold wind coming off the lake, I plunged into the past, back to Oakville and my youth.

It's a mill town, and as with so many such places, it grew around the river that fueled the mill. In our case, the river ran right through the middle of town, dividing it in two as surely as a wall. It wasn't even two hundred yards wide, but it might well have been two hundred miles.

On one side, the north shore, were spacious brick homes, emerald green lawns and bright flowers, and the Oakwood Country Club, where bright umbrellas fluttered in the sunshine on the flagstone patio. At night the golden reflection of lights from these houses danced on the dark water, and music floated across the river on the breeze.

These were properties with tennis courts and backyard pools, towering oaks and maples, arching across the roads, lining driveways, and paths neatly laid out in flagstone or cement blocks. Elegant, spacious homes with full length draperies and oak flooring, in neighborhoods that spoke of prosperity, where Mill management, and the small coterie of Oakville elite lived. This was Richard's world.

On the other side of the river, the south shore, a narrow rutted road hugged the bank, lined with tired triple deckers. A row of buildings, once the thriving woolen mill where my dad had worked for many years, and the reason Oakville existed at all, now stood empty, four stories of red brick studded with hundreds of windows, most of them broken.

A little further along, past a few weed filled empty lots, was Sal's Pizza Parlor, and on the corner of Porter Street was Vinnie's Market. I lived around the corner.

No towering oaks here. Our yards were filled with vegetables and fruit trees, with no space wasted on useless flowers or ornamental trees.

I don't know if one way of life was better than the other, but I know my friends and I were envious of the people who lived on the north shore. I can't imagine that any of them envied me.

It was all one town, but I grew up on

Porter Street, and Richard on Kingsley Road, in Edgewood Park. Worlds apart.

The only reason I ever came to know Richard was that Oakville had only one school system, and if there were social differences between us, we were totally unaware of them in our school days. The expectations of our families with respect to higher education, careers, or the correct mates for their offspring may have differed, and our parents certainly did not mingle, but in general all the kids simply hung out together, regardless of where they lived. We had our share of snobs, and anti-snobs, but there were many couples like us.

Richard and I had been seeing each other regularly since ski season, but we went public at the "Spring Fling" dance, in our junior year. We went together for five years—until the summer we broke up, just before his senior year at college.

God, how I loved that boy. Dark eyes, bright and alive, that constantly changed with his moods. He would roll them mischievously, adding a rakish smile, inviting you to share a joke . . . they changed in an instant from a penetrating stare to soft, sexy warmth. Just remembering gave me a joyful flip inside. Eyes that melted into deep pools, glowing with a warm light that brightened his face and lit up my life.

He used his long, slender pianist's hands, still only in reflection, when it was his habit to rest his chin on his palm as he gathered his thoughts, to add graceful expression to his words. And when those hands roamed over my body, I quivered in anticipation, thrilling at the inevitable advance from cozy warmth to total arousal . . . but never, never, going all the way.

First love. Exciting, trembling, with emotions ranging from gut-wrenching pain to soaring ecstasies of joy. And after the inevitable heartbreak, never again loving so freely, growing a shell to hide the exultant happiness and abysmal depths. First love. I wasn't alone in this. We've all been there.

Of course Richard went to college, a place as remote as outer space for girls like me. I stayed behind in Oakville, learning to type. If he had girls at school I didn't know about them. When he came home, our love flourished.

We usually went to the movies on Saturday night, necking in the dark, often sitting through the same show two or three times, then to Sal's for a Coke, eventually making our way to the Point, there to snuggle close, glowing with love. When he got his own car we found other, less crowded places to be alone, driving out to the back roads outside of town.

He cast a magical spell, but it was overshadowed by another, more powerful one. Reduced to simplest terms, I was afraid of my mother!

She had done her work well. Believing I would go straight to hell, get pregnant, be cast aside by a lover who had taken what he wanted, or all of the above, I preferred to wait. The physical act of making love required a big leap of faith and trust, and I didn't have the courage. Richard wanted much more than I was able to give, and called me a tease for holding him off, but Mother's warnings flashed like neon signs in the back of my mind.

"Give a boy what he wants and he'll throw you away in a minute. Behave like a slut, Andrea, and you'll be treated like one."

She didn't like Richard, not at all.

"I don't like all that long hair. Doesn't he own a pair of proper pants, rich boy from across the river? And those sandals!"

"Mom, he goes to college. Everybody on campus dresses like that! That's no reason not to like him!"

"And after college, what then? He'll go away, get a good job somewhere else, marry himself a college girl."

A college girl! Why wasn't I a college girl? God, life was unfair. "Just give me one real reason why you can't stand him, Mom."

"Andrea, I don't know how else to put this. He'll use you until the right girl comes along, then he'll forget you. He's no good, he can't be trusted! I know his type. Find someone else, Andrea!"

If I had been in her place I wouldn't have trusted him either.

Shivering with cold, I stood up and stamped my feet to get the warmth circulating again. This place was great in the summer, but in the winter . . . I looked around, but Moses was nowhere to be seen, and before I called for him something came to mind. It must have been summer . . . a Saturday afternoon . . . my parents had gone to the Springfield Exposition, the biggest fair in the state. Due to a serious oversight on Mother's part, Richard and I were alone in the house.

"Where is the dragonlady? Did she forget I was coming over today?" He backed me against the wall in the front hall and pressed close, kissing my ear.

Shy, nervous, though the tight jeans and tube top so popular at the time probably exuded wantonness, I said, "They've gone to the 'Big E,' Rich, they won't be back for hours." An invitation.

He closed in on me, and before I knew it we were in my bedroom peeling off our clothes. I had felt it before through his clothes, but had never seen it or touched it. He took my hand, guiding me. "Yes, oh yes, that feels so good, Andrea, just like that." It grew, and I pulled away.

He touched my breasts, familiar territory, bending to kiss them, sliding down my bed, planting burning kisses in the most intimate places, using his tongue, both of us aroused to fever pitch. He was on top of me, trying to part my legs. Oh, how I wanted him, but I found my wits and pushed him away, preventing him from going inside. He came all over my stomach, my bed . . .

I clung to him, but he stood up and moved away from me, disappointed. So was I, but I just couldn't do it. I was in tears, but he left me lying there, angrily slamming the front door when he left.

Trying to imagine the joy of making love, I touched my breasts, small compensation to be sure. My eyes closed, and with fingers outstretched, my hand snaked down my belly, gently, slowly teasing until a swell of peace and pleasure radiated throughout my body, my mind wholly absorbed, building to frantic climax, sad and lonely consolation for the pleasure I had missed.

I was overcome with guilt, knowing that what I had done was wrong, but doing it with Richard would have been infinitely worse.

In time, I thought, as the years passed . . . but we ran out of time. Others, it seemed, were happy to satisfy his needs, and he didn't have to wait for me any more, if indeed he ever had. After his slip that night in the car, he tried to explain, but I refused to listen.

"They were just girls! They meant nothing to me, Andrea, I never wanted to hurt you."

Girls! Not just one. I was humiliated. "You never meant for me to find out, you mean. I never want to see you again."

"I tried to resist, but . . ."

"Just how stupid do you think I am?" Lying, cheating bastard.

"Andrea, I love you, I want to spend my life with you. It will never happen again. Please forgive me!"

How I wanted to forgive, but I didn't dare believe him. Finally I convinced myself that he meant absolutely nothing to me. Mother's warnings rang in my ears. "Boys only have one thing in mind, Andrea, s-e-x—dirty sex. He's no good, he can't be trusted . . ."

Mother had been right. How lucky that I had never given in. Reputation pure, virginity intact; the important things were safe.

But I was humiliated and angry. He had made a fool of me and broken my heart. I would never forgive him. He begged me to reconsider, and I struggled to remain cold, when more than anything I wanted to run into his arms. I would *not* give in. He might do it again, but to someone else, not to me! I was miserable, but I slammed the door and shut him out of my life forever.

Years later, I wonder why he chose to keep on seeing me. He never had his way with me, and if other girls satisfied his sexual needs, then what did he get from me? Probably, as Ellen says, it was the thrill of the chase. Why didn't I have sex with him? I wanted it as much as he did. Was life so different then?

Today, in an age of guaranteed protection against unwanted pregnancy, with a relaxed belief in an all-seeing God, and no social stigma or punishment for behavior no longer considered sinful, we can afford liberal attitudes toward premarital sex. Old-fashioned moralities seem dated and stuffy. For me, at that time, the fears of hell, and pregnancy, and parental censure were real. Yes, things were very different then . . .

* * *

Moses crashed into me, chasing a paper bag as it blew in the wind, bringing me back to the present. I was frozen stiff! When he pressed his cold nose against my face I tried to burrow into my jacket, but he stuck his big furry head in deeper, making me laugh, and would not be ignored. I threw a few sticks for him to catch, but my heart wasn't in it, and eventually he got the message and ran off again.

I took the picture of Richard and me out of my pocket and looked at it once more, hoping to recapture the good feelings, but I was filled with sadness as I walked back around the frozen lake with my furry friend, totally engrossed in my thoughts.

I frequently talk to myself, and this seemed a good time for a chat.

Richard is just a memory from another lifetime, and can't hurt you now. You are happily married, with a fine husband, and it is idiocy to suggest you still love Richard. That was buried long ago, and the old hurts with it.

But suppose he didn't even remember me? The idea brought a sharp pang of disappointment.

If you meet at the reunion, I continued firmly, you meet as old friends. If he has forgotten . . . no, I couldn't believe that. Whether he's there or not, you had many friends in Oakville, and you'll have the time of your life.

This very important conversation ended with all my questions answered. I put my memories back into their little box and closed the lid. I whistled for Moses and left the park, a much happier woman.

God, I'm stupid when it comes to men.

Eight

We always planned our Christmas party around a central theme, and this year I wanted the warm ambience of an old-fashioned New England country inn. That called for pewter, and plaid and lots of greenery! And candles, multitudes of candles, to establish the mood, glowing in pewter candlesticks of every description on cloths of red and green plaid covering every table in sight.

We made swags and wreaths and centerpieces with the holly and juniper from the yard, and pine found in abundance in the forest behind our house, tucking in tiny sprigs of red berries, adding red and green velvet ribbons and bows. It was beautiful, and aromatic, the pungent scent mingling with the spicy mulled cider heating on the wood stove.

I used every pewter dish I could beg or borrow for the food. Along with contemporary finger foods, we served New England standbys like clam chowder and Boston baked beans.

The friendly bartender at the Wayside Inn shared his recipes for two authentic Colonial drinks. The ever popular Coowwoow, a potent mixture of rum and ginger brandy, and the Stonewall, another rum concoction, were powerful additions to the bar; they liked their whiskey neat back in Colonial times.

Stuart drew the line at costumes, so the Innkeeper and his "goode wyfe" wore contemporary dress. The party went on well into the morning; a good indication, we thought, of success.

Ellen and Kevin McGrath came early and stayed late, helping us set up, serve, and clear away afterwards. Around three-thirty we quit, leaving the rest until the next day, and sat with our feet up on the coffee table among the napkins and the nuts, finishing up the mulled cider, munching on the last of the cookies, talking over the evening.

Stuart surprised us all with the news that Fred and Julia were splitting up.

"So that's why she came alone. He really doesn't have the flu at all," I said, marveling at her poise as she lied to me.

"She said she found out he'd been cheating on her, and she just couldn't stand it. I guess she really didn't know."

"The wife is always the last to find out," said Ellen, expressing my thoughts. Everyone else knew Fred had been running around for years.

"I wonder why he fools around, though," said Kevin. "Julia adores him, waits on him hand and foot. Can't he see what he's got?"

"Sometimes people don't know what they've got," Stuart answered. "They see greener pastures, and they have to check them out."

"It's just possible," said Ellen, "that Fred wants someone more independent, less subservient, than Julia. I bet his mother didn't coddle him the way she does! Maybe he's become tired of it over the years. Maybe he wants someone with more zing!"

"People do surprising things," I observed. "They've been married something like eighteen years—you'd think they'd be settled and accustomed to each other by now."

"Tastes change," said Kevin. "I myself am looking around for a leggy young redhead—with more zing—to share my twilight years!"

"Good luck to you," Ellen countered. "Let me know when you find one. I'll be happy to go out to pasture!" They smiled fondly at each other as we laughed, and conversation moved on to other things until they left.

But Stuart's comment stayed with me. Maybe people don't always know what they've got, but how do they know that what they've got is what they want? What does it mean when people question what they have, and start dreaming old dreams?

An hour later, it was still bothering me.

"Stuart."

"Hmmm?"

"Stu!"

"What!"

We were finally in bed, physically tired

but not ready yet for sleep. It was after four o'clock, but we were reading—just a few pages—a habit of long standing.

I can't go to sleep without a little Leon Uris, or Dick Francis, even Agatha Christie and the delightful P.G. Wodehouse in a pinch! Stuart, naturally, reads to learn, and his idea of a bedtime story is a lofty tome on successful investing or motivational stuff about climbing the corporate ladder.

"Are you listening?"

Mmmm. I'm all ears."

"Stu, would you ever have an affair?"

"Oh, sure."

"Stuu-uu, get serious!"

"Well then, no, I would never have an affair."

"How can you be so sure?"

"Because I love you very much and an affair would hurt you and our marriage, and the consequences are too drastic to consider."

"Suppose I had an affair. Would you love me still?"

"Is this something you're contemplating?"

"Just asking. I'm thinking about Fred."

Carefully marking his page, he closed

the book he'd been reading and rolled over onto his back. I finally had his attention. I turned off my bedside lamp, and slid across the bed, and with my head on his chest, we settled into our favorite position for late night chats.

"Well, an affair of any duration would be a blow, but I could probably live through a one night stand; say you met someone and the chemistry worked and you found yourself in bed with him. Only for one night while you're changing planes in Madrid or something, and I never heard about it. Of all the possibilities, that would suit me best."

I chuckled. "Stuart, that is a lousy example. Obviously you'd have to know about it for it to become an issue!"

While he thought, he absently began describing lazy circles on my back; it was quite relaxing.

"Well, I haven't spent day and night worrying over this, but way back when we first met, and I didn't know how you felt about me, I planned fallback positions . . . Bet you didn't know you were a campaign!

"If you turned me down on one invitation, I had another one ready, hoping you couldn't refuse me too many times. Because I loved you so much, I also created a series of compromises that I felt would be acceptable, you know, the worst possible case type of thing."

"I had no idea you had given the subject so much thought." Stuart was not given to outbursts of emotion, rarely getting angry, never verbalizing his internal observations. "You had this whole plan laid out? Just in case? What would you have done if I said I never wanted to see you again?"

"I never allowed for that. You seemed to care for me, but you reminded me of a bird, perched but ready for flight at any moment. I wanted you to trust me, to know that almost anything you did would be acceptable to me as long as you loved me."

The slow circles widened, shifting gradually away from my back, gently grazing my breast, urgency building in the touch of his fingers. I could tell it was no longer unconscious, and felt myself beginning to respond.

"But we never talked about anything like this!"

"No, I had no intention of ever discussing it with you. But before we were married, I felt that you were hesitant, waiting for something bad to happen, and I wanted to be ready for any test. Gradually I thought you began to trust me, and I forgot about it. I haven't thought about that for years."

Amazing! I thought with surprise that in almost twenty-two years of marriage he had never expressed his feelings like this, not even at the beginning. It was probably a good thing I never knew, because I think I would have considered such vulnerability a weakness. He had to be strong and reliable for me, with no chinks in his armor. A solid backdrop for my emotional ups and downs. And now? Who knew? We'd been together for so long . . .

I would have had a difficult time expressing how I felt about him. I had never been passionately in love with him; we just seemed to fit well together. Stuart gave me security; I took it for granted. I rarely considered his feelings for me, and vowed to give this new dimension some thought.

"My guidelines, in case you're wondering," he said, continuing his thoughts, "were very simple. A one-nighter would be more acceptable than an affair, and an affair infinitely more acceptable than your leaving me."

How would I handle Stuart's having an affair? I couldn't be so open minded, but I was certain that whatever my reaction, it would be spontaneous. Stuart, true to form, had a strategy, a plan ready to execute. He took his time and analyzed everything carefully, which annoyed me. But in a highly emotional situation would he really be so dispassionate—if actually faced with a dilemma like my having an affair?

For the first time I realized that though I had never told him about Richard, he had seen my need to trust in someone. How perceptive of him, I thought, surprised by a side of Stuart I had never known. I certainly trusted him, but wasn't there supposed to be more than security and trust? Like passion, maybe? Excitement?

"What are you thinking about?" he whispered.

"Oh, nothing, really, just absorbing this new side of you that I didn't know."

"Well, since we are still on the subject," he continued, "I want you to know that I haven't changed. I love you, and I'll always be here for you, no matter what."

Romantic words, unlike anything I'd ever heard before from Stuart, but instead of warmth and love, I felt a rush of embarrassment. I was growing restless and uncertain of my love for Stuart, and I didn't want words. I wanted . . . what? I had no idea. I didn't want to be bored, or an old married woman, taken for granted. I had missed out on the bells and whistles, and wondered if maybe someone else could thrill me, excite me. These were the thoughts that filled my head and my dreams.

Hormonal, Ellen would have said.

Stuart's gentle touch became more urgent, and he pulled me towards him, filled with anticipation. He reached out and turned off the lamp, and we made love. *And I wished I was with someone else.* I couldn't help myself. I wanted more—a wild, passionate lover, a man who would take me over the edge of reality into a new dimension.

I didn't know much, but I knew that sex had to be more exciting than this.

Surely the raw, insatiable passion described in hot, steamy novels wasn't imaginary. Surely there were men who brought women to climax over and over . . .

With a sigh, I rolled over on my side, away from Stuart, now almost asleep, and imagined other voices whispering, other hands caressing me intimately, bringing me to heights of unimaginable delight . . . making me cry out in wild abandon . . . definitely the stuff of fantasy, but I wished it would happen to me, just once!

Gradually this fantasy lover assumed Richard's shape, his well remembered hands, his kisses, and I drifted into a dream of Stuart's one-nighter, Richard and I, stranded in some exotic port—Tahiti, maybe, or Zanzibar—where by a series of incredibly complicated coincidences we discover each other. Or even better . . . Richard, the captain of a pirate ship, an insatiable lover, and I his helpless prisoner . . . taking me into his cabin, ravishing me, inventing wild, incredible new ways to make love.

Nine

It was good to get back to school, to the more normal craziness of our life-style, to the studies that challenged and diverted my mind.

My paralegal course was taking me into the procedures of trial law, and I was up to the eyeballs in decrees and motions. We spent quite a bit of time at court, and Stuart and I saw less of each other than I could have thought possible, considering we slept in the same bed. Which is just about all we did together—sleep. He went from year end to tax time, putting in a lot of overtime, and any spare time he had was spent with Brian at the rink. I missed most of my son's hockey games that winter, as I learned to draft legal memoranda and attempted to clarify pleadings. Some of the information I gathered took painstaking research, but I thoroughly enjoyed the work, and frequently wished I were younger, so I could seriously go into law.

There were only three males in my class of eighteen, a balance I found appalling. In this room, I thought one day, looking around at my fellow classmates, are yesterday's legal secretaries. Young women today are still afraid to reach for the stars! I hoped Kelley would follow her dreams, whatever they were. I really had no idea; she was in a noncommunicative phase at the moment. She had a weekend job which she disliked, and from conversations overheard I knew she couldn't wait for the ice cream stand to open again for the summer—she liked her job there! She dated a bit, apparently no one in particular, spent a lot of time with Sue, and sat in the house staring off into space.

As the time for the prom grew nearer, the prom committee kept her busy, and she surprised Stuart and me one night when she burst in to tell us that the parents of committee members always volunteered to chaperone the dance.

"Always?" Stuart asked, home for a change and reading by the fire.

"Well, yeah, unless they expect to be out of the country, like Mary Beth's parents, or something like that!" Stuart and I exchanged glances. We had no such plans for the end of May, and she seemed so anxious. We did little enough with her, each of us wrapped in our separate lives.

"Of course, honey, we'll be happy to act as chaperones."

Every year during February vacation I took the kids to Oakville for a few days. It was a good chance for them to spend time with their grandparents without all the bustle that surrounded our Christmas visit, and it was a welcome change in our routine.

I looked up old friends, catching up on the latest events in their lives, going out for lunch or dinner, sometimes getting together with the few who still lived in the area.

Or I visited with Lorraine. Now that children's schedules ruled our lives, we saw too little of each other. Even though she was over forty, and I was older yet, when we got together we acted like children, playing pranks on each other, laughing and talking well into the night. There was a gap of five years between us; Mother had miscarried twice, and the doctor advised her after Lorraine was born not to have more children.

The February visit had become a family tradition, and many of our activities were repeated year after year. The annual skating party down at the river was a great way to spend a couple of hours, afterwards walking back to Mom's to warm up over hot chocolate and cookies.

This year it seemed the weather was not going to cooperate. January had been very warm, and we'd had a lot of sleet and drizzle, but by early February it was finally cold enough for the river to freeze thick and solid. After a couple of dull, dismal days, we awoke to sunshine. The kids were excited, and as soon as everyone was well bundled, we headed to the river with our skates.

Conditions were nearly perfect. The rain of the past few days had frozen into an expanse of ice so smooth and clear we could skate a half a mile or more in any direction without a stop.

Brian skated away as soon as his laces were tied.

"He skates beautifully," said Lorraine.

"I should hope so, with all the hockey he plays!" I answered, watching as he propelled himself smoothly, with no visible effort.

"How about you, Stevie? Are you going to be a hockey player too?" I asked my eight-year-old nephew.

"Over George's dead body," said Lorraine, her voice muffled as she tied Steve's skates.

"Hockey's too rough, Aunt Andrea," he answered.

"Oh give me a break!" I said with a pained expression directed at my sister. "George should watch Brian play sometime—those kids are protected better than any kid on a Little League field!"

Kelley had ten-year-old Maureen by the hand, helping her to get started, and Lorraine wasn't finished with Stephen.

"You guys catch up," I announced, skating away as fast as I could. That George! What a wimp! But my annoyance was blown away in the rush of cold wind as I warmed up. I used to be really good, in the days of my youth, but skating once a year was not quite enough training! Though I liked to pretend the passage of time made no difference, I was older now. A few minutes later, laughing at my foolishness, I threw myself into a snowbank to catch my breath.

The scene before me might have been taken from a Currier and Ives print. I looked across to the north shore, where dark pines grew to the water's edge. Ice coated vines gleamed in the sunshine, draping and softening exposed boulders, and holly bushes, bristling with berries, bordered the bicycle path that ran along the bank on that side. Couples glided smoothly against a backdrop of soft rose colored brick homes, a few boys had started a hockey game, and children shrieked with glee.

I turned to look behind me, at the more familiar south shore, but by comparison the view on my side was disappointing. I chuckled to myself; about the only consolation for living on this side was that we had the better view!

Turning to search out Lorraine and the kids, I thought I recognized a familiar clearing a couple of hundred feet away where the river turned, and I skated closer. It was the Point, our old hangout, which I had never seen from this perspective. Suddenly it was another winter long ago.

No matter how cold it was, there was always a warm spot for me nestled against Richard's chest. We would steal away by ourselves to our favorite hide-away—if memory served, that little hollow right there, where we pretended the rest of the world did not exist. We went in all seasons, but in the cold of winter we were usually alone.

Geese flew overhead, honking loudly, triggering a memory so clear it could have been here and now, of Richard and me standing close together, the icy wind whipping the long plaid scarf wrapped around my head and shoulders.

"What are we doing here? It's so cold my cheeks are freezing! My fingers are blocks of ice!"

"We came here to be alone, just you and me, with no one else around. So I can hold you, kiss your eyes, your fingers, your breasts to make them warm."

He rolled his eyes in his comic way as

he said "breasts," and we both laughed. I turned in the circle of his arms and he hugged me closer, kissing my frozen cheeks, my eyelids. Happiness surged through me. I must have been twenty or so then, and crazy about him.

"Rich, I have to get home—she'll be wondering where I am. You know she doesn't trust us alone together."

"With good reason! Wait until we're together always," he whispered. "No one to question, to interfere . . . I'll be able to strip you right here in this public place and make love to you!"

I laughed aloud, the sound snapping me back to the present.

Here in the stillness of another winter day I felt the sadness of loss creeping over me. Foolish girl, thinking things would go on forever just as they were. Foolish woman, for wanting those days back.

Lorraine and the kids were skating toward me, shouting and laughing, and I turned just in time to be knocked right back into the snowbank. They giggled with delight, and I laughed with them, determined to catch their happiness and high spirits, to remain in the present.

But I couldn't hide my melancholy mood from my sister.

"Everything okay?" Lorraine, concerned, looked closely at me. "You look like you've seen a ghost."

"No, I'm fine, I was just thinking about someone I knew a long time ago."

The combination of the reunion and this location brought memories to life, but there was sadness hidden there, and I was dragging more than memories into the present. If the last few months were any indication, Richard seemed to be haunting me. There was no denying I had been thinking an awful lot about him.

Dreaming was not going to change anything. I chose my life, now I had to get on with it. Trying to shake off this unwelcome depression, I attempted to lighten my mood.

"You can tell I'm over forty—I mean forty-five!"—beating her to it—"sitting around in a snowbank dreaming about old boyfriends!"

She looked at me inquiringly, but I waved off any more questions. I picked myself up and brushed the snow from my jacket. "C'mon, you guys, let's race back to the bench over there!" And I skated away without looking back, leaving the two young lovers and their unfulfilled dreams, behind me.

Ten

The first two weeks of March had been cold and rainy, a continuation of the lousy winter weather. The sky looked like a dingy gray blanket thrown over a soggy wet world. But at last, around the middle of the month things started to dry out, and though it was still cloudy, a haze of green was rapidly becoming visible on distant willow trees, and this morning the air was tinged with the damp earthy smell of growing things. The hyacinths were breaking through the ground, and the azaleas were blossoming their little hearts out. Spring was here!

I poured Ellen another cup of coffee. It was one of those rare days when neither of us had to work, and she had come over for a quiet chat. She helped herself to another muffin while I took a sip of coffee.

"You don't drink your coffee black!"

"I do now. Today is the first day of my new diet. I have to get rid of some of this fat. I look disgusting."

"Don't be silly, disgusting! How much do you want to lose?"

I had it all figured out.

"Thirty pounds. I've gained that over the past thirty years—a pound a year! If I set my mind to it I can lose it in a couple of months. I'm going to start with one of those milkshake diets, or the old faithful grapefruit. If they don't work, I'll try starvation! Maybe I'll look into liposuction, or that business where they wire your jaw shut."

We laughed, but I was not entirely joking. The invitation to the reunion had come in the mail a few days before, and the date was July 9th. Only a few months away, but plenty of time to lose weight, slim down, improve!

"Maybe I'll go to a fat farm!" I said.

"Come on, Andrea, get serious. You're not fat! Lose a couple of pounds if it makes you feel better, but I think you look fine."

"Easy for you to say, Ellen. You probably haven't gained two pounds since you finished high school. I hate people like you, skinny Scandinavian stringbeans! Here I am, short and chubby—look at these ponderous breasts! I'm going to look awful!"

"Ponderous! Listen to yourself! Andrea, everybody there will be thirty years older too. You're not the only one who has had children, maybe gained a little weight. I know this is your first reunion, but I've been to a few over the years, and believe me, you look fine. Just find yourself a spiffy new dress. I think you look terrific," she said, dear and loyal friend. "No wrinkles, nice smooth skin."

"Right," I agreed, "acres and acres of lovely smooth skin! This is so depressing! All I have to do is find a drop-dead outfit, lose a ton and a half, and have my boobs reduced. Before July 9th! Piece of cake!"

"Sounds to me like there is someone you want to impress."

"And just what do you mean by that?" I asked innocently—like I didn't have that someone on my mind, day and night.

"Oh, the old flame, maybe?"

"The old flame? Are you nuts! Of course I had a boyfriend in high school, but he was no big deal. Certainly no one I'd go out of my way to impress." I felt myself blushing hotly as I lied, and rushed on, improvising as I went. "He was very quiet, one of those deep-thinking sort of guys. Wears glasses now, I'm sure. Probably fat, and bald, too. I suppose he'll be there," I continued casually, "but I'm not out to impress him or any one else. I just want to look my best."

"Oh sure," agreed Ellen. "How's school going?"

"I may be on the right track at last," I began enthusiastically, glad of the change of subject. "This is the kind of work I could really enjoy. God, I wish I had gone into law when I was young."

We talked for about an hour or so, and when Ellen left to run a few errands, I plunked down in a rocking chair in the sunroom, asking myself immediately why I had felt it necessary to lie to her. Certainly there had been a boyfriend, and of course I thought about him, and was anxious to see him, wanted to look my best for him. Instead I denied he even existed, wanting to keep him hidden away, like remembering him was something to feel guilty about.

Seconds later, as his well-remembered face came into focus in my mind's eye, I realized that my thoughts about him were somehow improper. I wasn't behaving like a middle-aged matron remembering an old boyfriend, but rather like a young girl in love for the first time.

If this was a warning, however, it went unnoticed, and I gave in with a cozy swell of warmth tinged with a thrill of guilt. I felt myself drown in the memory of his eyes, his smile, recalling the deep, resonant sound of his voice, with its delightful trace of French accent, picked up from his European mother.

It was damp and cool on the porch, and I burrowed deeper into the overstuffed chair, pulling an afghan over my shoulders. I shut my eyes, trying to imagine how he might look today, and dozed off with the light patter of raindrops drumming on the skylight overhead, surrounded by the heady perfume of blossoms drifting in the open windows, and dreamed of my old lover.

* * *

Determined to lose weight, I embarked on a program of dieting and exercise guaranteed to make me fit for the next Olympics! I jogged around the park now on my outings with Moses, and although he looked at me in some surprise, he took to it with gusto. In just over a week I'd starved off almost three pounds, and would lose twenty-seven more if it killed . . .

I really didn't look that bad! I usually felt entitled to have gained a little weight, excusing it with the passage of time, the bearing of children, or water retention when I wasn't more inventive, but I plodded on with the dieting. I was certain that everyone else would be slim and gorgeous, if not naturally, then by hard work. One could certainly expect Stephanie Miller to be slim and svelte—she was so vain she would probably have had a face lift! Maybe I would have my nose fixed.

Toast, dry. Coffee, black. Half an apple. That's breakfast, brother!

* * *

"What's for dinner, Mom?"

"Broiled skinless chicken breast, carrots and broccoli. And no dessert!" Cheers and applause from the family? Not in my house! Actually, they were very supportive, as long as I brought home corn chips and dip with the cucumbers and celery. They celebrated with me, pound by pound, provided I buried their share of the zucchini in a cake. And they were behind me 100% sitting in front of a dish of Fettucini Alfredo while I munched on carrot sticks.

Raw carrots give me indigestion.

"Hi, my name is Andrea. My High School Reunion is coming up in a couple of months. I have to lose twenty-four pounds."

Chorus of sympathetic sighs from thirty or forty women, all thirty to a hundred pounds overweight, gathered in the church basement hall for the diet group meeting.

Diet group philosophy is great. After weighing in, rows of chubby women sit through meetings filled with amusing anecdotes and stories of inspiration, comparing recipes, convincing each other that chicken divan with half the meat and no cream sauce is delicious. The meetings were uplifting and supportive, with weight loss records being broken on all sides, but I'd get home to find the kids stuffing their faces with tortilla chips and salsa.

"Who bought this junk?"

"There's nothing to eat in the house, Mom."

"You're going to get zits from eating that crap!" I'd threaten, stealing a few chips slathered with dip, while viciously mixing up an ice cube and melon shake in the blender.

"The green salad looks great today! I think I'll have that, with lo-cal dressing. And black coffee."

Lunch.

The toughest thing about dieting is eating. Think about it! How simple it would be to stop eating for a week or two. Press a magic button, and your appetite, along with the body's need for food, disappear! No wracking hunger pains, no violent headaches. Dieting makes it hard not to feel deprived, no matter how good the cause.

"Congratulations, you've lost 3/4 of a pound. How about a big hand for Andrea! We're all so proud!"

Dieting is a long and lonesome business.

Eleven

Brian was growing in ways more subtle than outgrown clothing. He had discovered girls, one specific girl, to be precise, and he spent hours talking to her on the phone, or lying around gazing at nothing, unless someone disturbed him, breaking into his adolescent fantasy.

"Hardly adolescent, Andrea," his father admonished me when I mentioned it. "He's fifteen. His fantasies are all grown up!"

"Maybe it's time for the father-son talk? What do you think, Stu?"

"Trust me, we've covered it all over years of driving back and forth to hockey games. He knows whatever there is to know."

"Everything, Stuart? Like AIDS and stuff?"

He nodded, returning to his paper. I sincerely hoped so, because from what I heard kids were sleeping around at fourteen and fifteen. My concerns were not only the moral issues, or the equal responsibility boys and girls had to prevent pregnancy, but disease. I hadn't left that important discussion to the possibility that Stuart had covered it, however, and had progressed beyond morals in my lectures to both Brian and Kelley.

"It isn't about good or bad any more. It's whether you live or die! You have to be careful, and talk to me, or Dad, without being embarrassed!" I could only hope.

When Brian was not preoccupied with Janet he dreamed of buying his own car. He invented the most creative repayment plans; if we gave him a loan, he'd repay us with his lawn mowing money! Or, draped over my shoulder, he'd plead with me to visit used car dealerships, so he could drool over his ideal wheels.

His body was growing in all directions

at the same time, causing clumsy accidents. Arms too long knocked things off shelves, feet suddenly big squashed flowers and backed into furniture. His voice cracked at inopportune moments, to his mortification, and dreaded acne spots covered his cheeks, sending him to the bathroom mirror to check his condition hourly. I would be very happy indeed when this adolescence was over.

"Mom, I told you about the dance. You said you'd take us down to the school, and Janet's father is going to bring us back home." Brian raised his eyes to heaven, his patience tested to the limit. "You never pay attention any more!"

"Have pity, son, it's Alzheimer's! I've been meaning to tell you, but I keep forgetting!"

"Very funny, Mom, but you have to drive us there. You promised!"

I really didn't remember the conversation, but no doubt I had made the commitment. I was a little light-headed these days, probably from starvation, drifting in and out of reality, my head filled either with some technical point of law that had to be memorized by the following Tuesday, or daydreams of Richard.

My children noticed, observant by nature and wary of any changes that might impact on their lives. Stuart seemed oblivious, as usual, but I was quite positive that I could shave off all my hair and serve dinner naked and not get so much as a raised eyebrow from him, intently reading the evening paper, or watching the news or some sporting event on television.

Is there a woman in the world who watches sports on TV? I think not. But Stuart and Brian would park themselves on the couch to watch a day-long baseball game, or spend an afternoon cheering Boris Becker or Yvan Lendl in some tennis match in France or New Zealand. During the seemingly endless hockey playoffs they were glued to the screen, criticizing every play, discussing better angles for shots, Stuart with pointers, Brian positive that he could outplay the pros, cheering raucously when their favorite scored.

"Must be some form of male bonding," Kelley remarked.

I didn't begrudge them their relationship, though I was a little jealous. I'd never been a sports fan, and after I became a mother we stopped going to tennis matches or hockey games together, except for Brian's games. And after one of his games, all the way home from the rink they discussed the game while I sat mute, left out, contributing nothing, a mere woman with no knowledge of the intricacies of the sport.

"I played some hockey when I was in school!"

"Yeah, Mom. Girls' hockey."

Enough said.

I remember once, at the US Open, Stuart and I sat in the pouring rain at Longwood, huddled together under an old golf umbrella, his arm around my shoulders, not leaving until the players conceded the match. Then running to a nearby bar, splashing through puddles, giggling like children . . . a few moments shared together. Stuart would say that in typical female fashion I found it romantic, with the rain and all. He would be right, I guess, but sweet moments like those were long gone, buried under children and budgets and daily wear and tear and overall boredom. These days I wished for a little romance, some spontaneous fun.

Our marriage was *boring!* I often wondered if our friends were bored with each other. My life was so stale I couldn't even remember a time when it had been fresh and exciting. There was a hole where my soul should have been. I felt wistful and lonely, without an explanation for it, except that Stuart simply didn't notice me any more.

I would have been very surprised to know that Stuart was fully aware of the changes in me, that he observed and worried, but said nothing. Perhaps if he had talked about it then . . .

We celebrated our twenty-second anniversary on the nineteenth of April, not one of the landmark years, proving only that I had been married a long time and was fast becoming a middle-aged woman. Ellen and Kevin hosted a surprise dinner party for us. It was a lovely tribute. Mom and Dad, the kids, a few close friends. It should have been delightful, and I think I behaved graciously, but I felt dissatisfied, strangely out of sorts. My discontent when we got home was apparent even to Stuart.

"Maybe you're in your change of life," he suggested.

"Change of life? You mean *menopause?* Thanks a lot!"

"How would you feel about a vacation without the kids this year," he mentioned a few nights later, "to celebrate our anniversary. Just the two of us . . ."

I looked at him in surprise. "Now you can't say I never get romantic," he said.

Remembering our honeymoon, I didn't find the idea exactly intoxicating, but we hadn't gone away alone since the kids were born, and it might be nice for a change. A place with a beach, and sunshine, terrific food, dancing . . . well, probably not dancing, but maybe we'd find whatever it was that seemed to be lost.

Poring over brochures, I began to see potential fun in the trip, and when we finally settled on a week in Bermuda at the end of May, I was excited. I had lost ten pounds, and my new bathing suit looked really good with less of me to cover. Stuart might find it sexy, and go crazy . . . Stuart and Andrea get down and dirty! Yeah! I booked our flight and started to make arrangements for things to run smoothly while we were gone.

It was Robbie Burns, I believe, in one of his poems, who warned that ". . . the best laid schemes o' mice an' men gang aft a-gley . . ."

Twelve

"Remember Pat Murphy? The twins, you remember them . . . she was the funny one, the older one, born four minutes before her sister, Jan. She's a flight attendant for one of the airlines, and she's arranged her schedule to fly into Logan on Friday and stay for the weekend!"

Janice had called, bubbling with news and arrangements. Interest in the reunion was catching on, and our classmates were responding in the most positive manner.

"Oh, and Grant . . . get this! Grant lives in Hawaii now, but he's arranging a business trip on the mainland to coincide with the reunion!"

The committee had put in many long

hours of work, and at last were beginning to see results.

"Is Stuart coming with you?"

"I think so, though I wish he wouldn't. He doesn't know anybody except you and Mike, and frankly I think he'd prefer to stay here with the kids. You know Stuart. He hates big bashes!"

"More fun for you if he doesn't go. I wish I could leave Mike at home, but that's hardly possible, since he graduated with us. I intend to behave like a seventeen-year-old schoolgirl, and I don't need him around to remind me that I'm not!"

"Right, Janice—maybe you can get a little action going with Tom! Remember the notes he used to send you in French class? Talk about romance languages!"

"I'd forgotten all about Tom!" She burst into giggles. "He always started his notes with 'Ma chère Janeece', like he knew so much French!"

We dissolved into fits of laughter.

Still giggling, she added, "But I never really went out with him. How about you and whats-is-name, the brain in Math! You two got pretty serious! You'll want to rekindle that flame!"

She was talking about Richard, of course, and my laughter faded.

"Janice, don't be silly. I haven't given Richard Osborne a thought in years!"

My heart pounded, loud in the silence, and trying to sound casual, I asked, "Heard from him yet?"

"Nope, but that's no surprise. You wouldn't believe how organized this is. Remember when I couldn't figure out why I was on the darn committee? It's because I'm in Chicago, and I've got every known body west of here. I've been tracking people down for months, but they're all to the west. He's not on my list, so you'll have to ask Marilyn Jablonsky—she's got everyone east of the Mississippi! We haven't heard from lots of people, but don't worry, there's still plenty of time."

"Oh really, Jan, what a thing to say . . ." Blood resumed flowing through my veins, my heart began to beat again, and in that incredible moment I realized how badly I wanted him to be there.

Suppose he didn't come? I had imagined our meeting countless times . . . me regal and aloof, he a bumbling fool, or both of us tongue-tied and embarrassed. Whatever the scenario, I had never imagined him not there. Suppose he didn't come—when would I get to see him? There might never be another chance! He had to be there. Over rising panic, I dragged myself back to Janice.

". . . to dig around, find some pictures, ribbons, anything you've got. You'll get it all back, but we're trying to get as many mementoes as we can."

"Pictures? Oh sure, I've got pictures." And memories. "I'm sure I can find some things to bring with me," I said. "I'll let you know."

I hung up the phone, sagged against the wall, and stared off at nothing. Until a moment ago I had imagined myself on a nostalgic trip down memory lane, but apparently I had been fooling myself. I was shocked at how desperately I wanted to see Richard again.

For so many years he had lived only in my dreams, but now he was so close to becoming real that I would be crushed if robbed of the chance to see him. I pulled out a kitchen chair and threw myself into it, my mind finally absorbing the incredible truth: I had to see Richard; I would go crazy if I didn't. At the reunion, if he was there. If not, I'd find him. One way or another, I was going to see him again.

A week later I was on the phone with Marilyn. "Of course, we'd love it if you brought snapshots. Those ski trips were a blast, weren't they?" Then she innocently fed me the next line. "Can you remember some names of the kids who went? I'd hate to think we'd forgotten anyone."

"I'm sure you've got the twins . . . how about Brian Novak, and Sally, his girlfriend—"

"They got married, did you know? They live in New York too, and sometimes we get together, though not very often."

"How about Richard Osborne?" My turn to cut her off. She consulted some kind of list, I heard the papers rustling, and an eternity passed while I waited for her answer.

"I haven't heard back yet, but he's actually on Michael's list to contact, so I guess he's somewhere up in your neck of the woods." Talk about efficient—they had the whole damned country cut up into little sections. "Hey, I remember now—didn't you two go together?"

"Yeah, for a while . . . how about Shirley Marsh?" I threw in, successfully diverting her curiosity. I let her babble for a few minutes, cut her soliloquy short and quickly said goodbye, off the phone before I realized I didn't know which Michael to contact. We'd had at least three, and Michael Burns was the only one accounted for. I'd ask Janice next time I talked to her, or I'd make up some new excuse to call Marilyn again.

Thirteen

The headaches were blinding, and nausea had taken up permanent residence in my stomach, but I was losing weight one agonizing ounce at a time. My diet, though short term, was appalling, but I considered the side effects a mere inconvenience as long as I saw results.

Today was so bad I barely got through the morning at work. Brilliant spring sunshine, fluorescent overhead lights in the office, and starvation had combined to create the ultimate headache.

At twelve-thirty I broke for lunch, toying with the idea of taking the afternoon off, but I had too much work to do. Instead I rummaged in my handbag looking for aspirin. Guess I used them up on yesterday's headache, I thought, and when I came up with none I detoured to pick some up at the drugstore on the way back to the office.

I stepped off the curb in the crosswalk and waited for the midtown traffic to come to a screeching halt, just for me. What a stupid idea these crosswalks are, I thought, as I always did. With no lights or stop signs, pedestrians crossed the road between two white lines painted on the pavement, providing target practice for inattentive drivers!

Traffic halted, and I started across, preoccupied with the terrific pounding in my head, my eyes squinted nearly shut against the bright noonday sun. I was looking to the right, holding traffic at bay with my glare, when suddenly on my left I sensed movement beside a large delivery van. Turning, I caught only the glare of reflected sunlight on a windshield . . . I didn't feel the impact, and in the dreamlike silence that followed I watched, completely detached, as my body sailed through the air over the hood of the car that hit me into two lanes of oncoming traffic. What a pity, I thought, she's going to be killed!

The gritty, pitted pavement rose to smash my face, I heard "Aw shit!", and suddenly the air shrieked with squealing brakes. Someone yelled as I landed in an untidy heap on the road, and the world went black . . .

I guess I was out for a few minutes, because when I opened my eyes, still alive, two men in blue shirts were busily working, stuffing padding and supports around me, adjusting Velcro straps, forcing a collar around my neck . . .

"Hey, Peter, she's back!" I heard someone say.

Another face looked down, but the movement of the clouds behind his head made me dizzy, and I shut my eyes again.

"Can you tell me your name?" he asked. "Do you know what happened?" asked the other one. "Do you know where you are?" They talked but never stopped working, sending shooting pains across my back, and when they turned me sideways, my left hip screamed in agony. I moaned, and apparently passed out again.

When I came to I was still lying in the street. My face felt sticky, and strands of hair were plastered to my cheek, but when

I tried to raise my hand to push the hair away, my arm didn't move! Same with the other one! My God, I must be paralyzed! Panic set in and it was several thudding heartbeats later before I realized I was strapped down on a stretcher.

I hadn't heard any sirens, but in my severely limited range of vision was an ambulance and a police car—make that two police cars, with lights flashing. In a loud rumble and screech of tires, a fire truck pulled up, and the street was suddenly crowded with men in black and yellow slickers. A fire truck? What the hell for? What did I do . . . ?

The sky directly above me was framed by a ring of concerned faces, and I suddenly knew how life looks from the goldfish's point of view. I was surrounded by people! Where did they all come from? Good grief! This was too humiliating. Suppose someone knew me! Maybe I could die quickly!

"How's the head, ma'am? Any headache?" The one called Peter, I thought.

Headache? Very funny! I'd laugh if I could. A headache! But, while attempting to nod, I made an amazing discovery.

The massive headache that got me into this mess was gone!

"No, no . . ." I mumbled.

Someone shoved my handbag under a strapped arm, oddly prompting me to notice that my feet were bare. My shoes were missing. Where could they be? I wouldn't leave without my shoes! Speech was virtually impossible, with my jaw and neck padded and stuffed and strapped, but my grunts caught someone's attention.

"Shoes," I mumbled. "Where are my shoes?"

The one with blue eyes stared, concentrating, and then, as understanding dawned, he flashed a smile. God, he was young!

"Nobody took your shoes, ma'am. The shoes always come off. It's the muscles contracting real tight does it. Got 'em right here."

Puffy white clouds were spinning, twirling dizzily above my head, and I closed my eyes again, as they raised the stretcher, locked the legs in place, and rolled me to the waiting ambulance. Pain shot through my back again.

The stretcher was hard and so narrow

I expected to roll off as we bumped across the street. But then, maybe most accident victims didn't notice the discomfort. I was hoisted into the ambulance, tipped so far backward that the reason for all the belts became nauseatingly clear. I tried to settle my bones as the doors slammed shut, but my head began to spin, and pain clamored from somewhere else, so I rigidly held the same uncomfortable position.

Blue-eyes was on a walkie-talkie speaking to the hospital. ". . . female, Caucasian, thirty-nine-ish!" He raised enquiring eyebrows and grinned, trying to coax a smile from me . . . Oh, he was cute!

We rolled away with sirens shrieking. Brian would love this, I thought, and I was out again before we had gone half a block.

Stuart saved the newspaper clipping. They even had a picture! Some damned creep in that crowd had taken a picture of me unconscious on the street—it was horrible! According to the article, I had "stepped unheedingly from the curb directly into the path of" what was purported to be the most cautious, careful driver on earth! The article went on to inform all and sundry that "Ms. Walsh, a woman in her late forties (!) had been taken to Union Hospital, and had not sustained grave injury."

Ms. Walsh was, however, "the third victim of an auto-pedestrian collision at this particular crosswalk within the past two months," and the paper went on to editorialize that something would have to be done to make these pedestrian walkways safer . . .

Automobile accidents are a bloody mess, and mine was no exception. I was released from the hospital after three days of exhausting rounds of X-rays, cat scans, twistings and probings by people in white jackets.

I was ugly, black and blue and yellow where the bruises were beginning to show. Thanks to a separated shoulder, I couldn't use my left arm at all, and it was strapped to my chest, completely immobilized . . . for weeks. The bones that had been broken in my leg would mend eventually, and my left hip was badly bruised, but not broken. I was very lucky, but I didn't give a damn. I was too dizzy, and hurt too much, to appreciate that.

Physical therapy was recommended to reduce joint stiffness and prevent permanent disability. But that was for later. Meanwhile, I had to lie around doing nothing.

My head and face were straight out of a horror movie. I cried the first time I looked into a mirror. Scratched, bruised, puffed up beyond recognition, I don't know how anyone else could stand to look at me. I was sentenced to bed for a week because of the concussion, then paroled to the house, first floor only, with a minimum of activity, for the next three.

Time hung heavy on my hands. Vertigo made my head spin, while bright lights flashed and little black spots danced in my vision. My mind refused to focus. It was ironic—for most of my life I wanted more time to read, and now that I had all the time in the world, I couldn't get interested in anything. I had three books going; one was a historical novel, another was science fiction, and something from Ellen that was full of raunchy sexy stuff. Not one of them suited me. My frame of mind bordered on suicidal. If I hadn't felt so crappy, I'm sure I would have appreciated the fact that I hadn't had a headache since the accident.

Staring at the walls in my bedroom, I counted the repeat of the large blue flower as it marched across the wall—fifteen times. Next I picked out all the little acorn-looking things, but soon I ran out of the pitiful amount of energy that required, and I fell asleep.

I was taking drugs; anti-this and anti-that, and they made me dopey. Time lost continuity, and hours passed unnoticed. I would fall asleep, not knowing when I woke up if I had had a nap or slept through the night. People moved in a dream, thoughts drifted like cobwebs in my mind, disjointed and meaningless. After four days I had my first coherent thought. I was hungry!

But when Kelley found something for me and put it on a plate I lost interest in it. My only consolation was that I was losing weight. Dopey me! All I had to do was get hit by a car! Why hadn't I thought of that sooner!

I napped, and thought about life, and stuff.

I played a little game I called "What if!"

What if I were rich?

What if I had stayed single?

What if I were dead!

This frightening thought began about a week after the accident. I'd fall into an uncomfortable sleep, get struck by the car, fly through the air, hit the pavement, and be dead . . . everlastingly dead.

The dream was clear and final, and I'd wake up in a sweat, filled with dread and afraid to go back to sleep. I'd waken Stuart, too terrified to face the dark alone. He wasn't much help; he'd pat my arm in his sleep, but he provided a barrier between me and the nightmare, and it was better than being alone.

It bothered him to see me lying around, bruised and broken. He didn't say much, but he would come into the bedroom and sit on the edge of the bed, smiling his crooked smile, looking at me with eyes filled with love and pity. I found it annoying.

"I might have lost you," he'd say. "What would I do without you?"

Your own laundry, I'd think, for a start!

Ellen sent flowers, prepared meals, came by to chat, and was treated to my convalescent bitchiness. Among other things, she learned that I wasn't exactly satisfied with my life.

"I've had all this time to think, and I realize Stuart and I have nothing in common," I complained. "We don't communicate unless it's about the budget or the kids. We probably would have been bored to tears in Bermuda."

Conversely, now that we couldn't go to Bermuda, I saw it as a golden opportunity missed, the chance to solve our problems.

"Of course, in Bermuda, alone in a hotel, away from the kids . . .

"Ellen, I'm forty-six years old. I'm not an old lady, and I'm not having any fun. Stuart has no idea how boring our life is! I didn't really notice myself until I was forced to lie here counting the damned flowers on this ugly wallpaper!"

Ellen listened patiently, and wisely counseled that I should get through this recovery period before I rushed out to look for a divorce lawyer.

"You'll make a better catch when you look less like a rainbow and can walk without stumbling. Stuart deserves a medal for not running when he gazes on this lovely face," she joked.

Of course she was right, but lying around was dull, and I had too much time to feel sorry for myself. The longer I lay around the more convinced I became that my ennui went deeper than the boredom of waiting to mend.

What did I really want? I wanted things to be different. I couldn't define it any more clearly.

I had dreams. In just a couple of months I'd be seeing Richard, and there were times I could barely breathe around the swell of anticipation in my chest. My heart thudded and pounded as though he were there with me, the handsome young man of twenty-five years ago.

Compared to my imaginary Richard, Paul Newman would have fallen short, and poor Stuart didn't stand a chance. Looking at him sitting across the room watching the news, or reading the *Wall Street Journal,* this quiet man with bifocals and thinning hair, and dark pouches under his eyes, I'd feel disillusioned, as though I had been tricked.

Depressed, inactivity both the breeding ground and the perfect shelter for my unhappiness, I retreated into a shell, uncommunicative and morose. "No, Stuart, I don't feel like talking right now. I think I'll sleep for a while." What was there to say? Stuart, leave me alone, I don't love you any more?

But when I recovered, life would be different, I vowed. I had wasted enough of it, and now that I had seen the dark face of death I was going to make the most of the time I had left.

Stuart withdrew, and I had no inkling that he was eating his heart out. He consulted with Doctor Fagan, the neurologist, who said depression was common after the kind of shock I'd had, but Stuart was not to worry; he was keeping close tabs on me.

Apparently trying to follow this advice, I heard Stuart tell Lorraine he was trying not to hover, giving me all the time and space I needed to get better. It was a bad combination: my inborn inability to see things from any perspective other than my own, aggravated by pain and discomfort, and Stuart's reluctance to pry or to put his own fears into words. Inevitably, we grew further apart.

Fourteen

Mother came to visit for a few days, spreading cheer and dust as she whipped through the house, tidying for me. She had come to help me after both Kelley and Brian were born, and each time she had spent most of her day cleaning and dusting. Maybe it's fun to clean other people's houses, I thought, new dirt in new nooks and crannies to discover. Well, whatever turned her on.

I came into the kitchen one morning to find her rump sticking out of the refrigerator, jars and containers of jam and salad dressing all lined up on the floor, ready to be returned to their rightful spot after she had polished them, no doubt.

"Mom, what on earth are you doing?

I didn't want you to get into housecleaning. The house is fine, now that the kids do their share. I wanted to sit and talk with you. I'm lonesome up there in my room; it feels like a prison. Stop that stuff and talk to me!"

"Oh, Andrea, I'm sorry for making you feel left out. But when I put the ketchup back in the fridge this morning it looked like the shelves could use a little spiffing up."

She had no business in the fridge: I never keep the ketchup in there—the damn stuff is obstinate enough at room temperature.

"The fridge is fine, Mom. Forget it for a while."

"Sit, Andrea, sit right there . . . when I put these few jars back in their places we'll have a nice cup of tea."

Yes, in my mother's refrigerator jars had their own assigned spaces, and woe to the one who put the horseradish in the wrong spot! She had many other idiosyncrasies, which I refused to dwell on at the moment, but one of her quirks was that she never drank coffee after nine in the morning. I filled the kettle with water for tea and set it on the burner to heat.

I almost tripped over her as I took two cups out of the cabinet, but eventually I got the tea things together and she got up off her knees long enough to sit with me.

"So, I guess you're feeling better, coming down cranky like this. Just like when you were a little girl, whining in your room when you had a fever and had to stay in bed. Mamma, come read to me . . . color with me . . . sing to me . . . I couldn't get my housework done then, either. Your face looks better today."

"Yeah, I looked at my face in the bathroom mirror. It's a different color every day but I don't really care about that—this dizziness bothers me too much. Right now, as I sit here, you and the room are spinning around me . . . I feel like I'm on the ferris wheel."

"Or the Turkish Twist," interjected my mom.

"What's that?"

"A ride . . . they used to have them at the carnivals. People stand around the sides of a big round cage, like a big hamster wheel lying on its side, and it spins. There are handles to pass your arms through, and when it gets going really fast the floor disappears and you are left standing on nothing . . ."

"I don't remember anything like that. Does this thing go up and down, or tilt?"

"No, it sits there and spins around, and when the floor disappears you are pressed against the side by . . . by . . . you know, that fancy word for squashed!"

"Centrifugal force. That's how the washer spins your clothes almost dry, and you find everything all flat and tight against the drum."

She didn't care about the washer, she was pursuing thoughts of her own.

"Your father took me to the carnival, in Springfield, when we were courting. I remember the first time like it was yesterday . . . ah, it was special. It was magic."

Her eyes glowed with happiness as she searched her memory.

"The lights, they were everywhere, on the booths in the midway, and outlining the ferris wheel . . . up on the roller coaster. And the music—every ride played a different song. We stopped to play some of the games in the midway, throwing dimes into saucers, hitting little metal ducks at the shooting gallery. Your father bowled and bowled until he won the biggest blue teddy bear for me—we must have been there for an hour! Then he had to borrow money from me to buy cotton candy!

"We rode on the salt 'n' pepper shakers . . . I don't think they have those any more, either—I threw up in the bushes when we came out. We went to the Tunnel of Love . . . Leo asked me to marry him . . ."

"In the Tunnel of Love! Mom, that's incredible! How romantic! I bet you were thrilled!"

"No, I turned him down. We came out of the boat ride very unhappy."

"Why did you say no? I thought you were nuts about him right from the start."

"Oh, I had lots of reasons. We knew each other a long time, but we weren't going out very long, only a few months, and I thought maybe he was being kind, doing me a favor. Our families knew each other, he was a friend of my brother, and I thought . . . I thought maybe he knew . . . about me. I wasn't ready."

"Knew what about you, Mom?"

But she continued, not hearing, or ignoring my question.

"He said he wouldn't take no for an answer, and would just keep asking until I said yes. I said no in the Laugh in the Dark, and in the House of Mirrors. I refused him at the hot dog stand, and when he walked me home, I had to say no at the front door, too. My, he was persistent."

Again her thoughts turned inward, and she sat silently with a little smile on her lips for a few minutes. By no means a beauty, at this moment she looked quite pretty, and very young, her features softened with memory.

What was there to know? And what did she mean by "he was being kind"? I didn't remember how old she was when she married, but I know they got married young back then, especially in the Italian community. A girl who was unmarried at twenty-one was considered an old maid. I remember my grandmother having a fit because I was twenty-three and not yet taken! Who would want me when I was old and dried up?

"How old were you—" I began, but she didn't hear, and went on.

"And then he didn't ask any more. He came to visit, we sat on the swing, he took me dancing and we went to church together, we went for long walks . . . All through the spring and summer we were together, but still he didn't ask."

Shrewd old fox, Dad, I thought. "You wanted him to ask again?"

"Not at first, but as time went by and he was so quiet, I began to worry and wonder what was wrong with me, that he didn't talk about marriage. Was I wasting myself on this man? Did he think I was only for dancing, a party girl? I wasn't good enough to marry and have his children?"

She chuckled. "Finally I had waited for him long enough. In September it was, Labor Day weekend, we went to the amusement park for the last time before it closed for the season. We went back to the Tunnel of Love. And this time I asked him to marry me."

We laughed like children together. "What did he say?"

"He said, 'It's about time! I thought I would have to wait forever for you to ask!' "

"That's a great story, Mom. A wonderful memory. Did you ever regret asking him to marry you?"

"After I set my cap for him I never looked back. We have a wonderful life together. It's not easy—we don't have lots of money, and we can't buy the kinds of nice things that your father wishes he could give me. But I have him, and he is like a brick. He gave me a reason to live, and he makes me very happy.

"When you brought your Stuart home, the first time, I told your father, 'Leo,' I said, 'he is just the same as you, a man to depend on. He is the right man for our Andrea'. And was I right?"

I couldn't answer. I had a lump in my throat, and no words to express what I felt. My mood crashed in seconds from lighthearted and happy for my mother, to sour and depressed for myself. I'm glad someone is pleased with my choice, I thought. What did she see in Stuart that I was missing?

I stood up with cup and saucer in hand, walking to the dishwasher, but she took them from me, tut-tutting that I shouldn't be bending and doing housework. "Sit, sit—I'll take care of it."

"I guess I've been up too long, Mom, I've got a headache and I'm dizzy again. I think I'll go rest for a while."

Before I was halfway up the stairs she was back in the refrigerator, humming happily at her work, and I went to chew over my misery.

Stuart and Brian took my mother home on Sunday morning. She had stayed with me five days. The house sparkled and shone like never before, and we had enjoyed each other's company for a change. But this was long enough to be parted from her Leo. "He has eaten up everything I prepared for him. There won't be any sauce or meatballs left, and he doesn't think to get bread from the bakery for sandwiches. The hamper will be overflowing, and I can just picture my kitchen!" She rolled her eyes in mock horror, but there was one thing I knew for sure. Dad might not wash socks or cook meatballs, but he wouldn't dare leave her kitchen a mess!

She bustled off with Stuart, waving and blowing kisses from the car. I stood at the window, waving back enthusiastically, and heaved a sigh of relief. After almost a week of cheery bustle and orange juice first thing in the morning—freshly squeezed and sour (which she knew I hated but made for me anyway)—I looked forward to some quiet and solitude. Mom was happiest taking care of people, running things her own way, and as long as I was more or less helpless she was able to play her favorite role. For a change I appreciated all her help, whereas normally I would have resented her take-charge attitude, her good advice. Stuart says I'm like her. Stuart doesn't know what he's talking about.

The house was empty. No games on TV with the boys out, and Kelley had slept over at Sue's, so the house wasn't thumping with the muffled blast of heavy metal. I put on my favorite George Winston CD, dug out the P.D. James mystery that Ellen had brought over a few days before, and settled on the couch in the family room. With my feet up and two cushions behind me for comfort and support, I read almost twenty pages before I fell asleep.

When I woke up, the afghan was spread over my legs, and Kelley and Sue were whispering and giggling on the porch. They knew I was there, so I continued to lie there with my eyes closed, just in case I needed to be found asleep for some reason, and listened hard. I would never eavesdrop on my daughter on purpose, but I had no choice, lying here asleep and all . . .

"My mother would just die!" I heard her say.

Great! Did I really want to hear this?

"What did he say then?"

"He said . . . well, like, he smiled, and put his arm around my shoulder"—squeals of delight from Sue—"and he stared right into my eyes"—squeals from both of them—"and he goes, 'You keep getting into trouble. Guess I'll just have to take care of you from now on.' "

Heavy sighs. "Wow, too much!" offered Sue.

Who? Who was this person? Was I going to find out? Would I be happy when I did?

"Where did you go after work?"

Kelley had a job for the summer at TasteeTreet, the local ice cream spot. Maybe this was a boy she worked with?

"We stayed right there when we finished cleaning up. Mr. Kaplan let us have a frappé for nothing, and we sat outside at one of the picnic tables and talked for, like, ages!"

It was someone at work, so she had to be talking about Friday night, because last night, Saturday, they had gone to a party. I was enjoying myself immensely.

"Lucky for you he was there last night," said Sue, dashing my high spirits to the ground. What went on last night?

"It wasn't just luck . . . he wasn't invited, you know . . . I think he crashed the party just to see me."

Lots of ooohs and giggles, but the consensus seemed to be that he had indeed gone there only to see Kelley. *Who?*

"So, I guess he followed us outside? I was real happy to see him out there when that jerk started feeling me up! I was so drunk, I could hardly . . ."

I couldn't take any more. Groaning and creaking, I made a production of getting up from the couch and ambled slowly into the porch, rubbing my eyes.

"Hi, girls, how was the party?" I asked, in a voice thick and groggy from sleep.

"Oh great, Mrs. Walsh. Wasn't it, Kel?"

"Yeah, it was pretty good, nothing much to talk about though. Sue, let's get something to eat."

They wandered into the kitchen to raid the fridge, and I stared out at my garden, wondering if I was ever going to find out who saved my daughter from the clutches of some filthy Lothario. I'd like to thank him myself.

I didn't have long to wait; Kelley was dying to talk about her new love, and she did, as soon as Sue left.

His name was Phil. Philip Marsden. Sue's brother.

They had known each other forever, but recently she had noticed some subtle difference in his attitude toward her. He didn't treat her like his baby sister's friend any more.

"It all really started the morning he found me sitting on the front steps at his house. And wasn't that the luckiest thing! If he hadn't come out when he did, and stayed to talk to me . . . well!"

And the party clinched it, as I found

out after dragging a few details out of her. "It was at the Maxwells', so of course there was a lot of drinking going on . . ."

Of course there was? "Did you get drunk?"

"I usually only have a couple of beers, but everybody was talking about how good the punch tasted, so I tried some. After two glasses I felt strange, and then I heard a guy say it was doctored up with liquor, and soon after that things started getting out of hand. There were people jumping into the pool with all—or none—of their clothes on, and some weirdo was trying to talk me into stripping . . . no, I didn't," with a sigh at my anticipated shock, "and anyway, suddenly Phil showed up. He told the jerk that I was his girlfriend, and why didn't he go find someone else to bug!"

She smiled, starry-eyed. "He called me his girlfriend! Oh, Mom, isn't he perfect! He put his arm around me and made me feel terrific. It was kind of like having a big brother, but . . ." a shy smile . . . "it's a lot better than that."

"He's working at TasteeTreet too, at

least until he gets a real job. So I see him every day!"

She was really smitten, and since I only knew Phil by sight, I decided to make it a point to look him over carefully next time I saw him. As it turned out, my opportunity came later that very day, when he came to pick Kelley up. He had a quick smile, nice white teeth, dark wavy hair, a medium build, and brown eyes that looked her over hungrily—or did it just appear that way to me, her mother? They went off in his car, and I waved goodby, smiling, making a mental note to talk to that girl about protection, and soon.

Fifteen

I couldn't go to Kelley's prom, which depressed me so much that I was quite indignant when Stuart tried a little joke, accusing me of orchestrating the accident to get out of my duty.

"What did you pay the guy?" he asked, and at the sight of my long face, added, "And couldn't you give him enough to take care of us both?"

I laughed, a little, and he went without me, both of us agreeing that it would hardly set the appropriate tone for one of the chaperones to be wobbling around in circles like a drunk. A drunk who had been beaten up, at that!

I missed her graduation exercises for much the same reason; I wasn't up to explaining my condition to everyone there, and I didn't want to steal any limelight from the kids graduating. Better to stay home and hear about it all from Stuart and Brian. Kelley was bitterly disappointed that we had to shelve plans for her graduation party, but there was no possible way to put it together.

I missed out on Kelley's big day, I missed Brian's team winning the playoffs for their division, but I missed my classes most of all. The studies that had started with me out to prove something had begun to give me a personal dimension, an identity separate from Stuart and the kids. I was adding something to myself, and because of it I felt more real. It broke my heart when I called to cancel.

"We're very sorry about the accident, Ms. Walsh, and of course we'll refund a percentage of your course fee," said the sweet little voice on the phone, "but surely you'll be back next year for the second semester? We'll hold a space for you," she chirped.

"Yes, that's probably what I'll do," I answered, "I'll let you know." But would I go back? Now that the pattern was broken, I wasn't sure it was in me to try it again.

* * *

"That was the best steak I ever ate!"

"Brian, you say that every time we barbecue," said his father.

"But it was great! Thanks a lot!" he repeated with relish. Stuart and I added our thanks to Brian's compliment. We were sitting with Kevin and Ellen on their backyard patio, finishing dessert, thinking about digesting our meal.

"C'mon, Dad, you said we'd play volleyball!"

Kevin and Stuart rose, grunting and groaning, and followed the boys across the yard.

"Glad I'm not anyone's dad," said Ellen, as she began to clear away the debris of our meal. "Go and park yourself in the shade. I'll bring out a couple of wine coolers."

I hobbled over to one of the deck chairs by the pool, twisting in my seat to absorb the sight and sound of the noisy game, the scent of the roses in the garden, the lingering smell of barbecue spices in the air. A Saturday afternoon in June, and now the last warm golden sunbeams danced and sparkled on the water in the pool. Each sensation registered clearly, separately, and a rush of happiness filled me as I thought of how lucky I was to enjoy all this.

It had been almost two months since the accident, and things were definitely looking up. I didn't lose my balance as often, and the constant vertigo was less intense though my eyes never quite focused clearly on anything. The ugly bruises were fading, and I could go out in public with people wondering only if someone had blackened my eye, not thoroughly beaten me up.

I was driving again, excited as a sixteen-year-old behind the wheel. Nothing exciting, just to the hospital for checkups, the chiropractor for what he called "adjustments". But it was good therapy. I felt less isolated, part of the living world. I was very cautious, keeping to myself the violent bouts of vertigo when the world spun out of control, driving only along familiar streets, stopping the car when I became nauseated.

I still tired easily, and household chores were impossible at present (and with luck unto eternity) but life was more or less normal. I was more interested in other people, and concentrated less on internal aches and pains.

"Made any plans for the summer?" Ellen asked, handing me a frosty glass as she settled into the deck chair beside me.

"Nothing definite yet, but it looks like I'll be allowed to get away from the doctors for a week or so. How about you?"

"We're going to Disneyworld to suffer the heat and humidity of Florida in July. What we do for our kids!" Jeff, their younger son, had never been there and they were going to treat him to its wonders. We went north every summer, where the relatively cool air and lower humidity made a pleasant change.

"Stuart wants to go to Vermont, or one of the lakes in upstate New York. Maybe by the end of August I'll be able to go a whole week without therapy. I'll test my travelability in July, when we go to Oakville for my reunion."

"You're still going, in your condition?"

"Why not? It's not like I'm in a wheelchair. I'm improving daily, and I really don't want to miss the fun."

"And Stuart will be there." A statement, as though I needed a keeper.

"He's driving me nuts! Since the accident he hovers over me, like something might happen if he's not watching. So yeah, I suppose he'll go."

"You don't sound too thrilled."

"I'm getting around just fine on my own. Stuart has never gone to his own reunions, high school or college—he hates parties like that! He doesn't know any of those people, he'll be left out, and I'll be stuck introducing him all night."

"Wow! Have I struck a nerve! Afraid he'll cramp your style?"

I forced a grin. "Ellen, you are so amusing!" I said, taking a sip of my drink. She was just being funny, wasn't she?

"Planning to misbehave?" she persisted.

"Out with it, El. What are you trying to say?" I had nothing to hide. All I had to do was stay cool and say nothing.

"Of course it's none of my business, Andrea, and you shut me up last time I hinted at this, but whenever you talk about this reunion, you get all dreamy-eyed, like there's someone you're anxious to see. Am I right?"

"I guess so," I mumbled, demonstrating my ability to keep my lips sealed.

"Someone Stuart doesn't even know about?"

"Well . . ."

"This can only be an old flame—look at you blush! I knew it! You've been so uptight—are you afraid for them to meet, or are you afraid to meet him yourself?"

"Afraid?" No, just wildly excited. "Ellen, I think you're reading more into this than there really . . ."

"Do you think you still love him?"

It landed with a thud, the very question I'd been running away from for months.

"Oh God, El, I don't know. I'm so confused. I haven't thought about him in years, though I *do* dream about him once in a while—isn't that weird? Anyway, I broke up with him long before I met Stuart, but lately I've been imagining—since I heard about the reunion I haven't been able to get him out of my mind."

It was impossible to speak of my wild fantasies—the passionate kisses, then making love with him . . .

"Imagining?" she asked softly, honing in on my dilemma.

"Oh, imagining things like—like having him around instead of Stuart. What would my life have been like? More exciting, I think. I must be nuts!"

"Don't be silly! With your reunion coming up he's on your mind, and when you aren't happy,"—I looked at her sharply, but she went on, "when things aren't going right, the old times always seem better. I'll bet some of this is middle age—pardon me!" she added as I grimaced. "You say you're bored after all these years with Stuart, and you think of the old boyfriend, who still looks terrific, which, by the way, is not surprising—he's still the handsome teenager you were in love with! Or maybe you never got over him, and you have residual feelings that you've never faced. Or maybe . . . oh, I don't know, there could be so many reasons . . ." she trailed off, and I must have looked stricken, because she went on. "Don't you think you should deal with this before you see him? If you need to talk, Andrea . . ."

She was anxious to help, but I was too confused and miserable. How could I tell anyone, even my closest friend, about my silly fantasies? In the blink of an eye I threw away the chance to share my confusion. "He wasn't really that important.

I'm just nervous. It's been such a long time since I've seen that crowd and I'm excited! That's all!"

Ellen gave a small, uncertain nod of her head, the look in her eye still questioning, her expression skeptical.

"Really, that's all it is!" I repeated, emphatically.

I nearly changed my mind about attending the reunion. Nobody wanted me to go.

The neurologist didn't recommend the drive, the alcohol, or the late hours, a bad combination for my scrambled brain.

"My husband will drive, Doctor Fagan. I promise not to drink, and I'll leave early!" I insisted.

The orthopedic surgeon and the chiropractor both frowned on the idea. "Motion is good for you, perhaps a walk around the block," said the surgeon, "but . . ."

"Dancing is out!" said the chiropractor!

I had to agree that a two hour drive might be uncomfortable, since my hip was still, as I admitted in the privacy of my mind, very painful.

"I'll take painkillers, I'll lie down in the car, I won't dance, whatever! But I'm going!"

Stuart tried to argue me out of it.

"How could a party with people you'll never see again be so important?" he demanded.

I tried to keep the hysteria out of my voice and answer reasonably. "I know it would be wiser for me to stay home, but there are people I liked so much in high school, people I haven't seen in years and years. I promise I'll take care of myself! I really want to go, Stu."

Behind my bravado and insistence I was scared. After all, if the experts frowned on it, maybe I should listen. But those worries were overshadowed by a far greater fear: this might be my last chance to see Richard again, and I wouldn't pass it up. I simply had to go!

Even with all this carrying on, I still didn't know if he'd even be there! Janice had given me Mike Baranoski's number in New Hampshire, but he'd been no help at all.

"Sorry, Andrea, he got his invitation

same as everyone else, but I guess he can't be bothered to answer. And he's not the only one, there's lotsa people like that. Jeez, it's tough trying to coordinate this thing."

"Is he married, Mike?" I breathed, surprised that he heard me over the rush of blood in my ears.

"Married? How the hell should I know! You think those guys from the North Shore bother to keep in touch with the likes of me! They're all too busy with their big careers."

I'd forgotten that Mike was one of the reverse snobs in the old days. He apparently had never overcome his childish jealousy. "Well, you've heard from me, and my husband and I are really looking forward to it. We'll see you soon, Mike. Bye now."

And I hung up, none the wiser.

Decisions and arrangements were made. In the end Stuart opted not to go, surprising me by deciding to stay home with Brian. "We'll get some yardwork done—right son? You don't mind, do you, Andrea?"

Did he really think I wanted him there? "I'll be fine, Stu. I'll have Mom, of course, and Janice'll be right there . . . Don't feel guilty. Really. I know how you hate these affairs. Stay."

Phil, still without a job, volunteered to be my chauffeur, so I could stretch out, and Kelley, of course, came along for the ride. We bundled into the car amid a flurry of hugs and kisses and warnings from Stuart to take it easy, to behave myself . . .

I stretched out in the back seat, grinning from ear to ear as Phil backed carefully down the drive. Stuart was already forgotten, anticipation a hard knot in my stomach, as I went out looking for trouble for the first time in my life.

I found it, and I've wondered a thousand times since then what my life would be now if I had stayed home.

Sixteen

The term "better half" annoys me, but as I walked alone through the panelled and thickly carpeted hallways of the Oakwood Country Club, I definitely missed my "other" half. The last time I was here was my wedding day. I'd never been to a dressy function without him, and tonight I was goosebumpy and cold, though the temperature was in the nineties. Nerves, of course.

Janice and Michael had offered to take me with them, but they had to be early since they were one of the couples orchestrating the event, and it seemed wiser for me to spend as little time on my feet as possible. So Phil drove me across the river from Mom and Dad's house, and I arranged for Janice to take me back.

In the lobby of the Ludlow Ballroom I saw a few middle aged people standing around, looking lost, and was suddenly overcome by dread: I didn't know them. Two couples standing in the doorway were the only other people around, and I didn't recognize them, either. I detoured into the ladies' room.

I had made a mistake; this was the wrong party. Nervous hands, cold and damp, twitched my skirt and patted my hair. Ellen and I had raided the stores in Boston, and I had found an outfit, something in aqua that she swore suited me well, and though I hadn't lost the anticipated thirty pounds, I was nineteen pounds lighter. I looked pretty good I thought as I checked my lipstick for the tenth time, then smiled mechanically and forced myself back out the door.

By the double walnut doors a table had been set out, covered with name tags lettered beautifully in calligraphy, but I didn't see a Walsh . . . it took a few seconds for me to realize that I'd skipped over the one proclaiming "My name is . . . Andrea Corelli." I picked it up with a chuckle. I had been Andrea Walsh for most of my life, and seeing my maiden name added to the unreality. I pinned it on, hoping it would help create the illusion of stepping back in time, and coaxed myself into the room, praying for a familiar face. There had to be someone here I knew!

My lips were dry, and I wondered if it would be gauche of me to go to the bar. What did women do with no husband to get their drinks?

Terror and excitement churned in a combination that made me want to throw up. I told myself to relax—it was just another party! But it wasn't the party. Faced with the possibility of seeing Richard, I hung on the edge of panic. I had discreetly glanced over the other name tags at the reception desk, and his was still there. It didn't tell me whether he'd be here or not . . . but he wasn't here yet.

Silly, I thought, building up this big fantasy thing. You're going to feel so stupid when he doesn't remember you, or turns out to be a bald, paunchy old coot, peering nearsightedly at your chest to read your name tag. I could just hear him. "Corelli? Seems vaguely familiar . . . were we in science together?"

Just have the good sense not to laugh out loud, I cautioned myself, if that's how it is. It would serve me right I thought, after all this idiotic daydreaming, if young Lochinvar turned out to be a wrinkled and stooped old man . . .

I looked around for a place to fit in. I should know just about everyone here. Our school had been very small, housed in a building built before the turn of the century, holding only about two hundred students in all. It closed the year after my graduation to merge with three other towns into a huge regional complex complete with an indoor Olympic-sized pool, gigantic cafeteria, track and playing fields with lights, an impressive media center. My sister Lorraine had gone to Central, along with about a thousand other kids, but I graduated in a class of fifty.

Mementoes, grouped and carefully labeled were displayed on long tables against one wall. Trophies and ribbons were scattered among photograph albums provided by classmates, and scads of pictures, including the class photo I had delivered to Janice that afternoon, were hung on the wall alongside banners and posters. I wandered over to get a closer look, hoping not to be observed as I fumbled in my evening bag for reading glasses.

Some things were so familiar! A copy of *The Voice* our school newspaper, where for one year my name had been proudly displayed as Senior Editor. Arrowheads and pottery shards dug up from the ancient Indian burial ground, discovered on school property when the septic tank was replaced, transported me back to the day the site was found. I remembered the reverence we felt for these ancient artifacts as they were dug up.

There were posters protesting the war in Vietnam, and several photographs of schoolmates killed there. Doug Rhinehart would never have the chance to go bald like his dad, I thought stupidly, finding his picture there. He had been dead all this time, and I didn't know. Though I hadn't seen him in thirty years I felt a sharp pang of loss.

I moved along slowly, my vision blurred, noticing some Kennedy memorabilia, saved all these years by politically active students, I guessed. Like most of the world, I had been totally enamored of John Kennedy and devastated by his senseless assassination, but had never thought to save or collect pictures or newspaper accounts of his death.

On the lighter side, displayed in a shadow box frame for all the world to see, were lacy panties—the panties that Steve Hoffman swore he had stolen from Darlene, his girlfriend, while she was wearing them! He had worn them like an armband on his shirt for a week. Why had he saved them all these years? Assuming he had married, I wondered how his wife felt about it. I laughed . . . Darlene would be so embarrassed! I couldn't wait to see her face when she saw her panties up there on the wall!

Memories, I began to realize, could be happy or sad, and both kinds were treasures.

Other things were totally unfamiliar, and I wandered down the length of the table trying to identify some of the items. Pinned to the wall were the words to the school song. I didn't remember any school song! Who wrote it? Who sang it? We didn't even have a Glee Club!

Someone called my name, smiling as she walked toward me. "Andrea?" I had no idea who she was, and panicked. I looked frantically around the room like a scared rabbit, and pretending that I had spotted someone I knew on the far side of the room, I waved, and escaped, the bar my ultimate goal. I really needed a drink now.

The room was filling up, and I squeezed between groups of people hugging and kissing, scanning faces for someone I recognized, furtively searching for one in particular, yet dreading the moment.

Rip Van Winkle felt like this, I thought, awakening from his long nap. Some faces were vaguely familiar, but had been transformed in an Alice in Wonderland way into older, padded, lined versions, with grey hair or dyed hair or no hair at all. Slowly some of the changes made by time began to fall away, like looking at someone's baby pictures, and here and there a face emerged that I recognized.

Now I had to give them names, and

terror struck again; my memory for names is appalling. I had so many embarrassing incidents on my record that my fear of drawing a blank was very real.

Maybe it was pent-up tension, or simply bad timing, but suddenly I was having an attack of vertigo, and I leaned against the wall while the room swooped and spun around me, totally out of sync with the merry-go-round whirling crazily inside my head. I was a veteran of such attacks now, and I closed my eyes, praying I wouldn't be sprawled out on the floor when it was over. I was pleased to find myself still on my feet, and waited a few minutes, panting and sweaty, while the haze slowly cleared. I badly needed to freshen up and headed gingerly for the ladies room. I never made it. Great hammy arms wrapped me from behind, and a gruff voice whispered in my ear "I been lookin' for ya all night!" Oh no, I thought, it can't be—it wasn't. It was Paul Grilli, football star and Romeo, who grew up around the corner from me and wasted a lot of time and effort writing me love letters. I still saw him once in a while when I visited my folks. I was thrilled to see him—someone I knew, at last.

"Paul, you big moose, you scared the pants off me." That remark drew the expected reaction, and turning in his grip I returned his hug. When I came up for air, I recognized a pair of bald guys as Frankie and Johnny Ruffino, and chuckled as always at what their mother had done to them. They looked like identical twins, though Frankie was a year older than Johnny. They'd always been pudgy, but now they were two round butterballs with big brown eyes buried in chubby faces shiny with perspiration. Still single, they told me, living together in the old house they'd grown up in. Momma and Pop were both gone, and they ran their father's paving business. I was smiling broadly now, feeling more and more a part of the scene. This was going to be fun!

Paul finally left my side when I begged him to get me a drink, and I had a minute to scan the crowded room. Still no sign of Richard, or the bald, fat person he might have become. People were finding old friends, and the noise level had picked up perceptibly.

At the center of an especially noisy group stood Janice's husband Mike, and I made him my next stop. He was surrounded by women, each trying to outdo the others with her giggling and flirting. God, I thought, some people never grow up! But he had been quite handsome in his day—he still was—and I was secretly pleased when he singled me out with a huge bearhug and a kiss.

A woman standing next to him was wearing a totally unsuitable dress, intricately ruffled and frilled, strained across her ample bosom, brilliantly printed with colorful pansies, or maybe anemones, the whole business topped off with streaked blonde hair and huge amber-tinted glasses with her initials in the bottom corner. I stared at her for a moment, waiting for something to click . . . and from this apparition slowly emerged the formerly dark-haired, formerly painfully thin, and surely formerly flat-chested Sharon Stevenson, her whole face a welcoming smile.

"Got a weed?" she asked. Squealing with laughter, we hugged each other. They . . . her chest . . . was . . . enormous! I couldn't help it; I commented on the change.

"Yup, had'em improved years ago, and never regretted it," she stated adamantly.

"Care to slip into the 'Girls' for a puff or two?" I asked. More shrieks when we discovered that neither of us had smoked in years! We were about to get down to the nitty gritty of thirty years passing, but a heavy-set man who had been standing nearby looked up and, wearing a huge grin of recognition, was now heading our way. I had no idea who he was.

"Oh God, Sharon, the guy coming over here, on my left, what's his name?" A whispered plea.

"How could you forget? That's Gordie McDonald." My mind filled in red hair and removed about eighty pounds, and I was looking at the best quarterback our school ever produced. Arms raised for the customary hug, I trilled, "Gordie! You haven't changed a bit!" grateful to Sharon for the tip. He bent forward to enfold me, and over his shoulder, at long last, I recognized Richard.

Frozen with my arms around a totally forgotten Gordie, while the rushing sound of silence filled my ears, and my stomach fluttered nervously.

He leaned against the wall, his arms folded across his chest, head tilted to one side, in a pose achingly familiar. He was paying close attention to someone I didn't recognize, but I sensed that he knew exactly where I was, though he hadn't even raised his eyes. Something in his expression, the exaggerated way he concentrated on her every word, clearly told me that. I can't explain it; I just knew him well.

Tan, lean, his hair still combed in the same style but magically frosted with silver, he was in profile to me, and looked wonderful. I had time to take all this in before he slowly raised his head and looked at me across the room . . . across the decades.

A smile spread over his face, touching his eyes, and the well-remembered glow began, like redhot coals in the embers of a fire. My heart swelled in my chest.

Demonstrating remarkable restraint I tuned in to Gordie, anchoring myself to his arm to keep from running over there and then. A pleasant smile of recognition would be sufficient, and I bared my teeth in a tight grin. *He's happy to see me!*

I continued to circulate, hugging and kissing and shrieking and smiling till I was tired. There were so many people to catch up on. Classmates were spread out across the country, some had gone to various cities in Canada. Some were married, others unmarried, still others once married. A few were little changed, others became clearer on closer investigation, and there were some I can't recall to this day ever having met before. I glanced at Richard a few times, to see if he had a woman attached to his arm, but I saw no one who might be his wife.

I finally caught up with Steve Hoffman, whose wife turned out to be Darlene after all. "We ran into each other at a wedding, about five years after we finished school, and something just clicked," Darlene said. They had married that same year.

"How about the underwear?"

"Not the originals, but we thought it would be really amusing." They thought correctly.

We turned the clock back thirty years, to a time of innocence and youth, an irresistible pleasure for anyone over forty. Time passed in a blur of renewed acquaintances, amusing anecdotes and laughter, for me verging on hysteria whenever I caught Richard's eye, acutely aware that he had been watching me.

An electrical current arced across the room between us, and I felt feverish with excitement. I kept him in my line of vision as I moved around the room, afraid to get close, yet inevitably drawn toward him.

We finally met in this strange dance. We shook hands, politely pleasant. I searched his eyes for hidden messages, then moved away quickly. Agitated, breathing unevenly, I acted like a young girl on her first date. Maybe that's what it was all about; he made me feel young again, a feat of no mean proportion! Or maybe not.

Denise DiSarro was there, but with a new husband. Louie had passed away after a heart attack a few years ago, but she had met Bernie, and was apparently very happy with him. There were tears—many of us hadn't known—and again I felt that queer sense of loss, as though something had been taken from me when I wasn't looking. My past, I thought.

There were a few couples who had married straight out of high school, growing into the rest of their lives together.

"Umm," said Pat, when I asked, "I never wanted anyone else, and Bill has never looked at another woman, and it's been that way for twenty-nine years." Lucky Bill, and lucky Pat, genuinely content, their pleasure in each other obvious to all. "There's nothing magic about it," she insisted, his arm draped comfortably around her shoulders. I wasn't so sure.

I scanned dozens of pictures of children, anxiously hoping to identify the proud parent in the child. "Oh, she's beautiful! She has your eyes!" I said again and again. Yet I was totally wired to his movements, sensing when he was near, absolutely certain that his eyes could see into my soul and the exquisite torment of confusion there.

Angela had two daughters, as slim and coolly attractive as their mother had been at that age, but she herself was a delightful surprise. She was still beautiful, though no longer slim, with short curly hair framing her face and a warm, vibrant personality that had emerged from the lacquered shell of assumed sophistication. Her husband was with her, and he was obviously responsible for the smile that never left her lips.

"Love is lovelier," she sang in my ear, "the second time around . . ." Falling in love with a new love had worked wonders for her, I mused. What was I doing, I chuckled, gathering data?

I found him in a group showing the inevitable photos, and I snagged the picture of his two beautiful children, while I smiled and wondered about their mother, his wife. We spoke, in stilted sentences, unwilling to bridge the gap from past to present. It was like nibbling at something, never really taking a good bite.

The sound of his voice was a warm caress, and when he spoke he leaned close to my ear. Was there really that much noise? Who cared! He leaned, I tingled; my mind brimming with salacious thoughts.

I didn't dare touch him, but I yearned to feel his lean body against mine. I knew precisely where I fit if he put his arms around me, held close against his chest, listening to his heart softly pounding. I knew the gentle strength of those arms, I knew where he was firm and I was soft, and I knew I was aroused like never before in my life. I could hardly breathe. His effect on me was wilder than even my fertile imagination could have dreamed up. Having sexual fantasies about a man I had not laid eyes on in almost twenty-five years! I think I looked normal, though I was practically drooling over him.

I had promised the doctors I would stay off my feet, but I hadn't counted on the pull of the music. The lure of the good old stuff was too much, and I shuffled around for a couple of slow dances.

First it was the Sonny James hit, "Young Love" that got me to my feet, dancing with Kenny Stephenson. His wife looked at me very oddly when I grabbed his hand and pulled him to the floor, but I'd had a crush on Kenny when that song was popular. He'd been in love with someone else, and I had adored from afar . . . I didn't bother to explain, I would have felt silly, but his arms holding me firmly for that dance made up for many months of teenage heartache.

Then it was the Everlys' sweet, innocent, "All I Have To Do Is Dream," because I couldn't refuse. Bob, the man who asked me to dance it with him, told me with a shy grin that he would have liked to ask me out, but I had Richard . . .

Dennis Monaghan, Irish brogue thick as ever, though he'd been in this country since the age of seven, sat with me for a while. Always an odd sort of guy, he had a very simple philosophy, he said. "I am what I am, and I don't pretend to be anything more than that. Look at these people, exchanging cards, boasting about how well they're doing. I'm just an ordinary fellow, with an ordinary life, an ordinary job."

"You're married, aren't you, Dennis?"

"Sure, and she's great, but she stayed home with the kiddies. I couldn't see dragging her all the way back here, showing her off like a trophy. Like I said, we're ordinary people."

Were they happy people, I wondered? I couldn't ask, it felt too much like prying. He sounded sincere, but this ordinary happy leprechaun routine didn't ring quite true. If he was acting, I was afraid to expose what might be beneath.

Mulling that over made me wonder if this whole show wasn't a kind of deception, all pretending to each other that we had flawless lives, our spouses and homes and children were beautiful, that our little worlds were perfect. In that case, did the dozen or so people who hadn't shown up have something to hide? Were their lives less than perfect, I mused? Were they afraid of our collective scrutiny? Would I have come if we lived in a slum and Stuart was a degenerate alcoholic? Probably not.

I drank a lot of water and Diet Coke, but not a single gin and tonic. I didn't need alcohol. I was drunk on nostalgia, sixteen again . . .

We smiled and posed for hundreds of pictures before dinner was finally served. I sat down starving, but I couldn't eat a bite.

Richard had chosen a seat two tables away, and he watched me over Judy McMorrow's shoulder, smiling his enigmatic smile. His attraction was magnetic, and I watched him back, blushing and grinning like a fool, ignoring the lively conversation at my table. I felt overwhelmed with emotion, as transparent and easy to read as a book.

Maybe it was infatuation, the magical illusion of youth, the memory of love. Had I been transported back in time, among all these now-familiar faces, eighteen again? Whatever the reason, it didn't matter. Long before dinner was over, I had fallen helplessly in love with him. Again.

After dinner, before the serious partying began, I wandered over to the wall to see if there were any photographs of us together. I wanted to recapture those memories, take them home with me and treasure them. Quite acceptable, given this mood of nostalgia, or idiocy.

I came to an array of pictures entitled "Olympic Ski Team" and paused to flip through them casually, surreptitiously searching, when his voice at my shoulder said, "Here we are. Here's the one you're looking for." With a flourish he pulled a picture from his breast pocket, the same shot of us at the ski hill that I had at home, and he grinned wickedly.

"Are we going to circle around each other all evening? I came tonight only to see you, and I won't leave without talking to you. Come, sit with me over there, away from this crowd."

I nodded, unable to trust my voice. At last. He took my hand and led me to a couple of chairs in a quiet corner. He immediately set the tone for our intimate chat.

"Do you have a dog?"

I burst out laughing, breaking the tension.

"Well, yes! A sheepdog. Moses. Why do you ask?"

"You used to say you wanted a big furry mutt. I guess you have one."

"What a memory!"

"I remember everything about you."

I glanced up sharply, but if there was special significance in the words it didn't show in his expression. I was keyed up, hearing things that weren't there. Relax, Andrea! Chill out! I would die of embarrassment if he saw the effect he was having on me. I took a deep breath and went into a long story about Moses.

"Do you have any pets?"

"No, my wife thinks dogs are too much trouble, too messy, and the girls are allergic to cats. We have tropical fish." We discussed his fish.

"Tell me about your work." He laughed, a wry chuckle, "I can answer questions as long as you're willing to sit and listen. There's nothing much to tell, really. I have my own software company, called TechTron. Small but solvent."

"Quite an accomplishment," I said, prompted by the pride in his voice.

"The hours are long, but the money is worth it. On the whole my life is good, I guess, though I've always regretted . . . no, I can see that makes you uncomfortable." He stared at me searchingly, then, thankfully, changed direction.

"Now, tell me about yourself. What kind of law do you practice? You always talked about law school . . ."

How did he remember these things? I couldn't even remember his birthday.

"No, I never went to law school. I was a legal secretary until I had the children though I finally got close last fall—I started a paralegal course, but the accident stopped me in the middle of it."

"You'll get back to it. Nothing keeps you down for very long."

"What makes you think you know so much about me?"

"The same instinct that you have about me. I understand how your mind works. At this moment, I know you are feeling a very strong attraction to me. We are like magnets, Andrea. I think of you often . . . I don't say that to frighten you—I just wanted you to know."

He thought about me often. I had to ask him the question that had been burning inside me for months, and I plugged the gap in our conversation cleverly with "You have beautiful children—is your wife here?"

He paused to phrase his answer, just the way he used to.

"No, she didn't want to trail around behind me meeting people she doesn't know, has nothing in common with, and won't ever see again. My wife is not very sociable, and we don't go out together very often. She divides her time between the business and the kids."

He gave me a rueful smile, inviting sympathy, and I wondered if it was self-pity I heard behind the sarcasm in his voice. I smiled back, saying nothing, refusing to be sidetracked, though I must remember to ask about this business she had . . .

"She . . . we, uh, it's not a perfect union, Andrea. My wife has a very good head for business, she loves the children, and that about sums it up. She doesn't like to dance, parties bore her, she wouldn't know the difference between Mozart and the Beatles, and she has no *joie de vivre* . . . she's not at all like you." He stopped talking, and his eyes met mine. "She doesn't know anything about you, Andrea."

My heart lurched against my ribs, and I looked down, away from those probing eyes. *He had married someone just like Stuart, and they weren't happy either.*

After a long while I looked up, a fatal mistake. His smile was friendly, superficial, but shining deep in his eyes, unguarded and exposed, was love for me. It hit me with a certainty that was physical, and the question in my mouth died on my lips. He loved me! No matter the hurt, the passage of time, he still loved me! I was not imagining things. He loved me.

"Why did you marry her?" I almost whispered it.

"Why?" He gazed at the hanging streamers while he gathered his thoughts. "I was at a very low point in my life. I finally realized how much you meant to me, but when I went back home I heard you had run off and married. You didn't give me much time, my love."

Oh my God!

Again that wistful little smile. "She reminded me a little of you, not in looks, but enough to make her interesting enough to pursue."

There were so many things I wanted to say, but I settled for, "Did you love her?"

"No. No, I did not." No hesitation there, I noticed, chilled by the coldness in his voice.

"I finished school with a degree in electrical engineering and a great interest in mathematics. The computer industry was in its infancy in the sixties, and IBM was the leader. I went to New York and got a job as a computer analyst, putting both skills to work in a very satisfactory way. We were a dedicated and serious group, on the cutting edge of an exciting new science. All work, no time for fun. Do you know I lived in Manhattan for four years and was never inside Radio City Music Hall? Nightclubs like the Copacabana were all the rage, but they never made a penny off me. Computers, and the burgeoning software industry of the future, took up all my time. I dreamed that I would one day have my own company . . .

"Valerie had the same dream. She's a couple of years older than I, and one of the very few women working with us—not too many women interested in the intricacies of programming in the sixties. She was ambitious, we were excited about the same things, and talked for hours about how best to gather data to be converted into useful information. No diskettes then, everything was punched into cards and stored on huge reels of tape. She is very intelligent, with a quick mind for mathematics and logic.

"I wasn't a recluse. I went out with a few other women"—(No surprise there, I thought)—"but they just smiled uncomprehendingly when I talked about the things that interested me. Val absorbed and understood and made contributions of her own. She asked me to her apartment a few times for dinner, and, one thing leading to another, we . . . we . . ."

He seemed to be looking over pages of his past, and I let him ramble on, wholly engrossed in his story. He took a deep breath, then continued. "She became pregnant. I'll never forget her face when she told me. Triumphant, as though she had finally met a goal. She was twenty-nine, and as they say nowadays, her biological clock was ticking very loud! She had chosen me on the basis that any children we had would be both clever and good looking, and that was enough for her."

His eyes focused again, and several emotions crossed his face. Surprise, maybe, that he'd told me any of this, and relief that I knew . . . and once again, that wistful smile.

"My children are the best part of my life, and I love them dearly. Valerie is a founding partner in my company. Her money—her father's money, really—put us in business. We're a good team, but we don't love each other, Andrea."

He had this way of pronouncing my name, with a slightly foreign accent.

Aund . . . Aundray . . . I said it under my breath, over and over . . . but I still heard his next words, though they were whispered.

"I wish I had you in my life, Andrea."

I melted like butter . . . What romantic fool wouldn't? He missed me, he longed for me . . . this was better than anything I had ever dreamed. I didn't know what to do. Fighting the urge to reach out for him, I found my voice.

"Maybe we should join the others," I suggested, though I really wanted to stay here with him.

"Just one minute more. Please, Andrea."

"That sounds like old times at the Point, doesn't it?" We both laughed, my voice sounding shrill and artificial to my ear, but it served to break the tension between us.

"Not to change the subject, but what kind of car do you drive?" I asked, recalling his love for English sports cars.

"What else," he replied, with laughter in his voice, "but an old Austin Healey."

No surprise! The one he drove in the old days was barely roadworthy and definitely would have failed today's sticker system. It was dark green, with tan leather upholstery except where the stuffing was coming through holes in the seats. In that car, along with many other things, I learned to drive.

I remembered sundrenched fall days when we took the back roads out of town, lurching along rutted dirt roads to find a secluded spot, lunch forgotten, wrapped in each other's arms, enjoying the thrill of getting close to the edge. And as much as I thought I wanted him then, my desire was like a candle compared to the bonfire burning in me tonight!

I wanted this man, this oddly familiar stranger, to crush me to him, to kiss me, make passionate love to me until . . . ! Good Lord, what had come over me? I snapped back to the present.

"Sorry, what did you say?" The band was playing, and I leaned closer, pretending I couldn't hear, wanting to feel his breath on my neck. We talked on, weaving memories into the fabric of our lives. As our conversation became more animated, I began to punctuate words and phrases by touching his arm or his knee, resting my hand on his thigh, right next to mine . . . Good grief, I couldn't keep my hands off this guy! I wanted to feel the warmth of his body through his shirt . . .

"Let's dance!" I said, at last, unable to sit still any longer, pulling him out to the dance floor, where I could touch him, a legitimate reason to be in his arms. I had no idea what music was playing, and lucky for me, it was a slow dance. I prayed that my hip would behave for a few minutes, though I suppose it would have given me an excuse to cling to him.

The dance was disappointing after the intimacy of our conversation. We didn't fit together. He held me at arms' length, and we stayed rigidly apart. I've been more intimate with seventy-year-old uncles at weddings!

When the music ended, he chastely kissed my cheek. "Goodnight," he said, very gravely. "It was so good talking to you." The only thing missing was the bow! Turning quickly, he walked across the room and out of my life. Again.

No! It couldn't end like this! I had waited too long—we had so much to say. I started to follow him, but someone stopped me to ask about Lord knows what, saving me from embarrassing myself. I felt cheated. After the agony of months, waiting for this night, our time together had been incredibly short, and now it was over, he was gone. How could he just up and go? And why, why did it matter so much?

The night ended with pledges to keep in touch, old friends swearing never to lose track of each other again, exchanging phone numbers and addresses, vowing to call each other soon. I joined in, but the only one I wanted to keep in touch with was gone. Smiling, hugging, kissing, I went through the ritual, but I was hurting, and would hurt long after that night.

Seventeen

Back home I rambled on interminably about the reunion. I was excited, nostalgic, and talking concealed the confusion generated by my meeting with Richard. No one, not even Ellen, seemed to notice my agitation. Cool, composed, I cleverly handled Stuart's questions in a calm and confident manner.

"Did you have a good time?" he asked.

"It was okay," I answered. "You didn't miss much."

"Meet any high school sweethearts?"

"I had no sweethearts in high school, so there were none to meet." My heart thudded against my ribs, but I kept my turbulence well hidden.

"No boyfriend, at all, Andrea?" He peered into my face, as if to read the answer on my nose.

"I just said no, didn't I? God, you'd think I was lying!"

He turned away, apparently satisfied, and I exhaled at last. Stuart didn't bother me after that—in fact, he didn't express any interest at all. Kelley, fortunately, was a willing audience.

"This is Angela—I told you about her, remember? Some people just don't change. She's not thin any more, as you can see, but there's still something charming and attractive about her . . . and here's . . ."

I sent six rolls of film out to a rapid photo place, and when the pictures came back I pored over them, with Kelley, my faithful companion.

"Mom, this is a great one of you!" A picture with three men, Richard one of them, and I beamed like a fool. "Oh, Kelley, I take lousy pictures," I said, quickly shuffling that one to the bottom of the stack. She seemed fascinated, or was I too enraptured to let her get away? Out came the graduating class picture and I compared the old with the new.

Richard was in several photos, but when she asked about old boyfriends, I pointed out a few men in the crowded photos, passing over the one special face. Safely hidden in one group or another, he smiled out at me, and I hugged to myself the knowledge that he had been there only to see me. When I was alone, I took the pictures out and gazed at him to my heart's content.

Days became weeks, and dreaming no longer satisfied me. I had seen him, and touched him, and I wanted more. "If I don't see him again, I'll die!" echoed over and over in my mind. Just once, and then I'd know. Know what? I had no idea, but daily the conviction grew that seeing him again would make things right.

This grew into an urgent need, pushing all sane thoughts out of my head. I'd run our conversation through my mind, like a tape, embroidering shamelessly. Surely he said "You look wonderful to me," and not the mundane "You're looking good!" Our conversation took on a dreamlike quality, until I couldn't remember what had actually been said. I must have made things up, because he couldn't possibly have said he wanted me back in his life! In memory he reached for my hand, and held it tightly in his, though in reality I had taken his hand as he spoke, interrupting a graceful gesture so painfully familiar I had been compelled to stop it.

He was never out of my waking mind, and when I slept he dominated my dreams. The warmth of his smile, the gleam in his eye when he looked at me, the glances filled with love. I listened for that trace of French accent in other men's voices, and would have seduced on the spot the first man I heard with a voice like his.

He became an obsession.

Strangely enough, my accident was a blessing in disguise. People had become accustomed to my lapses in concentration when I had an attack of vertigo, when entire conversations were drowned out by the rushing sound of water running or a strong wind blowing in my ears. The worst of that was behind me, thank God, but the memory served me well, an iron-clad excuse to be far away whenever it suited me.

Meantime Stuart waited and watched. He talked to Ellen, a conversation she repeated to me much later, hoping to discover what was wrong with me.

"Andrea seems hard and brittle to me, like she'll crack if she relaxes. Have you noticed? Has she said anything to you?" he asked her.

Ellen, who had her own suspicions, kept them to herself. No, she said, she had noticed nothing strange lately.

"This behavior is not normal for her, Ellen—it's like an act. The doctor said to expect some temporary changes after the accident, but I think she's getting worse, not better. I'm worried about her. I want my Andrea back."

A plea guaranteed to pull the heartstrings, but when Ellen reported to me months later, he sounded weak and pathetic.

"Why didn't he come right out and ask me what was wrong? If he'd had the guts to bring it up, things might be different now!"

Poor Stuart, uncomfortable about prying into other people's privacy, had done his best.

"Everything okay, honey?"

"Sure, I'm fine. Why?"

"You look like you need cheering up. What do you say to dinner out tonight?"

Alone together? "I don't know,

Stu . . . I really don't feel . . ." My answer trailed into nothing, and he dropped the invitation.

"Feeling alright, sweetheart? Can I get you anything?"

Yuck, I thought, why is this man bugging me?

He even spoke to Lorraine, and when she asked me if anything was wrong I cleverly put her off with vague words about the nature of concussions.

Meantime, on the home front, life went on. Kelley was in love, she glowed with it, but I thought it was too soon for them to be so serious about each other, and Stuart agreed. They were talking about marriage, and she hadn't even started college yet!

"Phil might be perfectly suitable in five or six years," I shouted at her, "but you're too young to make a lifelong commitment. You're only eighteen years old!"

Like all parents, we wanted the best for Kelley. In four years she'd have a degree, earn some money, take the opportunity to travel a bit, be free for a while before settling down with children and laundry and not enough money to spend on herself.

"There's so much to do, so many places to see, honey," tried Stuart, more calmly. "A girl your age can do anything she wants, your life is just beginning. Indulge yourself, enjoy the freedom. These days don't come twice, you know."

"You can be a marine biologist," I added. "A lawyer, a doctor—you name it! But even if you don't want a career, don't settle for such a small piece of the dream. Not yet."

Kelley would be going away to school in September, in my opinion a ridiculous time to form a lasting relationship.

"You'll meet new people at school, not . . ." stopping her before she began ". . . not that I want to discourage your interest in Phil." That was a lie, of course I wanted to discourage their relationship! Phil, a senior at UMass School of Business, was already searching for a job, hard to find these days in the Boston area. If a tempting offer came his way, he said, he'd relocate. Suppose he moved somewhere else. Did this child intend to follow him?

"He seems perfect for you now, honey, and of course I want you to be happy, but . . ." How to warn her people that change, that comparison shopping would be wise, foolishly wanting some kind of guarantee that she would never feel trapped, or uncertain, thinking that waiting and looking around would prevent a mistake.

But my ideas were not my daughter's, and when it came to Phil, we disagreed.

"Mom, did you ever love anyone besides Dad?"

A humid Sunday afternoon in July, and I was in the kitchen making hamburger patties to barbecue for dinner. Kelley picked up a knife to slice onions and tomatoes—to help, and to talk.

Love certainly agrees with her, I thought, taking in the smiling face, her sparkling eyes. I figured she was comparing our marriage to her relationship with Phil, trying to imagine them twenty-two years down the road.

"Why?"

"Well, you two seem happy together.

Is Dad the only man you've ever loved? You know, the way I love Phil?"

I wondered how many there would be after Phil. But she was serious, and I wanted to be honest with her. She should be aware that first love sometimes is a testing ground, and things are not always as perfect as we want them to be.

"No, honey, he was not my first love. I once loved someone else, probably as much as you love Phil."

"Mom, don't get into that puppy love stuff!"

She must have been talking to her grandmother about Phil, because she was the only person I knew who used that term. Obviously it annoyed Kelley as much as it had me.

My mother made a point of belittling "first love," treating this emotional milestone as cute and childish. It made no sense to me, since she proudly said that she had married her first love, my father. Theirs was an example of first love that had lasted, but everyone else's was just puppy love. I would never understand my mother.

"I suppose Grandma has told you the story about the princess who kissed a whole bunch of frogs before finally finding her prince? I guess it was made up to comfort those poor girls whose first love affairs don't work out. Somewhere there is someone for you, if you keep looking! And they don't all work out, you know. Before I met your Dad, I was very much in love with someone else. I'm sure you think nothing will ever change or come between you and Phil. Maybe you'll be lucky, and your love will last. It wasn't like that for me."

"What happened?"

"I'm not sure if I can put my feelings clearly into words. I found it hard to understand myself, really."

Her eyes were bright with interest; mother had a "past"!

"We went together for almost five years—yes, it was a long time," answering her look of surprise. "During that time we had our share of arguments. You know the sort of thing. Nothing really important, but you don't speak to each other for a few days, and build up that delicious agony that makes making up so great!"

She grinned, understanding perfectly, and I went on.

"I broke up with him because he had been seeing other girls, and it was more than I could forgive. I didn't understand why at the time—I just knew I never wanted to see him again—but later I realized that it was about trust. I could never trust him completely after that."

She waited quietly, starting to slice a tomato, probably hoping for more.

"I thought I knew him, and when I found out I felt like a fool, but it was much more than that. I had trusted him to love me, and my trust was misplaced. It wasn't so much his actions, but my reaction, that changed everything."

"So you just dumped him? Wow, Mom, you were a tough cookie! I can't imagine never forgiving Phil for anything!"

"You can't imagine Phil doing anything to you that you can't forgive. Maybe someone else could have lived with it, but not me. I was certain of his love and fidelity, and when I found out it wasn't so, my world collapsed. I'm not explaining this very well, but if I couldn't trust him to love me, then I couldn't love him."

Back in the past, feeling the pain and humiliation again, wondering how I could have forgotten it all when I saw him again at that damned reunion. Twenty-five years of hurt, pouf! To cover my confusion, I changed course, adding brightly, "When I met your dad, I knew right from the start that I could rely on him to always be there for me."

"What was his name?"

"His name? Why?"

"I don't know. He just doesn't seem real without a name."

"Richard. His name was Richard Osborne," I answered with a heavy sigh, for the first time opening the door to my past just a crack. I never mentioned him after I left Oakville. Richard belonged to the past, and just saying his name would have brought him back to life. But now, since the reunion, he had moved into the present, and . . .

"Was he at your High School reunion?" She had to ask.

"No, he didn't show up," I had to lie.

I watched her pondering my heavy story. Mothers had no life before their children were born, and now hers had a secret love affair buried in the past.

"And you just stopped loving him? How?"

A question I had asked myself so many times during the long dark nights of desolate, hollow loneliness. How would I turn the love off?

"It took a while, but eventually I stopped loving him, yes. He had betrayed and hurt me, and I clung to that, forgetting the good times. Life goes on, and I got over him. I was very fortunate; I met Daddy, and you know the rest."

"But how do you know who to love, and trust?"

"I can't answer that, my dear, it's something you learn for yourself, part of the reason I feel so strongly that you and Phil should see other people—no, let me finish," heading off her objections before she got started.

"It isn't so much that I want you to go out with other people, but if you and Phil continue to see each other, get married, spend your lives together, you won't develop as an individual. Right now you're half of a pair, and quite pleased with the arrangement, but you're giving up your identity, the right to make your own choices. You give up the right to be independent, to make decisions on your own. Maybe it's because I'm older, but I think independence is something to value."

"But you, and your . . . Richard, you went out with him for four or five years!"

"Maybe that's why I'm against you and Phil being so serious. He wasn't right for me, and finding out after all that time was devastating. I guess I don't want you to face the same pain. Maybe you and Phil are a perfect match, but it isn't always that way, and I'd hate for you to wake up ten years down the road and wonder if there is more to life." Or twenty, I added to myself. "The happy bubbly feeling you get with Phil doesn't last forever, and when that fades, you're left with companionship and trust in each other. I was so lucky to find Stu—your dad. True, he isn't the most romantic soul on earth, but deep down . . ." I trailed away. Deep down, what? How did I know what he had buried inside? We never talked about love, maybe he was as bored as I was! Maybe—

"Mom?"

"Oh, I was just thinking . . . I was saying that deep down I know he loves me, and I guess that's what makes us such a good pair."

A lie? Not really, but I wasn't sure about things right now.

"Looks like we're all set here, thanks to your help. Go tell Dad to light the grill."

Long after dinner was over, as I sat on the screened porch watching fireflies darting around in the back yard, the questions, like tiny mice, came creeping back. I worried about Kelley being stuck for life with the wrong guy, yet after all these years I was worried about the same thing.

The tingling and bubbly feeling I remembered had been with Richard, never with Stuart! We were comfortable together, but lovers? Was our marriage a habit? Was I in love with him? Had I fallen out of love with him? Maybe we had never been right for each other. Was I really in love with Richard?

This was ridiculous! My marriage wasn't perfect, but after all these years I couldn't believe it was a mistake. Kelley's questions, her new love for Phil and that stupid reunion were bringing back old feelings I had long ago put behind me. But hiding something doesn't eliminate it, and apparently I had not exorcised Richard. Until a month ago, he had existed in the safety of dreams, where embroidering on the past added fantasy to the present, but my dreams were threatening to become reality.

I had to face it. It was time to start behaving like an adult, not a moonstruck teenager. If Stuart and I had problems, I would have to come to terms with them in reality, not in dreams.

Eighteen

It didn't rain for weeks, and the town put a ban on watering lawns. The grass dried up and turned brown, the flowers withered and fell, and though I illegally watered the vegetables every day, using empty milk gallons, they shriveled, and I gave up on a tomato crop. The air conditioning died one night, and it was ten days before someone could come to the house to fix it. Stifling hot days followed stuffy, airless nights when I suffered periods of vertigo so acute I couldn't lie down, but spent the night sitting up, with no escape in dreams for me. I was overtired and miserable. The kids got on each other's nerves, they got on my nerves, and when Stuart came home and tried to soothe frayed tempers, fresh from an air conditioned drive from his air conditioned office, he got on everybody's nerves!

July trickled into August, as it does, with no discernible change in the weather, and we were more than ready to get away by the end of the month, though by then no one was talking to anyone else.

We drove to Lake George, a beautiful mountain resort in New York, for a week. We had spent several vacations there, and never failed to have a good time. I was exhausted when we finally arrived. It was the heat, I thought, and hours of packing and loading the wagon, the discomfort of the long drive . . . and something more. With Kelley going away to college in the fall, our time together as a family was coming to an end. Fragile ties, perhaps our last vacation together, and I vowed to make it special. It was special, all right.

Ten minutes after we checked in, Brian was checking out the parasailing schedule, Stuart was getting a starting time at the golf course, and Kelley was changed and ready to jump into the pool. So much for togetherness.

"I hate to leave you here alone, Mom. Are you sure you can't play tennis? We can lob the ball gently, give you a taste . . . "

"No, thanks anyway, sweetie, it would be just my luck to hurt myself, and then what would I tell the doctor! I'll take a short walk—I'm stiff after the long drive—and catch up with you at the pool."

"I'll walk with you then, and go for a swim later."

"You don't have to—" she was passing up the pool to take a walk with me, and I was refusing! "That's great!" I amended. Stupid woman. I picked up the cane I used for walking, and we went off together.

After a ten minute tramp through rolling meadows I needed a rest, and we took a path through the pine trees that led back to the condo. "There are the tennis courts," she said. "Maybe there's a bench where we can sit for a few minutes." We had walked another hundred feet when the trees thinned, and suddenly . . . "Mom, a pan-o-wamic vista!" We laughed, remembering when Brian, just a little guy, used that phrase to describe the view as we drove along the Interstate in New Hampshire. Stuart and I figured he learned it from Sesame Street.

We stood high above the lake, at the edge of a meadow, and spread out below us was nature at its magnificent best. The sky was clear, with a few puffy white clouds scattered around. Many miles to the north stood the Green Mountains of Vermont, gray in the distance, and the lake at our feet was completely surrounded by the Adirondacks, with ranks of dark, scented pines marching down the hill to meet the brilliant blue lake below, dotted with a multitude of islands, large and small.

One was so tiny there was room for only a single tall pine, with a tent pitched at its base. Others were quite large, and evidence of The Invasion of the Condo could be seen on one of the largest. Green barns of buildings sprawled in all directions, studded with Palladian windows and rows of balconies, the whole surrounded by yachts in their slips, tiny in the distance, like the lace edge on a doily.

"Gross!" was Kelley's comment.

My feeling too, but we could afford to be smugly disgusted only because the condominium complex where we were staying had the sense to hide in the pine forest overlooking the lake, not plunk right down in the middle of it.

We found a bench strategically placed to shut out the sight of the offensive mass.

Kelly sat hugging her knees to her chest, a wistful look on her pretty face. "Phil would love this. I wish he was here."

"Were," I corrected automatically.

Phil had found his first job, working as a clerk at a life insurance company in Boston. Their policy precluded vacation in the first three months, so he had no break this summer. "He'll be here for the weekend," I answered, sympathetically, I hoped. Now that she had brought his name into the conversation, and given me an opening, I thought it was the perfect time to have a "talk" with her.

"You and Phil are pretty serious, considering you're going away to college in a few weeks."

I had hoped she'd go off with no

strings, away from home and free as a bird, but she had different ideas.

"Mmmm, he's great. He's perfect for me."

As I saw it, close behind perfection came sex, and I wanted to address the subject, hoping I was not already too late.

"I thought we could have a heart-to-heart, you know, about . . . things. I know we've had this chat before," I went on, feeling the wall come up between us, "but they were more or less hypothetical discussions, and I think reality may be here."

"I know what you want to say, but we're not doing that."

I believed her. She had no reason to lie to me, but if they weren't doing "that" yet, they probably would be soon. I was positive I'd never hear her crying that Phil had tried to fondle her breasts or touch her against her will. Those days of innocence were gone, and protection, both from pregnancy and disease, was foremost in my mind."

"I just wanted to say that when you're ready, you can make an appointment with Dr. Wray, and talk to her about contraception."

Her face flushed with embarrassment, and her lovely gray eyes, inherited from her father, filled with hurt.

"Honey, I'm not prying into your life, but if there is going to be sex you have to be protected."

What a conversation! A mother urging the Pill on a girl who apparently didn't want it. But I wanted to make sure the barn door was closed before the horse got out! An old line of my mother's, one I had heard a hundred times though she would have locked me in a damned barn if she thought I was fooling around. I refused to pass this fear and guilt on to my daughter.

"I'm not judging, honey. I just want you to know you can talk to me anytime, about anything, okay?"

"Sure, Mom, I will . . . Let's go back—Dad will be looking for us." She skipped ahead, anxious to put some distance between us, and I followed along slowly, hopeful that I had done the right thing.

* * *

Toward the end of the week, Stuart took me out for dinner to a rustic log cabin restaurant he had spotted while fishing on the other side of the lake. Apparently Kelley and Brian had other plans, and we went alone.

"I thought the kids were coming with us," I said in the car, disappointed.

"Nope, they preferred the game room. Anyway, I wanted you all to myself for a change." He took my hand, and I let it sit, limp and unresponsive, in his palm. I wasn't comfortable with him any more, with thoughts of another man on my mind.

Our cozy little dinner was filled with long awkward silences and the conversation of strangers, but at last it was almost at an end. Stuart nibbled at his dessert, and I sipped my coffee.

"Aren't you ever going to tell me what's wrong with you, Andrea?" God, what a shock. I tried to conceal my surprise.

"Nothing, um, there's nothing wrong. Dinner was lovely, this is a really cute place, and I'm glad we came here."

"You know I don't mean tonight. You haven't been yourself for a long time."

"Oh, you know, since the accident, I don't always feel . . ."

"No, not the accident. This is different. Sometimes you seem edgy, restless, like you can't settle, or withdrawn and silent, not like you at all. You've started grinding your teeth again in your sleep."

I had done that many years ago—tension, the dentist said, and he'd made a special appliance for me to place between my teeth during the night. "Guess I'll have to break out the mouthguard again," I said, laughing.

"You don't seem very happy."

That neatly shot holes in my theory that I could hide from him.

"Do you want to talk?"

"What about? I really don't have anything on my mind." When in doubt, lie. "I'm disappointed that we didn't get away to Bermuda," I went on, trying for a diversion. "That accident spoiled a lot of plans."

"That bloody accident again. I'm disappointed too, it would have been nice, but that was last spring, and we can go next spring if we want to. We don't have to go away to be happy together," he said, "and we aren't. Happy, I mean."

"So you've noticed!" Sarcastic.

"Hard not to. We don't talk to each other, you don't tell me those stupid jokes you hear on the radio. The last time we made love was before you went away in July, almost two months, Andrea. A long time."

I had managed to put him off, blaming vertigo, my period, pain, discomfort, anything!

"There's something . . . you've changed somehow, and I think it all started with that reunion in Oakville. I hoped you would tell me about it."

"The high school reunion, Stuart? Oh, really, I think you're imagining . . ." I smiled, a grimace filled with false pity, the one I give the kids when they've said something utterly foolish, and ducked my head, sipping cold coffee. He settled the tab, and we went back to the car.

Driving back to the condo I blathered about dinner—wasn't it great we must go back there soon too bad we were leaving this weekend had he noticed the lovely herb wreaths and country things on the walls in the restaurant and oh look how pretty it is with the moonlight shining on the water!

Stuart maintained complete silence.

"Brian and Kelley must still be in the game room," I said, suddenly nervous, as I opened the door on the dark, empty unit.

With his arm around my waist, Stuart walked me into the dark living room, turning me toward him. "Let's make out," he invited, gently kissing my neck from behind, reaching around to unbutton my shirt, finding my breasts, his fingers teasing unresponsive nipples.

No! Oh God, no! I didn't want him to do that. I didn't want him to touch me—the thought of him inside me was revolting! He backed up and sat on the couch, pulling me down on top of him.

"The kids may come in any time," I hedged, but he laughed at my hesitation, his voice smothered as he bent forward to nuzzle the breast he held in his palm.

"Not until all the money I gave them runs out! We won't see those guys until we drag them back in here!"

"Stuart, I'm so dizzy suddenly, sitting down so fast, you know I still have these spells . . ." I slid from his lap to sit on the couch beside him, pulling my shirt tightly around me.

He stiffened, angry. "This is not about your accident. You don't want me to touch you, you don't want to make love!" He was shouting.

"Stuart, I . . ."

"Andrea," more quietly now, "I can't figure you out. I may not be the best of husbands, but you must know how much I love you. I can't stand to see you unhappy—no, don't turn away—you've lost the vitality that I love so much about you. You're sad and melancholy now, like when I first met you. Those beautiful eyes, dull and lifeless . . . all the sparkle's gone. Sweetheart, please talk to me."

I sat stiffly silent, caught up in amazement that he knew about my unhappiness so long ago. He seemed to notice a lot more about me than I thought.

"C'mon, honey, you can tell me anything that's bothering you. If it's you, I'll make it better. If it's me, I'll change. I can't stand to see you like this."

A good time, one might say, to try to communicate my unhappiness, share my troubles, but I couldn't find words for the feelings churning inside. The spectre of Richard loomed large in my mind . . .

he was here now, between me and Stuart. Talking might have cleared things up before the reunion, but now, telling could only make things worse. How could I possibly confide in Stuart when I didn't know how I felt myself? I couldn't even imagine his reaction. No, I thought, brilliantly! I can handle this alone.

"Stuart, it's nothing, really, you wouldn't understand."

. . . and passed up a perfect opportunity.

He'd had enough. He had twisted around on the couch until he was kneeling on the floor, and he rose from his knees beside me, an angry dark shadow standing rigid in the middle of the darkened room.

"You're right, I don't understand at all. You're shutting me out, building a barrier between us, pushing me away. I thought you loved me, trusted me to love you, care for you . . . Why are you doing this to me?" His shoulders slumped, then he turned, with a heavy sigh, and slowly went out the door, leaving me alone to cry in the darkness.

What was the matter with me? Of course I knew he loved me, cared for me, so why was I wallowing around in romantic dreams of someone else? Here was romance. What more could I possibly want? This quiet, thoughtful man loved me, asked nothing more than love in return, and I couldn't give it to him. Of course, I reasoned, he didn't know about Richard. If I told him, he might feel differently. Richard had been the cause of my unhappiness those many years ago, and Richard again was the reason for my present confusion and misery. I needed Stuart to help me, but I couldn't ask him. I'd been sucked into a whirlpool—and how was I ever going to get out?

Huddled in a tight knot in the dark room, I cried until I fell asleep.

Nineteen

The splendor of fall in New England had returned, in glorious, riotous color. Trees that had worn refreshing greens all summer now donned brilliant coats of scarlet and gold, while falling leaves created a bronze carpet. The dazzling reds and sparkling whites of summer's blooms changed to the rusty oranges and muted wines of chrysanthemums. The days were still warm, but were followed by cool, comfortable nights.

In most homes life returned to normal after summer's respite. School was back in session but Kelley, now a college freshman, had left the nest. Apparently she missed us as much as we did her, if we could believe the phone calls which came almost daily. That, I was assured by friends with older children, would change.

"Soon the only time you'll hear from her is when she needs money!"

"Stuart will have a heart attack over the phone bill first!" I would answer.

She must have been lonesome, because she and I had long conversations late at night, something new in our relationship. Of course, most of her conversation was about Phil, or college people I didn't know, but it was nice to hear her voice, to feel that she was becoming a friend. Alone now in a house of men, I missed her company. At night I waited for the sound of her key in the door, disappointed when I didn't hear it, realizing she wouldn't be home at all. Saturday nights just weren't the same any more.

She was still in love with Phil, his name in her mouth surrounded by hearts and flowers, her voice glowing when she spoke of him. She was very serious about him, and invited both her dad and me to pass judgment. She wanted our approval, but we preferred to keep this love affair low key.

"You're very young," Stuart warned her, "and in love for the very first time.

Sometimes feelings and circumstances change."

"There are so many new people out there for you to meet, honey, and though we like Phil . . ." I really had very little to say in view of the mess I was making of my life. What could I possibly say that was wise and motherly when I was behaving like a fool!

She was no longer a gawky high school girl, but a mature college woman. I wasn't sure if it was Phil's influence, but she had grown up a lot over the summer, settling nicely into the kind of groove we had hoped for her. She had come up with a desire to be a pharmacist—out of nowhere, I thought, since forever, she said. Anyway, it seemed she no longer butted her head against authority, she didn't do drugs, rarely attended campus keg parties unless Phil was there with her, and had very strong opinions on love, which she thought we should accept as those of an adult.

Phil was her life, with a little biology on the side. "You can't imagine how it feels to really, truly be in love with someone," she would crow, childishly. Smiling at her enthusiasm, I wished her happiness, and hoped things went as she wanted. As Stuart had said, things could change. No one knew this better than I, but everyone deserves the thrill and romance of her first love.

Brian, now a high school sophomore, was growing and changing in many respects, although still somewhat shy with adults. He had developed a strong, well-built body, with incredibly broad shoulders, and a wry, common sense view of life. His warm brown eyes shone with intelligence, and his delightful sense of humor kept us in stitches. Right now he wanted to become a lawyer, but we couldn't take him seriously; by next week he'd probably be interested in pathology!

He had a girlfriend, Kathy something-or-other, a bright, attractive girl with the tiniest waist I had ever seen. She hardly spoke to us, but they spent hours on the phone, and if the giggles coming from his room late at night were any indication, he enjoyed her company.

I spent more time at home. I hadn't worked all summer, and since Labor Day I went in three days a week. The house was very quiet with everyone away all day. For a while I enjoyed it, and accomplished more housework, read more books, and was able to visit the few friends who didn't work.

The summer crowd was finally gone from the park, and Moses and I returned to our long walks, free to wander anywhere we wished. He raced around, showing off, rolling in the leaves, splashing through the water, thoroughly pleased with his life.

I was not so carefree.

Richard was constantly on my mind. If I talked to him I might find out why, so long ago, he threw my love away, as though the answer might have some bearing on my life, or change my future.

Since the reunion the intervening years had disappeared, and I needed him to convince me that he loved me. Once I knew that, I thought, this heartache that I couldn't understand, that was driving me crazy, would stop. I wanted to see him.

Did he want to see me? Remembering the look in his eyes, I knew without a doubt that if my need was so great, his must be the same. The memory of his voice made me shiver, I had to hear it again. Relentlessly the desire to talk with him became a consuming need.

My obsession grew.

Did I consider my marriage? Not for a moment. I hid in daydreams. Fidelity, love, trust, had no place in this nightmare fantasy. I took no one into my confidence, certainly not Stuart, and still hesitated to pour all this out to Ellen. I was alone in this hell.

I began to imagine bumping into him on a street in town, or in a bar or restaurant, pretending the meeting was accidental. His company was called Tech-Tron, a name now etched into my brain, and it could easily be arranged. Tech-Tron was in Boston, right here, no more than twenty miles away. Not in Los Angeles, or halfway around the world.

Many people from Oakville lived in this area, and after the initial shock, I wasn't at all surprised that he was here. Oakville sits midway between Boston and New York, and the ambitious, the corporate-minded, gravitated to such large cosmopolitan centers. In the past twenty years, Boston had become a major center of computer technology. God, I thought, how could you do this to me! Of all the cities in all the world . . . !

I worked near home, in Marshfield, still a legal secretary. After I married Stuart it seemed silly to pursue my dream to become a lawyer. I remained with Markham, Markham and Doucette until Kelley was born, when we moved from the city to this beautiful coastal town near Plymouth. I stayed out of the workforce for the next twelve years, preferring to be at home with my children, able to make that choice thanks to Stuart's more than adequate income.

Later, when I wanted to rejoin the world outside, I was fortunate to find a job where I could use my old skills while learning the intricacies of the computerized world, and last fall had made the move to something new, taking a job working for Bob Murphy. Although out of the mainstream of the business world, my work was interesting, and the office was a convenient ten-minute drive from home. Just a few days ago my boss had called me into his office to ask how the paralegal course was coming along.

"Oh, I thought you knew, Bob—I had to drop out. My head was so messed up by the accident last spring that I couldn't concentrate."

"That's too bad, Andrea, we have a spot opening up with Hansbury leaving us, and her job might be just the thing for a fresh new legal mind."

"But I'd only be a paralegal . . ."

"That's enough, at least at the start . . . who knows how far you might want to go?"

"Well, I *had* planned to go back and finish . . . when is Leona leaving?"

"End of the year. You think about it, and get that course completed. We'll talk again in January."

If I needed incentive to sign up for the second semester, that was it. I promised to think about it. Meantime I had other things on my mind, like how glad I was not to be working in the city, near temptation.

Fortunately, we had settled in suburbs far apart. At the reunion I learned that he lived near Andover, an inconvenient drive of almost two hours from me, thank heaven! Imagining him living nearby sent me into convulsions, and only the distance kept me from driving over to check out his house.

A foolish notion, as silly as running into him downtown, but another idea took hold and spread like a disease: I didn't have to see him. I could phone him.

During the next few weeks my idea that everything would be resolved if I spoke to him became a certainty. Questions would be answered, my ridiculous yearning would fade away, life would settle into its stable old pattern and I would be content with what I had instead of churning constantly in this agony of indecision.

I had faced the issue at last and I was pleased that I had come up with a solution. One morning, after weeks of agonizing, I screwed up my courage and picked up the phone.

I made it easily past the receptionist, had no trouble at all with his secretary, but almost hung up when I heard his voice!

"Hello!" Firm, confident. Same old Richard.

I was tongue-tied.

"Richard Osborne here. Can I help you?"

". . . H-hello . . ." hesitantly, a great beginning.

"Who is this?"

". . . An old . . . um, a friend . . . I think . . . maybe you don't recognize me . . ." For some reason I was afraid to identify myself. What a start!

"And—of course I remember you. How may I help you?"

I remembered his voice as warm, mesmerizing, but he sounded remote, and cool. "I didn't want to bother you . . . I thought if you had a few minutes, we might talk . . ."

In the cold silence my stomach churned with the horrible nausea that comes whenever I'm nervous. I felt rebuffed and was quickly running out of courage. "Look," I said, "I'll go now. I'm sorry I—"

"Hold on a moment, please," he said.

A few muffled words, the sound of a door closing, and he was back.

"Sorry, I had someone in my office. Andrea, I can't believe it's you!" Now came the voice I remembered, pitched low, warm and intimate. "I've wanted to call you so many times, but I didn't think you would want to hear from me. I've imagined the sound of your voice a thousand times . . ."

"I shouldn't have called, it was a silly notion, really, but it seemed so important for me to talk to you! I'm really embarrassed," I said, anxious to get this over with, "I'll say goodbye now."

"No, oh no, Andrea, please don't hang up. I know exactly how you feel. That reunion brought back so many memories. Dancing with you, I was afraid to hold you—I wanted only to crush you in my arms . . . I had to get away quickly!"

That explained his abrupt departure. I didn't know if this news was good or bad, but my heart leaped and raced.

He seemed pleased to hear from me, when I had expected him to laugh at my foolish fantasy. He would have, I was sure, if this had been a figment of my fertile imagination, a romantic idea created out of boredom. Lucky me! This was much worse than I had envisioned.

"I thought talking to you might clear a few things up, resolve some confusion . . . I'm really sorry I bothered you, I'll just—!"

"How about lunch," he broke in. "Downtown."

See him again? Isn't that really what I wanted? "No! I, really, I couldn't . . ."

There were people in his office again, I heard voices in the background. "I'm about to start a meeting," he said, his voice cool again. "Glad you called. How is your schedule Thursday?"

No more waffling. "I can make Thursday. Okay. Yes. Thursday's fine."

We settled on a restaurant, and hung up. I had to be crazy! Insane joy filled me to bursting, and for the next couple of hours I vacuumed and cleaned house, washed and folded laundry, ran with Moses, trying to burn off this furious energy. Nothing worked, but one thing was certain by the end of the day; I'd have to juggle my schedule, but I'd make this lunch Thursday if I had to quit work to do it!

It was only Monday—three more endless days until Thursday. I'd be dead long before then.

If only I could tell Ellen, I thought, but how could I talk to anyone about this! I was acting like a lovesick cow, a total fool, and I knew just what her reaction would be. She'd tell me to act my age! Did I want to hear that? Absolutely not. So to hell with Ellen! I broke our lunch date Wednesday. On Tuesday I told them at work I had a dental appointment Thursday afternoon, and switched my days to Wednesday and Friday.

At night I lay awake next to Stuart, sleeping soundly, innocently unaware that his wife was having fantasies of another man. Fantasies! Slightly more than that, my dear. I had a date with a man I'd seen once in a quarter of a century! What a joke! In other circumstances, Stuart might have seen humor in the situation, put the whole mess into perspective.

I tried to figure out why I had called Richard, what I wanted from him. Hear his voice, I said, talk to him again. But I was lying, and I knew it. I wanted him to sweep me off my feet, to make passionate love to me. This notion was so crazy I laughed out loud, but there was a hysterical edge to the sound. I wanted him so badly I ached—I throbbed with it. The yearning had taken over my body and mind, and if something didn't happen soon, I'd lose my mind.

Why this great need for him? Objectively, I thought, as I lay listening to Stuart snore next to me, my marriage was boring. Life with Stuart held no passion, no surprises, no thrill. We made love once or twice a month. Maybe. In bed. In the dark. Recently even that ritual has been suspended. We were like strangers living in the same house.

So was this about thrills, a need for diversion? S-e-x? A middle-aged housewife's fantasy had come alive. How many forty-six year old women met an old flame who turned out to be better in the flesh than the fondest memory could possibly create? If that was it, I could easily stop this from going any further with a simple phone call. Tomorrow I'd call him and cancel lunch! This calmed my racing mind and heart, but once again, on the edge of sleep, the craving need in my body swelled, becoming a physical pain that I couldn't brush away, and I knew I wouldn't cancel.

The week slowly ground along, and by Wednesday morning I was knotted up so tight I could hardly swallow toast and coffee. I called in sick. I didn't give a damn. All day I lay around on the couch, the tragic heroine in a Victorian novel, alternating between nausea and erotic dreams.

Wednesday night Stuart surprised me by making half-hearted advances, but I turned away. I had enough on my mind without adding to the confusion and guilt. I wasn't ready to make peace with him. Since our fight in August we had a public truce, but in private I stayed far away from him. I didn't want to know how he felt, didn't care if he worried about me. I cut him off every time he approached me. He acted like a father, I brooded, not like a concerned lover. His patronizing attitude annoyed me, though once I had found it reassuring and depended on it.

We had established a bedtime pattern. I stayed over on my side of the king-sized bed, pretending to be asleep, and Stuart hauled out one of the huge volumes he kept by the bed, crawling between its pages, absorbing more knowledge.

At 3:30 Wednesday morning I had given up hope of ever falling asleep, but I must have, because I woke up Thursday morning feeling tired, haggard, and old. When Stuart left for work I took a long, hot shower, then spent over an hour on my face and my hair. After four cups of coffee and two hours of trying on just about every piece of clothing in my closet, I finally left the house wearing a white silk shirt and batik woven vest in golden autumn colors, a dark skirt, and flats, well-dressed on the outside but filled with quivering Jello.

It was a beautiful fall day, sunny and warm, trees wearing the reds and golds of early October, a promise of the incredible show of color to come. The drive into town, an easy forty-five minutes, had a calming effect on me, and by the time I parked the car and walked the half block to the restaurant, I was completely in control, a woman meeting an old friend for lunch.

Twenty

Soaring ceilings, hanging plants and potted trees, oak tables draped with dark green and rose chintz cloths. I had never eaten here, but I was willing to bet their salads would be fabulous, the portions would be small, and goat cheese and sun-dried tomatoes would be liberally sprinkled over anything I ordered.

I was early, hoping for a few minutes to get settled, but I saw him immediately as I entered, in a booth across the room, the cosmopolitan male, one arm draped casually over the back of the seat, suit jacket unbuttoned, looking over the lunch menu. I started to cross the floor inconspicuously, but hostesses in fine restaurants don't miss a trick. She cornered me as I tried to slink by, braying loudly, "May I show you to your table, Ma'am?"

At least thirty pairs of eyes turned towards me, and I flushed, hotly embarrassed.

"I'm meeting someone . . ." I said, trying to slip past her. "Oh, I see him," I said, softly, with my best smile, "over there by the wall," nodding in his general direction.

She consulted her book. "Ah yes, that will be Mr. Osborne's table. He's expecting you," she announced to the restaurant at large. Now everyone within shouting distance knew about this clandestine meeting, and would watch to see exactly where I was going. "Right this way."

With eyes glued to the floor I followed her across the dining room to his table. Finally looking up, I caught the gleam of amusement in his dark eyes, and burst into embarrassed giggles. "Brother, I'm surprised she didn't ask me for I.D.!" I settled into the seat, taking a moment to appreciate this vision seated across from me.

He really was an exceptionally handsome man, even in the light of day. Composed, a business man at lunch, impeccably dressed in a lightweight navy suit and crisp white shirt and a mottled print tie. He showed no signs of aging, except for the silvery sheen in his hair, which added a soft continental touch to his tanned, smooth skin. Andrea, I asked myself, how did you let this hunk get away!

Feeling flushed and overcome with shyness—or lust—I dragged my eyes away from him and looked across the room from the shelter of the booth, fully expecting people to be staring at me, grateful not to be seated at a table in the middle of the room. I wondered if it was coincidence that we were in a semidark booth against the wall, far away from the windows.

Glancing back, I caught him looking me over, his expression registering approval, and he smiled. "You look terrific!"

A warm glow spread through me, and with a casual "Thanks!" I shrugged off hours of agony over what to wear.

"Welcome to our little assignation!" The words were flip, but there was a nervous edge to his voice. "I've ordered a Bloody Mary. What would you like?"

"A Bloody Mary? Mmm, I'll have the same. It's my favorite lunchtime drink—all that tomato juice and celery you don't even notice the vodka. You can drink two or three . . ." Shut up, Andrea. Babbling idiot.

I wound down and sat quietly staring at the grillwork behind his head, waiting for my drink. Nervous, awkward, uncomfortable, fidgety, with violent cramps in the stomach, would have described my condition well. I had no experience to draw on in a situation like this, and didn't know how to act, or what to say.

Me, silenced? Impossible! I heard the chiding voices of my children, and felt a stab of what must be guilt. But not for long. Whatever happened here had nothing to do with my family or my life. There were no words to explain the inevitability of this day, this meeting, this lunch. I had been programmed, manipulated by an unseen force, and like a puppet incapable of independent thought, I followed a predestined course, unable to resist the flow of events.

* * *

Drinks were served.

"Beautiful day," he said.

"Mmm," I answered. "Lovely drive. Lots of color."

He sipped his drink.

Menus were placed before us.

"How's the food here?" I asked.

"Very good," he answered.

I sipped my drink.

Conversation was exhausted. We hid behind our menus for a while, studying in detail each and every entree on the list. Bonnie, our perky server today, took our orders, and attempted to flirt with him. His mouth curved into a smile and his eyes gleamed, fully aware of her attention. Easy to see what Bonnie found so attractive, and I marveled that I knew his expressions so well.

"I'll have the green salad, with pine nuts and sun-dried tomatoes, cracked peppercorn dressing on the side," I said, breaking the spell.

Richard ordered grilled chicken, a dish that perky young Bonnie described for him in detail.

"What can I say?" he said derisively,

raising an eyebrow, when she finally left. "I'm irresistible." We laughed, then dove back into our drinks, waiting quietly for our meals.

Looking up at the hanging ivy and maidenhair fern, I took the uncomfortable silence as a good sign. I couldn't think of a single thing to say.

Seen any good movies lately?

How's the wife? Not quite the ticket.

Exultation bubbled, and I congratulated myself. No way in hell I was getting into trouble today! This might even be quite boring, I thought, wondering if Brian had remembered his house key. I was thinking of home, and he was probably going over some program for a client. I relaxed a little, positive that no harm could come of this simple meal, and flashed him a bright smile when he ordered us both another drink.

Slowly the uncomfortable chill thawed. The long empty silences, my silly giggles, the bursts of nervous chatter dwindled and stopped.

"Remember the french fries?" he asked, and another bond reached out from the past. An afternoon, a lifetime ago, when we skipped school and sat for hours in a booth over french fries and Coke. Shared laughter, warm and close, pulled us together, and I began to respond to the tenderness in his smile with a sense of flirtatious abandon, and an old happiness filled my heart, finally bubbling over. He was charming, and I was comfortable now, but was I aware of the danger in his charm?

No.

Yes. Oh my, yes! But the danger increased his attraction, made him irresistible, drew me to him.

"God," I prayed, "give me the strength to get up and leave right now, because things are going to get out of hand."

I didn't move.

We passed on dessert, but I ordered iced coffee, perhaps a significant choice. I sipped my drink and studied the man sitting across the table for the first time in twenty-five years, a stranger with voice and mannerisms poignantly familiar, and imagined us in a warp of time, poised on the threshold of a love that wouldn't be spoiled again because we were so much wiser than our former selves.

A maroon leather folder was discreetly placed on the corner of the table, and he smiled. On the back of the bill was "See u soon, Bonnie," with a happy face in the "O" of Bonnie. Our eyes met, but I didn't laugh. Lunch had been delicious, expensive, and nostalgic, but it was over and we had to move on. To what? A spasm clutched the pit of my stomach, reminding me that this was not a game, but a very precarious situation, and I shivered.

With fear? Nerves? Not at all! It was excitement, that fluttering in the pit of your stomach like on a roller coaster, dangerous, scary, but too thrilling to pass up. Throughout lunch, behind the banter and talk of old times, buried under an occasional twinge of conscience, lurked an underlying thrill of anticipation, the unacknowledged hope that lunch would lead to something more. Gradually I understood that this expectation was why I had come, and what kept me rooted to my seat, hanging in suspense.

"Have you made any . . ."

"I should . . ."

". . . plans for this afternoon?" he asked, glancing at his watch.

". . . be leaving, to beat the rush," I said, glancing at my watch.

We spoke at the same time, and it took a few seconds for his question to filter through the fuzz in my head. He wasn't looking at me, staring instead at his crumpled napkin, as though it held the answer.

"Nothing specific," was my whispered reply.

My limbs were leaden, and an ominous nausea filled my stomach. Plans? Who could make plans? Would life go on after this lunch?

"I have nothing on my calendar this afternoon, and it's such a lovely day, how about a little walk . . . ?"

His question hung in the air. Okay, Andrea, this is when you say no, lots to do, thanks so much for the lovely lunch, but I really have to run along now. The perfect opportunity to touch him, hug him, kiss him goodbye even! And get away from him. Now!

Soon.

"Sure, a little walk would be great before the drive home," I heard myself say.

Stupid, stupid woman! Ignoring the warnings, pretending that this was perfectly normal, that we were only friends, and worse, imagining myself in control!

We stepped out into the brilliant sunshine, and in unspoken mutual agreement walked straight to his car. Holding the door open, he took my arm to guide me into the low slung sportscar, and I caught my breath, pulling away as though I had touched something very hot . . .

Settling into the bucket seats, busily adjusting safety belts, we said nothing, looking anywhere but at each other. I waited for him to start the car, and when nothing happened, almost against my will I turned to look at him. He was studying me, dark eyes soft with love, a half-smile on his face, and I turned my head away to stare numbly out the window.

Oh God, I'm drowning! But I'd lost the ability, and the desire, to save myself. *Que sera, sera,* I thought with a sigh.

With a muffled roar we drove wordlessly into the beauty of the autumn day. Reaching over, he touched my knee, and after the initial shock of his touch, I clutched his hand tightly, listening to the sound of my heart pounding, deafeningly loud in the silence of the car.

We drove apparently without purpose for a few blocks, and on a street unfamiliar to me he whipped into a parking spot beside a wrought iron fence, enclosing a small city park. Another coincidence, or part of a strategic plan? Deciding it didn't make the slightest difference. I had come along willingly, and wherever this afternoon took me, I wouldn't dream of trying to change or prevent it. He locked the car, and in a state that could only be described as catatonic, I walked with him into the golden shade of towering oaks and maples.

"In a way this park reminds me of the place by the river in Oakville," he said. "You remember, Andrea—it was our favorite."

"The Point," I said, "yes, I remember . . ."

"There are more trees here, but just over this little hill you will see the water. I walk here often, when I finish work. I wanted you to see it."

Carefully planned!

"It's nice here all year round, but especially during the winter. There aren't many people around then, and the bare trees, the sunsets, all somehow remind me of you, of our good times together."

I wondered idly if there was any psychological significance in the fact that our fondest memories were of winters together, that we both skimmed over the other seasons. Perhaps our love was warmest in the cold weather.

But this was not winter, and the trees, crowded with leaves, created a shadowy canopy overhead, adding to the romance and excitement of being here with him.

He reached for my hand, and at his touch my knees grew weak, and I held tightly to his jacket. He wrapped his arm around my shoulder and we made our way into the refreshingly cool shade, once again in silence. It was early afternoon on a working day, a school day, and the park was virtually deserted. Surrounded by shrubs and bushes that added to the illusion of privacy, we walked down a gentle slope, toward a small pond where ducks floated lazily in the hazy heat of the afternoon. The only thing missing here were violins!

We found an inviting spot under the trees, and sat close to each other, but distinctly apart, on a carpet of bronzed moss. His eyes were on me but I pretended not to notice, and gazed off into the distance, barely breathing, waiting . . . then with a groan he crushed me in his arms, buried his face in my hair, hungrily kissing my neck, my nose, my lips.

My response was frightening. Overcome with an irrational need, I took his hand and held it inside my shirt, sighing when his fingers moved, burning the soft skin. My mind shouted to push him away, but I'd waited a lifetime for this, and I ached with the need to take him inside, soothing my pain, making me whole.

Gently pushing me back into the sweet autumn fragrance of grasses and ferns, he stretched out beside me, his face inches above mine, a smile on his lips, his fingers lightly running through my hair.

"I love your hair, Andrea, the weight of it, the color. This is how I think of you . . . I'm glad you still wear it this way."

Suddenly he clutched my hair tightly, and lowered his face to mine, eyes gleaming brightly with desire, a reflection of my own desperate need. His breath was hot on my face, and I kissed him with undreamed of passion, pulling him closer, my body and spirit exulting in total abandon.

He traced a line from my ear to the hollow of my neck with his tongue, and I shivered with anticipation. "Do you still hate to have your neck kissed?" he breathed against my bared breast.

"Hate it? No . . . I was scared, maybe, afraid I'd forget myself . . . break the rules," I murmured against his hair, feeling that way now.

His gentle, knowing hands moved constantly, now working at hooks and buttons, now delicately brushing my fevered skin. I caught my breath, all senses concentrating on his fingertips. Tenderly he kissed each rigid nipple, growing rougher with increasing urgency as his hands roamed all over my body, awakening a tremendous surge of desire that blotted out all hesitation. My body arched upwards in a frantic attempt to join his . . .

He hovered over me, body rigid, eyes burning.

"Should I stop now?" his voice a

hoarse whisper, "Do you want me to stop?"

"Oh no," I moaned, "not now, please don't stop . . ."

We were joined in a rhythm as old as time, yet fresh and new, each thrust filled with exquisite torture . . . seeking release yet wanting it to last forever . . . shuddering, rising to a climax of pure rapture, suspended in mingled ecstasy and oblivion, while stars burst behind closed eyelids . . . cresting slowly, slowly . . . leaving behind incredible peace.

Oh sweet, sweet love. With unbelievable tenderness he cradled me in his arms, wrapping me in a hug of the ultimate dimension. Totally, absolutely satisfied and content, I would die willingly here and now. Tears stream from my eyes, overflowing from my heart, he kissed my wet cheeks, whispers tender sounds. I smile through the blur of tears at the man I have wanted all my life. We lie still, holding each other while the storm of passion fades, replaced with the wonder and joy of love.

* * *

I stared up through the leaves, all sensibilities heightened, picking out their sharp, clearly defined edges, their subtle shadings, listening to the piercingly sweet calls of the mockingbirds, absorbing the peace of our surroundings.

Eventually we came alive, and walked down to the pond, watching the ducks placidly going about their business, catching flashes of tiny goldfish as they darted in and out of the shadows thrown on the water by the trees. I leaned against his chest, listening to the soft pounding of his heart, a sound that filled me with inexpressible joy. He was broad-shouldered, physically a bigger man than Stuart, and I felt tiny in the circle of his arms. We had barely spoken—there was no need to talk, but occasional wispy thoughts drifted through my mind and passed on. Stuart came and went without causing the slightest twinge of discomfort. In this dimension nothing was strange, like Alice, I thought, in Wonderland . . . but, I recalled, Alice landed with a bump, and eventually, so did I. I had just made love with a man, both a stranger and the dearest, most familiar person on earth. I had committed an act unpardonably wrong, yet in my present frame of mind, inevitable and absolutely right.

As with every dream, this one ran its course, and eventually the world of reality, of husbands and wives, of right and wrong, forced its way into my benumbed brain. Was this the end of an old love, or a new beginning?

"You have a wife . . . I have a husband . . ."

"Valerie and I . . . we have very little to do with each other. She has her interests, her life, and I have mine. But you?"

Me. And Stuart. No way did we live separate lives, and even though I was unsure of my love for him, this was not the moment to come to any decision about him, or us, or . . .

What happened now? Were we going to have an affair?

"This, um, this kind of thing is so new to me . . . I've never done anything like this before, never even fantasized such a thing," I said, hoping to explain, to understand my actions today. "I leave a lunch table with a man, a virtual stranger, and make love in the first remotely likely spot . . ." Words failed, I shrugged my shoulders in defeat, and I came to a halt. What had I done? Or more important, maybe, was why I had gone to meet him in the first place.

"Something happened at the reunion. I can't explain it, but I knew we would find each other." I stopped, remembering that I had set this meeting in motion. "Well, it sounds silly, I guess . . ."

He answered, his rich voice soft, caressing, "I knew when I saw you that night our story was not over. There are chapters still unwritten. We both know it started long before the reunion, many years ago . . . I've always loved you, Andrea. I love you still."

My heart took wing, soaring with pure joy, and the hurt hidden deep inside me slowly melted away. His eyes glowed as he looked straight into mine, a look of such intense love . . . and my eyes filled with tears. He loved me. A void had been filled, a circle completed, I was whole.

We stayed together while the shadows grew longer, reaching across the pond, and pink streaks in the sky heralded the coming sunset, wholly enraptured with each other, solemnly promising that this time we would not be cheated, that nothing, no one, would stand in our way.

On the drive back to the parking lot to get my car we held hands in childish innocence, talking about the future, making plans to meet again. It was easy to shut out the world for a few more minutes, not to worry about Stuart, thinking only of each other and the love we had found once again.

We were going to have an affair.

Now a pendulum swung back and forth, from absolute euphoria to abysmal loss. The reason for my happiness was clear, and I hugged it close, walking on a cloud, savoring the joy! We had found each other again, and after long years of thinking myself a fool, time had proven that he loved me. And yet, blissful highs were clouded by sadness, and a bewildering sense of loss, as though I had lost a lover, not found him.

I brooded about my guilt. I knew it was wrong . . . but I quickly, too quickly, dismissed it. Everyone deserves to be happy, I reasoned, and Richard made me happy. No one would be hurt. Stuart would never know. This had nothing to do with our life, our marriage, our long-standing belief in each other. I had been doing the right thing all my life; it was time to think of myself for a change . . .

I had more good reasons to go ahead than I had fingers! I wasn't thinking, of course—all I wanted to do was hop into bed with Richard, my dream come true, so I pretended the guilt didn't exist. I managed to justify having an affair with Richard, and refused to spoil it with pangs of conscience. But the Italian Catholic daughter of Antoinetta Corelli should have known better.

Twenty-one

On the Saturday after Thanksgiving, late in November, Stuart surprised me with tickets for *Cats*, at the Schubert Theatre. He had made reservations at my favorite restaurant, the Atlantic Fish House, where we went for a late dinner afterward. My broiled Cajun halibut was delicious, as always, and Stuart's swordfish was excellent, he said. With a green salad and a fine white Bordeaux, a perfect late night meal. We talked about the show as we busily munched through dinner, but by the time coffee was served, there seemed to be nothing left to say, and conversation lagged.

"What a great show!" I said for perhaps the fourth time. "And now this lovely dinner! It's been a wonderful evening, Stuart. Thank you."

"I thought you'd enjoy it, sweetheart. You haven't looked this bright and happy in months," he continued, his eyes filled with sadness. "Anyone would think we were out on a date tonight, not an old married couple—you look so young, and pretty."

"Oh, Stuart . . ." I began, ready to argue, but I stopped short. He was right, tonight did feel like a date, though I was sure we saw it differently. This was like a blind date, I thought, remembering nights, so many years ago, when my friends fixed me up with guys who didn't click, when the ice never thawed, when there wasn't a single thing to talk about. Dates who finally took me home, maybe after a quick feel in the car and the requisite kiss at the door, hopefully never to call again. No such luck tonight, however. Stuart would not be leaving me at my door, we would return to the same house, the same life. The same cold bed.

He was trying so hard to please me, but I couldn't respond. As I gazed around at other tables, it was obvious that some couples were deeply in love, while others seemed bored—probably married, I thought—and I wondered how we looked to someone watching us. Ill-at-ease, misfits, I would bet, thinking of our short bursts of conversation between long silences. We hadn't been alone together for ages, and keeping up a social facade was trying. We had nothing to give each other, no common interests other than the children, no separate pursuits to share. There was nothing new to learn about each other, and our lives were dull, Dull, DULL! I was mulling this over, placidly sipping my coffee, when Stuart threw me a curve!

"I ran into Ellen at the rink last night, at Brian's hockey practice. She said hello, that we should get together soon, and that she hasn't seen you in ages."

My stomach lurched, and I wondered if he had caught the significance of her casual remark.

"Didn't you two go out for dinner last week?"

Apparently he had, and he waited patiently for my answer.

Stuart had been out of town on one of his frequent business trips, Brian had hockey practice, and I made a date to meet Richard for dinner at a romantic little Italian restaurant in the North End, complete with checked tablecloths and Chianti candleholders. Inexpensive Italian decor out of the sixties, but in this place it worked. Unlike tonight's dinner with Stuart, we found plenty to talk about, as we gazed into each other's eyes and shared the warm intimate laughter of lovers. Richard wanted to go somewhere after dinner, but I didn't have the courage to stay with him.

Brian had gone to the rink with Ellen, and he was home when I arrived.

"Where you been, Mom?"

"Out for dinner with some people from the office. Mexican place, great food. How was practice?" I asked, changing the subject.

Stuart called from Cleveland the following night.

"Nobody was home when I called last night," he said."

"Brian had practice, and I went out for a bite with Ellen," I lied, without thinking. Afterwards I realized my mistake, but I didn't think it would come up again, and I forgot about it. Now I skated. "More like a couple of weeks ago," I grinned. "Time flies, doesn't it? Weren't you away? I can't remember now, but I think she canceled out at the last minute."

What had I really said when he called? I thought I told Brian I'd worked late, but maybe I said . . . no, he was with Ellen. I couldn't remember either story, and my mind darted through the possibilities. Suppose Stuart remembered, and questioned me on it? My panic moved into high gear, but he started talking about Brian's team, and a tournament after Christmas.

"End of January, up in Andover," he said. "They have three games, Saturday morning, Saturday night and early Sunday morning. We can find something to do during the afternoon, and stay overnight. What do you say?"

"Let me think about it, Stuart," I temporized. "Andover in January doesn't exactly sound tempting."

Picture me traipsing around Andover with Stuart and running into Richard at a mall, or in a restaurant with his wife . . . how amusing!

I pushed the reclining seat back, pretending to sleep on the drive home, and gave some thought to the unhappy turn events seemed to be taking. For the first time in my life I had deliberately lied to Stuart, and somehow I had been disloyal to my friend Ellen in the bargain. And though I enjoyed the hockey tournaments and the fun we had with our friends, I might run into my clandestine lover while out with my family. I would definitely not be going anywhere near Andover in January.

Never in my wildest dreams had I imagined that this could happen to me. This was not how our marriage worked. Stuart loved me, trusted me, until now with no reason to question that trust. Yet faced with temptation, I was telling lies and making up stories. What kind of person did that? Stuart, I reflected, you are living with a woman who lies to you, and I hope you never find out how deceitful I am. Oh God, what's happening here?

Richard had happened, reaching for me from far, far back in the past, with a hypnotic hold on me that surpassed the bond between Stuart and me. I had a chance at greater happiness than I thought was possible in this life, and I didn't have the strength to turn my back on it. And as long as I stayed cool and kept my stories straight, there was no way Stuart would find out, or my two wonderful children . . . suddenly I imagined their disappointment, the scorn and disgust in their eyes . . .

"Andrea!"

"Wake up, sweetheart." I rubbed my eyes, trying to erase the scene in my mind, while three fire trucks sped by, sirens still wailing in the night.

Stuart held my hand. "You were dreaming—are you okay now?"

"Umm, yeah, I'm fine . . ."

Again the same old questions went round and round the treadmill of my mind, and though the answers were there, I didn't want to listen. I knew I should stop now, but as long as they didn't know, it would probably continue. I didn't want the magic to end. I didn't want to think about it any more. Emotions would take me through the days and nights, living by the seat of my pants, hoping that everything would turn out right in the end.

* * *

A couple of weeks later, on a cold rainy Tuesday in December, a gloomy day that would have sent the happiest of people into a fit of depression, I found myself alone in the car, very low in spirits. The slapping rhythm of the wipers sang two words as I drove along; Richard, Stu-art, Rich-ard, Stu-art! I'd been pondering, wondering, agonizing for weeks and months and I was sick of the questions going round and round in my head, suffering from headaches that beat out the worst I'd ever had. Stu-art, Richard. Past and present were mingling together, the lines that normally defined the two were blurred. I was in perpetual turmoil, my mind a crazy tapestry of whirling images, creating improbable scenarios. Rich-ard, Stuart!

Sometimes I'd daydream, imagining Richard, Stuart and I, close friends, thoroughly enjoying each other's company. Hell, why stop there, we were worldly, sophisticated people—his wife would be there, too! Or I'd see Stuart and me at the mall, running into Richard, chatting amiably, as friends do . . .

Stupid.

Sometimes happy, my heart soaring

like a bird. Other times miserable, steeped in guilt, disgusted with myself, a sneak and a cheat. Sometimes I didn't care, other times I wanted to die.

Today, speeding along the expressway, already late for my dental appointment thanks to the traffic, I could see with cold clarity the utter futility of an affair, and I wondered how long it would be before Stuart found out. Or how long before someone saw Richard and me together, and asked questions . . . or how long before I went stark raving mad! Lost in thought, I was paying no attention whatever to the road, and I missed my exit.

Now came the scene in the dentist's office, where the receptionist, annoyed with me because I had screwed up her schedule, would send in other patients ahead of me. I'd spend the rest of the day in that hot, stuffy place! I felt a headache coming on, and decided not to go. I would call and cancel. No. I canceled my last appointment to spend time with Richard, so this time I really had to go.

While this perfectly stupid debate raged in my head I felt hot tears streaming down my face, and as soon as traffic permitted I pulled into the breakdown lane, laughing hysterically at the aptness of the name. The breakdown lane! By the time I finally stopped the car I was totally out of control, weeping and laughing at the same time, until the tears won, and I dropped my head on the steering wheel, crying long and loud in pain and despair.

I cried myself out of tears, and as I stared through the rain-streaked windshield, it came to me that this was definitely some kind of breakdown. I had to get help, talk to someone, and I could think of only one person I wanted to share this with. Relief surged through me as I started the car and drove back home, desperate and ready to unburden myself to Ellen, my friend.

God was with me; she was home. Crashing in unceremoniously, I threw myself into a chair, looked at her concerned face, and burst into tears.

"Oh Ellen, I don't know what I'm getting myself into!" I lamented after I explained some of the story to her. "I want Richard, I want him more than anything, but I can't imagine cheating on Stuart.

I deliberately lied to him the other night, and I've had nightmares about it ever since. My God, it would kill him if he found out!"

"Why should he find out?" she asked calmly. I stared dumbfounded, stunned at her words.

"Andrea, you've been complaining for years that you're bored with Stuart. Everyone craves excitement in their lives, some reason to greet each new day. If Stuart doesn't give you that reason, and you've found someone who does, then go for it!"

This was too weird! From Ellen I had been prepared for chastisement, lectures on how preposterous an affair would be, advice on how to get out of this predicament. Motherly advice. But Ellen is not my mother.

"Does your plan include leaving Stuart? Breaking up your marriage, moving in with this other guy?"

"Not even a remote possibility," I answered, not knowing whether it was true or not.

"With all the traveling Stuart does, I know how lonely you are when he's away three or four nights in a row . . ." She must have seen the shock in my eyes, and slowed to a stop.

"Seriously, Andrea, I think you need this. Take what you can for as long as it lasts. It will give you something to keep you warm on those lonely nights when Stuart is away, or when you get old."

More than shocked, now, I was horrified. And the horror was plain on my face.

"Ellen, this isn't what I expected from you at all. I thought you'd talk me out of this mess—"

"But this is what you really want, isn't it? To have an affair? What worries you is Stuart finding out and getting hurt. How could Stuart possibly be hurt if he doesn't know? And how will he find out if you don't tell him?"

Ellen must be putting something in her coffee, I thought. She was supposed to talk me out of my foolishness.

"Don't you think I'm nuts, or having a nervous breakdown, something like that?" I was pleading.

"Not at all. You're an attractive woman, facing middle age, with the opportunity to enjoy a wonderful sexual fantasy, no strings, with a man who loves you, a man you've dreamed of for years. Your marriage is run-of-the-mill and dull, but you have an opportunity for a last fling or whatever you want to call it! You're wrestling with guilt, but I think you should go ahead and have a good time for once in your life."

"But there's no stability or permanence in an affair, nothing to hold on to. I can't picture myself in some kind of sleazy romantic entanglement just for fun and excitement."

"Honey, I think that's exactly what you need right now. You're married to respectability and stability, you need the thrill of something new to refresh the old. If I had the opportunity, I'd jump at it in a second!"

We talked for hours, while I poured my heart out, my mood alternating between euphoria and gloom. I described Richard to her, shy as a sweet young innocent talking about her first boyfriend. I moaned about my boring marriage with Stuart, how unfulfilled and lonely I was, how wonderful Richard was, how boring Stuart was, around and over again.

"I don't want to lose what I have, and

I don't want to hurt Stuart. I really have a good life with him. But in some strange way this is right—like someone owes it to me, to make up for what I missed."

"You want to keep your money on the sure thing and take a flyer on something risky! I know, Andrea, I understand what you mean."

I laughed hysterically, finally explaining to her that my mother would have said "You want to save a piece of cake."

Hours later, I finally went home, thoroughly worn out but comforted. I wasn't alone. I had a friend who didn't think I was out of my mind. I was going to have an affair with Richard, and Stuart would never know.

On the way home I remembered that I hadn't called the dentist's office to cancel my appointment.

Twenty-two

Christmas shopping has always been one of the great pleasures of my life. The only exception was the year I was eight months pregnant with Brian, when walking the local strip mall became a challenge to equal the climbing of Mount Everest. Normally I enjoyed the crush and bustle of crowded department stores, the glitter and lights everywhere, the background sounds of Christmas carols a soft descant to the continual dissonant hum of voices.

Salvation Army santas made out very well when I was around; I couldn't pass one by without dropping a dollar bill into the kettle. Humming Christmas carols, threading my way through aisles jammed with overheated parents and slippery whining children, filled with peace and goodwill to all.

I take great pains over my list, carefully planning for months what I would buy for whom, shopping all year round to ferret out gifts I thought would be perfect for their intended recipients.

Until now. This year it was a tremendous burden, a chore without joy. I had put off my shopping until a couple of weeks before Christmas, and I hit the stores in a panic. Instead of chasing down the perfect pair of verdigris candle holders for Lorraine, an item that had been on my list since March, I picked up a silk scarf that I thought might do. And I did the same thing all the way down the line; the gifts I chose had no flair, and would certainly disappoint everyone, which added to my woes. But I had no energy. There was no room in my brain for anything more than the current mess.

The week before our annual open house serious hysteria struck. I hadn't wanted the party at all.

"Let's just forget it for this year, Stuart. It's too big, it's so much work, and I'm just not up for it." But Stuart, due to this peculiar aberration in his personality, couldn't imagine the holidays without it. The man hated parties, for heaven's sake, every party but this one.

"Come on, Andrea, you're only working part time now—last year you were in school, too, remember? You have more free time than ever before. Keep it simple, and it'll be terrific. You know you always enjoy it in the end. The kids and I will pitch in and help."

I settled for a buffet of cold sliced roast beef and a few salads and pasta dishes, and no theme. The Christmas tree says it all this year, I told the kids. I don't know how it went; my heart wasn't in it, my mind was somewhere else the whole time, and I truly didn't care if people had a good time or not. I had other things on my mind; an extramarital affair, to be precise.

When the family gathered at Mom and Dad's for Christmas dinner, Lorraine asked me several times if everything was okay. She thought I looked tired, and inattentive, as though my mind were somewhere else. "Are you losing more weight?" This from my mother, who also thought I looked tired.

"Don't I wish, Mom." What could I say? "Everything's fine. I don't know what you and Lorraine are worried about." Of course everything was great. Wasn't I having the time of my life?

The holidays finally dragged to an end, but still I couldn't focus on anything; the most ordinary tasks were burdensome, and I hated going to work, it cut into the time I could spend daydreaming, or worrying.

I didn't get around to registering for the paralegal class, and when Mr. Murphy approached me about Leona Hansbury's job, I lied. No room in the spring class, I said. Yes, it was a darn shame, but I was already signed up for the fall session. I was getting really good at making things up on the spot.

"Andrea, I am disappointed. I was counting on you to take over that job, commencing immediately."

"Maybe I can take a summer course, if thcy have such a thing. That would accelerate my diploma, and I'd have it by the fall," I said, with great enthusiasm. "I'll find out and let you know as soon as I can." But don't hold your breath.

* * *

I caught Stuart watching me when he thought I didn't notice. Could he guess what was going on in my head? Impossible. But I listened for hidden meanings in everything he said, sifting his words for a hint that he suspected something. The guilty mind at work, I suppose. Bothersome, but not enough to divert me from my plans with Richard. Nothing would stop me now. I was wrapped up in him to the exclusion of everyone and everything, and I wandered through my days like a visitor from another planet.

Richard phoned one day when Kelley was still home on Christmas break. She answered, yelled for me, apparently with no interest in who my male caller might be. But that call was the beginning of a nightmare, and every time the phone rang, I panicked. I lived in a state of continual anxiety from one phone call to the next, wanting to hear his voice, afraid someone else might answer. If he called again Kelley might remember his voice! Suppose Brian or Stuart asked who was calling. What would I say? I would be caught!

"Can't you call me at work, Rich? It's much easier for me. Nobody cares, but if I had to I could pass you off as my brother-in-law or something."

"But I love to surprise you at home. When you're in the office you don't say the things I love to hear—that's why I call you from the car phone. I can say what I like without my secretary bustling in with papers for me to sign. Now tell me, my love, when will I again kiss those sweet breasts . . ." That's all it took to sidetrack me into an erotic fantasy, anxiety forgotten for the moment.

I didn't dare call him; I didn't want any nosey secretary identifying my voice, so I had to bide my time, and the waiting and the anxiety were driving me around the bend. Once in a while, after only a couple of rings, the caller would hang up before I got to the phone, and I'd spend the rest of the day in a flurry of nerves, thinking he had called and I'd missed him.

One day when Brian was home with no school I had a stupid premonition that he would call, and spent the entire day ironing beside the telephone, pressing everything from shirts to underwear, praying he would call, frantic that Brian might get to the phone first. But there was no call, and I was devastated.

I was edgy all the time, introspective and self-involved, and no longer cared if anyone noticed.

We talked often, rambling conversations filled with longing and sexual overtones, but we had met only three times since the magical afternoon in the park, and always in a restaurant in Boston. The city gave me anonymity, crowds to get lost in, and surrounded by people in a darkened restaurant there was no chance of succumbing to his charm. Obviously I wasn't ready for anything more intimate.

Early in January Stuart went to Palm Springs to attend a four-day conference, from Thursday evening through Sunday. That Friday Brian had arranged to go straight from school to hockey practice, then to sleep over at a friend's house. I wouldn't see him until late Saturday afternoon. The stage was set. Richard phoned in the morning, before I left for work.

"There's a delightful little restaurant where they only serve chateaubriand for two . . . I'd love to share it with you," he said, in his most charming voice. "And then a nightcap, perhaps at The Black Cat?"

"That sounds lovely," I agreed.

"And finally, a suite at the Ritz?"

"Don't push your luck," I answered with a laugh. "See you at seven," I added, after he gave me directions. I raced up the stairs for fresh undies and my toothbrush, decided to give my conscience a holiday and see what transpired.

The restaurant turned out to be the most romantic little hideaway on earth. It was very small, Spanish, I think, or Portuguese, with an unpronounceable name, tucked away on a side street down near the harbor, in the oldest part of the city. Three massive stone steps led down from the street into an arched alcove, with a heavy oak door hidden deep in the shadows. Inside it was dark and cozy, with a fire dancing merrily in a huge fieldstone fireplace in the center of the room, defying the January cold outside. The walls were rough plaster, with heavy dark beams in the ceilings, and no visible electric lighting.

Tables were tucked away into nooks and alcoves, and candles glowing in ceramic pots on each one gave every couple the romantic look of illicit lovers. The atmosphere was enhanced by a strolling violinist who wandered around, playing something soft and plaintive whenever he stopped, supplementing the three piece combo playing soft Mediterranean music.

The chateaubriand immediately replaced every great meal I've ever had in my life. It turned out to be roast beef tenderloin, served with a rich dark sauce and a colorful bouquet of vegetables artistically arranged around the plate. We drank a bottle of a dark red Spanish wine, and for dessert we shared an incredibly delicious, sinfully rich waffle and strawberry concoction. I giggled when he fed me a little from his fork, recalling the sexy meal scene from *Tom Jones,* a movie we saw together many years ago. I did the same until our laughter subtly changed to sensual pleasure, and we dropped our forks to gaze at each other with eyes filled with smoldering desire, shocked at the eroticism in such a simple act.

The warm atmosphere, the floating murmur of conversation and soft laughter, the wine, conspired together as we sat in the secret embrace of a huge banquette, his hand resting on my thigh, his fingers teasing the skin beneath my skirt, while I drowned in the dark glow of his eyes, and fell even more deeply in love with him as I lived the romance that filled my dreams.

After dinner we went for a drink and cappucino to a cozy little bar in Boylston Place, the heart of the theatre district and convenient to several hotels in downtown Boston. Richard coaxed, I refused, though reluctantly. "Andrea," he whispered, "I want to spend the night with you, making slow, passionate love all night long. I want to wake up next to you in the morning, and make love all over again. You know you want it too."

His dark eyes glowed in the soft light, melting my reserve. "Am I right," he whispered into my hair, sending shivers down my spine. When I nodded, he grinned in triumph and reached for his coat.

But once outside, the January cold quickly chilled the warmth of passion. I balked on the sidewalk, rigid and unyielding. "Richard, I can't—I can't spend the night with you! Not tonight. Maybe some other night."

But his rich, seductive voice in my ear, his lips tickling my neck, sent a fluttering erotic response to the pit of my stomach. I wanted to make love with him again, and recalling the thrill of the first time, I finally gave up all resistance. I leaned against him, breathing in the warmth of him while he hailed a cab.

I was making little noises deep in my throat—I didn't give a damn about the taxi driver—while Rich kissed me and undid my coat and slipped his cold hands inside my jacket, under my shirt, icy cold hands burning my hot skin, hands that never stopped moving, touching, building and spreading desire and need and I was breathing in quick shallow gulps and thinking I was going to come right there in the backseat of this taxi and wanting nothing more than to make love to him that night, all night, every night!

Alone in the room with him, however, was a different story. After a chilling walk across the huge marble lobby, and riding thirty floors in the elevator with three guys, obviously drunk, laughing uproariously while one of them tried to remember a joke, I discovered I was very nervous. This is adultery, I said to the pale, scared face looking back at me in the bathroom mirror. I wanted to make love with him more than anything else in the world, but I dawdled in the shower like a virgin, as though he might leave if I took too long.

He didn't leave. Suddenly he was with me under the spray of warm water. Taking the bar from my hand he soaped my back, then his arms encircled me to reach breasts and nipples, one hand gently rubbing my belly while he kissed my neck and my ears, and I leaned back against his hard, taut body on legs too weak to stand alone. He bent to reach the mound of dark hair between my legs, but I couldn't take any more. I turned in his arms and kissed him while the soap clattered to the floor and he picked me up and he was inside me and we made love, standing under water that streamed through our hair and across our faces, the gentle hissing sound blending with the sighs and cries coming from me, a woman who had never uttered a sound in her whole life while making love.

Draping me in the huge towel he carried me to the bed, drying me off carefully, slowly unwrapping me, as though opening a gift, prolonging the pleasure by refusing to tear at the wrappings. He beamed at me, a radiant smile, then bent his head and took a nipple between his lips, moving his body over mine, ready to make love again. Oh my God, I mused, my last clear thought before I sank, I'm going to burst with joy!

Lorraine called me early one morning on a bright and sunny day at the end of January, the traces of snow in the back yard gleaming brilliantly. As I listened to her I watched a crowd of chickadees racing each other from tree to tree, dive-bombing through the air as though riding on waves.

"I need a hand to make new drapes for my bedroom," she began. In her best wheedling tone, she continued, "If you come and sew with me, I'll feed you lunch. I really need the help. It's only an hour's drive, and the roads are dry."

Sew with me, she says! Lord only knew why George, her husband, had bought her a sewing machine. At the age of twelve she conceded that she was hopeless with thread and needle, and had never bothered to learn.

"How long have you had that sewing machine?"

"Only six years. Not nearly long enough to learn how to use it!"

I laughed with her. "Okay, sounds like a great way to spend the day," I answered, and promised to be there no later than ten o'clock.

I measured and cut the material she had bought, and attempted to show her how to use the machine, but gave up at lunch time. "I'll sew them up after we eat," I told her, leaving the heaps of flowered chintz on a chair while we went into the kitchen.

Over soup and sandwiches, Lorraine and I chatted easily, and noisily, discussing her redecorating plans, Kelley's progress in college, laughing uproariously as she related tales of conquest about her son Stephen, who, at thirteen, was apparently winning the hearts of all the girls in his class. Conversation, as always with Lorraine, zipped along from one subject to another, and I saw nothing odd when she asked about Stuart.

"How's Stuart feeling these days?" she asked.

"Same as always, just fine."

"Well, he wasn't so fine when I talked to him at Mom and Dad's at Christmas."

"What was wrong?"

"You, I think, although I had a hard time figuring out what he was trying to say."

"Did he say something was wrong?"

"Well, no, not exactly, just that he was worried about you. He said you seemed far away and unhappy. He seems to have this wild idea that you might, um, have some other guy on your mind? Of course, I told him he was crazy!" Fear rose in her eyes. "You would have told me if there was anything going on, right? It isn't true, is it?"

"Lorraine, what did he say, exactly?"

"Well, he said you had changed lately, you're not attentive when anyone talks to you—which, by the way, is obvious to one and all—and he said you get this faraway look in your eyes, like you were daydreaming about something, or someone. That's when he said he thought there might be someone else."

I broke in casually, hoping to calm her fears. "Oh Lori, you know how I've been since the accident, I get dizzy, nauseous and sometimes I check out for a while with headaches and stuff. But I'm no less attentive to him now than I was before. Besides, Stuart wouldn't notice if I had an affair right under his nose. He never notices anything about me anyway. I can't believe he dumped all this crap on you without talking to me first."

"Andrea, he loves you a lot, and he seemed so worried, so scared talking about you, like he thought you were planning to leave him or something. Is everything all right between you?"

"Everything's just the same as always. Where is everybody getting the idea that something's wrong? Stuart and I never have any problems, nothing ever changes, life goes on day after day, same old grind. Nothing exciting, very dull. Very safe."

"What do you mean by safe? Are you afraid of something? Is someone bothering you? Is Stuart getting weird?"

"God, Lorraine, you've been reading too many women's magazines. Of course Stuart isn't getting weird. I said my marriage is safe, not scary. It's just something I've been thinking about lately. There is no excitement, or thrills, in my marriage. It's safe and secure. And boring. Are you bored with George?"

"Bored? Never thought about it. No, I don't think so."

They'd been married sixteen years. Maybe it was too soon for boredom, or maybe they had a great sex life.

"Anyway, don't worry about Stuart and me. We've stuck it out for twenty-two years, we'll make it twenty-two more! Everything is fine. Maybe it's me—I'm going through a stage, like Mom always says. I'll get over it, whatever it is."

I thought about this conversation as I drove home. What had given Stuart the idea there was someone else? I didn't think he was the intuitive type, but I could be mistaken. Or maybe I wasn't as good at hiding things as I thought, and cunningly decided to be more careful from now on. He had asked if I was unhappy, but we had never talked about another man. Of course we didn't talk much about anything at all these days, we pretty well ignored each other.

At Christmas, though, he had been pumping Lorraine for information, so obviously my distraction was noticeable, even to him. How nice, I thought, that he cares. Maybe what I took as mutual disinterest was really one-sided, on my side. Was I so out of tune with him that I didn't know whether or not he loved me? Or was I so involved with Richard that I didn't care?

Kelley came home for February vacation, but for the first time in many years, we didn't go to Oakville to visit my parents. Both she and her brother had made other plans, Kelley to spend as much time as possible with Phil, and Brian had been invited to a friend's ski shack for a few days.

He had grown since last winter, and his ski boots no longer fit. Fortunately, when he tried Stuart's on, they fit fine, though they were black, not fluorescent orange and purple stripes, or whatever was in this year.

"Can't I get new boots, Dad?" he wheedled.

"Not in February, son. Wait till next year." He whined a little, but after hearing the ultimatum that he would ski in Stuart's boots or not ski at all, he decided they looked just great. He was almost as tall as his father now, and Stuart's skis would work out well, even though they were longer than he was accustomed to.

"Good skiers wear longer skis," his father explained. "You can maneuver better, and with more surface on the snow, you go much faster." This pleased his fifteen-year-old ego immensely, and he went away happy with the borrowed equipment.

Kelley and I spent a day together shopping, but it was a half-hearted effort on my part, and though I tried to drum up enthusiasm, I spoiled her fun. We poked in and out of shops, where I barely looked at the merchandise, and at one o'clock we stopped to eat at Edgar's, a sandwich shop in the mall.

"You okay, Mom?" she asked, after we had ordered lunch.

"Sure. Don't I look okay?"

"It's just that you don't seem to be your usual self. You always have a bustling, full-of-stuff-to-do look about you, and since I've been home you seem kind of droopy."

"I do feel a little down. PMS, I guess.

"Dad doesn't look too great either. Is everything okay?"

Observant, my daughter. Annoyingly so.

"Are you guys fighting?"

"Your dad and I? Silly, what would we fight about? Don't you go worrying about us. Tell me about the movie you saw with Phil last night."

She started talking about the comedy they had seen, animation lighting up her face, excited about her date, and I stopped listening. I hadn't lied to her; Stuart and I were not fighting. We were doing nothing at all. Until now, whenever we had one of our very rare fights or arguments, something tangible, like a wall, would come between us, and we chipped away at it until it was gone. We didn't fight often, but we'd had a couple of good ones over the years, and that was the usual pattern. Each of us wanted to get through to the other, to get the argument behind us, and we'd talk until we found a way. But we hadn't had an argument in years.

Now there was nothing to overcome or break down, just a cold, stony void. I couldn't talk about my problems, so I remained silent, and when he probed, in his halfhearted way, I shut him out. Maybe he hoped in time that whatever the problem was would just go away. That would be Stuart, I thought, refusing to get emotional, insisting that a logical solution would present itself.

At night we slept far apart, and in the morning we'd shower one after the other, drink coffee in silence, and go to work.

Stuart frequently worked late, or was out of town, or at the rink with Brian, and I was often alone and lonely. This is all Stuart's fault, I'd think petulantly. If he wasn't away so much, I wouldn't be in this mess. But that wasn't true. I was solely responsible for the mess I was in, and honestly didn't know if I wanted to get out of it. Stuart and I had lived more than twenty years together, but for the thrill of a few romantic interludes with Richard my life was dissolving before my eyes.

Was our marriage worth saving? Was it over? If I stayed married to Stuart, and continued my affair with Richard, I could have my cake and eat it too. A moral dilemma, I thought ironically, but I was beyond caring about morals! I had lost my integrity, and as long as no one found out I was certain I could keep this deception going forever.

I wanted something to change, prayed for a change, but was emotionally incapable of realizing that any change had to originate with me. Instead, I wished for something drastic to happen; one of us might die, or we might be transferred far away. I desperately needed to be rescued from this ghastly situation, and belatedly remembering my God, I prayed for help, but if he was there, he wasn't listening.

Though I wasn't ready to call it quits, the thrill and excitement of my love affair had become burdened with guilt and deception, a weight I was incapable of getting out from under. I was cheating on Stuart, who trusted me, poor fool. Richard cheated on his wife, and though he said he loved me, I couldn't trust him. Guilt over one and distrust of the other simmered inside, and I was caught in a nightmare that would last forever unless something intervened.

It was inevitable, I suppose, that the precarious tower that was my marriage would finally crash and fall to the ground.

Twenty-three

Valentine's Day, in the best of times, came and went with a minimum of fuss and commotion in our house. If he remembered, Stuart would buy me a card on his way home from work, but that was rare. Way back, when we first got married, he used to bring me chocolates, in the red heart-shaped boxes, but after I had Brian, and worried about gaining weight, the candy stopped. He never thought of flowers, unromantic soul that he was, and I was used to being forgotten on this special day set aside for lovers. Given the current state of affairs, and the fact that we had not exchanged more than the necessary civilities in the past two weeks, this one would undoubtedly go unobserved.

When the doorbell rang at 5:30 in the afternoon, I was surprised to see a florist's delivery van out there, and in stunned silence accepted a huge bouquet of red sweetheart roses and baby's breath from the driver. It was beautiful, and I buried my nose among the fragrant blossoms, breathing in the fresh scent that always reminded me of raspberries. I looked at the card, and saw that it was signed only with an X. Oh, Stuart, I thought, as tears filled my eyes. What a sweet gesture! He never sent me flowers, for any occasion. Did he think flowers would get rid of our problems? Why be nasty, Andrea, the man feels bad about the way things are, he sends flowers, be grateful! And, I mused, as I buried my face in the fragrant bouquet, this may not be such a dumb idea. Here I was crying over a bunch of posies! Flowers might be a great way to start! I set the arrangement on the table in the hall, where he would be most likely to see it when he came in the front door, and went back to preparing dinner, humming softly to myself. Not a solution, it's true, but if flowers from Stuart could move me to tears, there must be hope for us.

He loved scalloped potatoes, and I had plenty of time to cook them.

He came in an hour or so later, looking deflated, as he so often did these days. I saw him glance at the flowers in the hallway as he hung his coat in the closet, but he said nothing.

"I left work early tonight, but traffic was terrible," he complained, rubbing his face with both hands as he does when he's tired. It made him look vulnerable, like a little boy, and always tugged at my heartstrings. I slowed down as I passed him on my way to the oven to show him what I held in my hands.

"Scalloped potatoes?"

I slid the dish into the oven to keep it warm. "I know how you like them, and it *is* Valentine's Day, after all . . ."

"Oh yeah, I guess I forgot. I drove right by the drugstore but I wasn't thinking . . ."

"Stuart, the flowers were enough. I don't need anything else."

"Flowers? You mean the bouquet on the hall table?"

I waltzed over, flirting with him. "Well, I don't see any other fresh, gorgeous red and white floral arrangements around. Thank you, they're beautiful," I said, reaching up to hug him.

He caught my wrists before they circled his neck, stopping me. "I didn't send you any flowers."

"Stuart, I know I've been a bitch lately, and things haven't been wonderful around here, but after such a sweet, romantic gesture, don't spoil it by denying it. I love them! Thank you, they're perfect."

"I did not send you flowers!" His voice was soft, but frightening in its vehemence, each word pronounced slowly and carefully spaced.

"Well then, who did?" As I said the words, the only possible answer struck me with such force I cringed.

"You're asking me? How the hell should I know? You should know who would be sending you expensive bouquets for Valentine's Day."

I chased my conclusion away. "Maybe the kids did it as a surprise. I should have known it wasn't you. You won't even send me flowers when I'm dead!"

"You know it wasn't the kids. They would have asked me for the money. So,

Andrea—who sent you the damned flowers?"

Frantic to keep my speculation to myself, praying nothing showed in my face, I continued foolishly, "It was probably Kevin, then. You know what a joker he is!"

"Kevin McGrath? Are you trying to pass Kevin off as your lover?"

"Where do you get this crazy idea that I have a lover?"

"Only lovers send flowers."

By now I knew there was only one possible answer to this puzzle. But only a truly stupid man, or a selfish, troublemaking one, would send flowers to the home of his mistress, so her husband could see them and get angry! Richard was not stupid, so he had to be trying to make trouble between Stuart and me. But why?

"Andrea, I didn't send the flowers. We both know that. I don't know what is going on. I've been trying to guess who or what is on your mind, I've been hoping you'd tell me on your own, but now I'm asking you point-blank. Are you having an affair?"

His eyes, those beautiful gray eyes,

haunted now, dark circled, stared at me from a face gone pale. He looked like he was going to be sick. My mind raced.

"An affair, Stuart, an affair? Me?"

He turned from me, his face crumpling. My God, he was going to cry!

"Yes, Andrea, an affair. You know what an affair is. It's when you have sex with someone who is not your husband. It's called adultery!"

"Oh, Stuart, what an accusation. How could you think I'd have an affair?"

He stared at me for a long moment, then turned and left the kitchen, head hanging, his slumped shoulders expressing his hurt much louder than words.

Too reasonable, Andrea, I scolded, not enough righteous anger there. If I had truly been outraged, I would have yelled. I had sidestepped his question, and he knew it.

Once didn't make an affair, did it? The first time in the park didn't count, and there had only been that one other night, in the hotel. The memory took my breath away! I couldn't pretend it hadn't happened, this sin had been committed twice! And I had every intention of doing it again. If that didn't constitute an affair, then what the hell did? I stood, guilty as charged.

The smell of scalloped potatoes burning made me realize I'd been standing there for a long time.

The phone rang, and I was there to snatch the receiver off the wall. It was rarely for me, but I had been hovering around it for two days, answering every call, praying I would be the one to answer when he phoned. I lifted the receiver, stomach churning.

"Hello?"

His rich, baritone voice, pitched low. "Andrea, it's me."

My stomach flipped and hit the floor. Another twenty-five years could pass and his voice would still send a thrill through me. I was in the kitchen, Brian was in the basement playing ping pong with a couple of friends, and with great presence of mind, I asked Richard to hold and went into the den, guaranteeing myself a maximum of five minutes privacy.

"Did you get the roses?"

"Why did you do such a crazy thing?"

"I wanted you to know I was thinking about you."

"I thought Stuart sent them, and we had a big fight over them. We never fight!"

"So, the wimp gets jealous!"

"What a nasty thing to say."

"Yes, it is, and I'm sorry. Did you like the flowers?"

"Richard, answer me. Were you trying to make Stuart angry, or jealous, or what?"

"Not really. I guess I didn't think it out very carefully. If it bothered you, or created trouble, I apologize. I just thought you'd be pleased."

"Pleased? Oh Richard, it was an irresponsible thing to do."

"Did you like them? Were they nicer than Stuart's?"

"Yes, I love roses. And no, Stuart doesn't send me flowers."

I couldn't help make the comparison. Richard, considerate and thoughtful, and Stuart, stodgy and prosaic.

"Tell me they were lovely, as you are." He had a timbre in his voice that would charm a mother bird from her nest, and I had to laugh.

"Yes," I sighed, "they were beautiful."

"I've been thinking about you . . ."

"Me too."

"Andrea, this is not enough. A phone call a week, dinner once a month. I want to hold you in my arms, make love to you again! We have to meet again, soon."

I was hooked. Anger and fear dissipated, the dreadful scene with Stuart behind me. More sweet talk broke down any further resistance on my part, and we were chatting gaily when the sound of my son's laughter in the kitchen penetrated my consciousness. My delight in the sound of his voice withered, and the enchantment of his call was destroyed by the thought that any one of them, particularly Brian, could pick up an extension and hear this conversation. I came back to earth with a thud.

"Brian's here with his friends. This is not a good time to talk."

"We have to make the time. I've wanted you for too long, Andrea. Let's find a place of our own, where the mundane world can't intrude and I can whisper into your ear, kiss your nose, make love to you in the shower . . . you liked it last time, didn't you?"

Liked it? Like didn't come close. Shivers ran up and down my back, but at this moment Brian came in for some paper in the desk drawer. Disturbed and embarrassed, picturing my behavior through the eyes of my son, I flushed with shame.

"Look, I've got to run now," I said into the phone lightly, as though to a girlfriend, while Brian stared at me, his eyes questioning. Guilt must be clearly printed on my face. I had to finish this conversation. I hemmed around until Brian left the room, eventually arranging to meet him, then sat numb for a few moments, to change gears, before I returned to my family.

I had put Stuart out of my mind so easily, charmed by Richard's voice, his words. If they had been calculated to stir me up, they had done their work, and now I sat daydreaming about our next meeting, imagination erotically flourishing.

But my feelings were mixed. Until Valentine's Day I had refused to recognize any wrong in my relationship with this man. We loved each other, and there was a certain justice in finding him again and setting things straight, like completing a circle. But his beautiful flowers, filling the house with their perfume, oddly enough had made me aware of reality, and on the morning of February 15th I had thrown the flowers away, their scent now reminding me of an overheated, heavily perfumed funeral parlor. I brazenly lied whenever it suited me, but I was a married woman, having an affair with a married man. I didn't like this image of myself, and banished it quickly, trying to rekindle the romance Richard's words had wakened in me. We had made another date, and I looked forward to seeing him again. Merely thinking about having sex with him again aroused me to fever pitch. So different from making love with Stuart.

Since Valentine's Day, two weeks past, there had been no contact of any kind between us. And every time I replayed that scene, I became more convinced that Stuart's accusation had been merely a stab in the dark. He was the least observant man in the world. He couldn't possibly know anything. Besides, I added childishly, an affair couldn't make this boring marriage any worse. Stuart might be willing to settle for this, but I was fed up with it. It was time for a change.

Once again pleasantly dissatisfied with Stuart, his intuition relegated to a dark corner of my mind, I switched back to Richard. He wanted to see me more often . . . he missed me. On that high note I marched purposefully into the kitchen to start supper, my head filled with naughty, delicious thoughts.

An easy man to underestimate, Stuart. Never a standout in a crowd, too quiet to draw attention to himself. But under that unassuming exterior, my husband was an ambitious and tenacious man. He set himself a goal and then proceeded in a direct line until he reached it. He rarely lost. Stuart had fought for the things he wanted all his life, and he wanted me.

My birthday comes at the end of the month. Stuart didn't acknowledge it in any way, and Brian probably didn't even know when it was. Kelley, away at school, had forgotten, I guess, because not even a card came for me in the mail. Her phone calls came less frequently; she had a campus life and was not dependent on her parents for companionship. For money, yes, and as predicted by our friends, we heard from her when she was broke.

Mom remembered, sending a card and phoning me on Sunday morning while Stuart and Brian were out at the rink.

"Happy birthday, Andrea, your dad and I send love and kisses. How does it feel to be forty-seven?" She had the gall to laugh.

"Not too bad, Mom. Probably feels better than being the mother of a forty-seven year old woman!" That put an end to that nonsense pretty quickly.

"So how's everything?"

"Just fine, Mom, terrific. How is Dad?"

"He complains of indigestion, says my spaghetti sauce is too spicy. Suddenly, after all these years, my sauce is not good enough for him. You drink too much wine, Leo, I tell him, it's giving you heartburn. Drink milk. But does he listen to me?"

A rhetorical question. Any answer there would be a mistake. On the one hand I would be contradicting her, on the other attacking her Leo. Either would begin an argument.

"Come to visit soon, come for Easter, bring the kids. You looked thin at Christmas, thin and nervous. And your Stuart, looking worried all the time. Is everything okay between the two of you?"

"Sure, I told you, Mom, everything's great."

"Did he give you a nice gift for your birthday?"

"Um, he's giving it to me tonight. It's a surprise."

"Have a wonderful birthday, Andrea, we love you."

"Thanks, Mom." Thanks, Mom, I repeated in a small voice. Would you still love me if you knew what your precious daughter was up to the eyeballs in? Another rhetorical question. I went to make myself a lonely cup of tea.

Twenty-four

". . . then you drive around behind the building. Unit 49 is about halfway down. I'll be there first, so you won't have to worry about a key." Richard's directions were clear and simple, and I'd had no trouble finding the place, on a side road off Route 1, off Route 128. How did anyone ever find a place like this, I wondered as I parked the car.

Richard didn't answer my first timid knock, and if he didn't hear the next one he must be dead in there. Obviously late, I fumed, leaving me standing out here like a dummy. The blustery March wind blew my hair around my face, and I decided to go back to the car. At least there I'd be out of the cold, and not hanging around here waiting. I turned and ran into someone right behind me. "Scuse me, Mrs. Fletcher . . . oops, my mistake," he said, as I pushed the hair from my face. "Thought you were someone else. Sorry, lady," he mumbled, rushing away. Richard came up behind me a second later.

"Who was that?" he asked, as he put his arm around my waist, squeezing tight.

"Lord knows, he thought he knew me."

While he unlocked the unit, I asked, "Did you use your own name when you made the reservation, Rich? Or an alias, like, uh, John Smith?" I laughed.

"Not Smith, but an alias, if you want to call it that. I told the clerk my name was Fletcher."

"But the guy out there . . . he thought . . ." The rest of my question was smothered by Richard's kiss, and I forgot all about it after he carried me over to the bed.

The bedspread smelled of mold, and I started to sneeze. I sat up and swivelled my head slowly, taking in the dark brown cheap cardboard paneling, threadbare carpeting, and dingy orange drapery. It wasn't dirty, but it was cheap. Suddenly I felt humiliated, like a ten-dollar hooker.

It got worse. Because of some glitch in one of his programs, Richard had to go back to work as soon as possible. But first, he joked, down to business. The urgency in his hands and his body didn't elicit any response from me. I didn't feel desire. I felt rushed, overwrought, overtired, and ashamed at being here with him, my lies to Stuart boldly etched in my mind.

There was no romance, no magic, here today, and I started to cry.

Richard held me in his arms, soothing me, covering me with kisses, and in the release of tears, I was swept up in the fever of making love with him.

Afterwards, lying on his shoulder, I tried to laugh at my apprehension. This was what I had dreamed of all my life. I couldn't let guilt or shame spoil the dream for me, not now when I held it in my hand. But not here.

"Have you ever stayed here before, Rich?"

"No, what makes you ask that?" he answered looking at me through the mirror as he adjusted his tie.

"The guy I bumped into outside, he thought I was Mrs. Fletcher, then when he saw my face, he said he'd made a mistake. I just wondered . . ."

"He probably assumed you were Mrs. Fletcher staying with Mr. Fletcher in Unit 49, you silly girl. Now, give me a kiss, I've got to get back to the office."

"I don't like this place, Rich."

"But it's—okay, you're right. We'll find somewhere else, a place of our very own, where you won't cry. Promise me, no more tears, okay?"

He leaned close until he caught my eye, and I grinned sheepishly. "I'll call you soon, love." Another kiss, a swift hug, and he was gone. For the moment, I was happy.

Dressing slowly, I pondered the clerk's reaction again. He took me for Mrs. Fletcher because I was outside Mr. Fletcher's room, but when he saw my face clearly, he knew he had the wrong woman. He knew a Mrs. Fletcher, and it wasn't me. That couldn't be a coincidence. Richard had stayed here before, using that name, with someone the motel clerk recognized.

That was before me, I said with a

forced smile to the woman in the mirror. But the words held no conviction. Richard said he'd never been here before, and though I desperately wanted it to be true, I was probably not the only woman . . . "other" woman I amended, in his life.

I loved him, but there would always be doubt in my mind when it came to Richard. I raised my eyes to the mirror to comb my hair. You're still a damned fool, Andrea Corelli, said the sad-looking woman there.

"Hi, Andrea, it's Ellen. Got a minute? I have to talk to you."

"Sure . . . what time is it?"

She laughed. "It's past nine, and you aren't even awake. I thought you'd be up, since the guys had hockey."

It was Saturday morning. Brian had a tournament in Billerica, about two hours away, and they wouldn't be home until four or so. "Stuart must have turned the alarm off when they left, and I slept in. Come on over, I'll get some coffee going." Twenty minutes later she arrived with bagels and cream cheese.

"So, what's up?" I asked as soon as we had settled at the kitchen table.

"Stuart, and he's upset."

"What do you mean?"

"He called me the other day and asked me to meet him for lunch in town. He said not to tell you, and I didn't, thinking he might be planning a surprise for your anniversary or something.

"I met him for lunch on Thursday, and I've never heard Stuart talk so much. He went on for an hour and a half. Andrea, he's sick with worry that you don't love him any more. I felt really bad, listening to him, knowing what I know . . . he was obviously hoping I might have something to tell him."

"Did you tell him anything?"

"Of course not. I told him he shouldn't worry, you're just going through a phase, that you've been depressed since the accident, that maybe he needs to pay more attention to you. You know, stuff like that."

"What did he say?"

"He says you've shut him out of your life, that you don't talk to each other any more, that something weird is going on and he's determined to get to the bottom of it. He also said . . . and I almost cried . . . he said he doesn't want to lose you. Andrea, don't you think this business has gone far enough? You've got Stuart's attention now. Maybe you should stop playing games?"

"Ellen, I didn't get involved with Richard because I wanted to play games, or to get Stuart's attention. There's something missing in my life, and I think I've found it with Richard. He's so attentive to little details, goes out of his way to make me happy. Stuart never bothers about little things. Did I tell you Richard sent me flowers? Laughs at my jokes? Listens when I talk? God, Ellen, the last time Stuart heard anything I said was 1979!" My eyes filled with tears of frustration, and I paused to collect myself, and then went on.

"I'll tell you what's wrong with Stuart. His lordship's life isn't running as smoothly as he likes it. A few days ago I was late getting home—I was shopping, El," I added, catching the look on her face. "He hates to be kept waiting. I don't flatter his ego by hanging on his every word any more, all that boring stuff about work and investments. He told you we don't talk any more! I don't listen any more, that's Stuart's problem! He's been spoiled, now he's not getting my undivided attention, and he doesn't like it! You don't think he misses the great sex we used to have, do you? No, it's just that his clockwork life is not running smoothly, so he blames me! There must be something wrong with me! Certainly there can't be anything wrong with Mr. Perfect!" I was shouting now, and burst into hysterical tears.

"Oh Lord, Andrea, look at you." She came around the table and put her arms around me, "Maybe you should see a therapist. You aren't very happy for someone who is supposed to be madly in love. You're nervous and edgy all the time, and you have everyone worried about you. Stuart thinks you're on the verge of a nervous breakdown, and I feel like I've contributed; if I had given you different advice the day we talked about all this maybe you wouldn't be in this mess."

I pushed her away and jumped out of my chair. I needed space, I had to get up and move around. "No, Ellen, it wasn't your advice, I was desperate to do something. You told me what I wanted to hear, but I would have gone ahead no matter what you thought. Don't make yourself responsible for my problems. I have enough guilt here without that too."

"I didn't want to upset you, I just thought you should know what Stuart told me." She glanced at her watch. "What time does the post office close today?"

"Saturday? Noon, I think, why?"

"I'd better get my ass in gear, I've got millions of things to do today, and I've got to drop the tax returns into the post office first. Stuart cares about you, and he wants to see you happy again."

"Sometimes I don't think I'll ever be happy again. I'm tied up in knots over this business with Richard. When I'm with him I'm on top of the world, but when he's not around, reality sets in, and I worry about lying to Stuart, and deceiving the kids, and wonder where it's all going to end."

I can't imagine what she reported to Stuart after this conversation, if anything, because no questions were answered that morning in my kitchen, and her intercession for Stuart did very little to change my behavior.

Richard did that.

After all this time I knew little more about Richard than I did twenty-five years ago. The time we spent together had no substance, other than sex. I had no idea if he liked music, ate Chinese food, or slept on the right or left side of the bed. Besides sex in the afternoon, we talked on the phone about once a week, whispering sweet nothings to each other, met for the occasional dinner in some out of the way place, arriving and leaving separately, and the conversation usually involved sex. We varied that routine only once, when, at my insistence, we went to the movies.

"*Dances With Wolves* is supposed to be terrific," I begged. "I'm so tired of being shut away with you. Can't we just once walk down a street together, arm in arm, or sit in a theater surrounded by people, as though we belonged together? Is that so much to ask?"

It was three hours long but we agreed that it was a Friday afternoon well spent.

I almost fell asleep the next night, however, sitting through it once again with Stuart, who had been dying to see it and wouldn't take no for an answer.

A stolen afternoon now and then doesn't allow for much casual chitchat, especially with urgent business to attend to. As soon as Richard kicked the door shut behind us we were on the bed, tearing off our clothes, anxious to stroke and touch each other. His lips brushed my skin, and I was all over him, damp with desire and shameless in my need to be filled with him, aroused and inflamed and finally sent over the edge to sweet fulfillment. I was a wild woman, and he was an amazing lover. We made love in bed, on the floor, standing in the shower, or sitting in a chair, and I was astounded at how little I knew about the intricacies of lovemaking.

We didn't talk about much of anything, and we never discussed the future at all. He understood me so well, I thought fondly. I was incapable of making any important decision about the future in my confused and topsy-turvy state of mind, and he was willing to wait, patiently, never pressing me to make a choice between him and Stuart.

But as time passed and I grew accustomed to this strange half-life, it became clear even to me that he liked things just the way they were. He had no intention of choosing between me and his wife, a suspicion abruptly confirmed the day I saw him with the other Mrs. Fletcher.

Jordan's was having a huge linen sale. We needed new sheets badly, and I decided to kill a few hours in the store at Dedham Mall rather than drive into Boston. I had just turned onto the ramp off 128 when I caught sight of an old-fashioned sports car a couple of cars behind me. My heart bumped, as it always did with anything related to Richard. I slowed, and with one eye fixed on the rearview mirror I watched the traffic behind me. It was Richard, but what was he doing all the way out here? A couple of cars went around, and he came right up behind me. But he wasn't alone, there was a woman with him, with long dark hair, wearing a camel coat, a lot like mine.

We stopped for a light, and in my rearview mirror he leaned over and kissed her. On the lips. A long, lingering kiss. Probably had his damned hand up her skirt, too! Not a business acquaintance, this, and probably not his wife. Then who? And where was the bastard going? Cleverly disguised in my innocuous Toyota, he passed me without a flicker of recognition, and I followed him, a quick glance at the gas gauge showing that I could follow him to New Jersey if necessary. But we didn't go far. Just beyond the Mall he took a right, and I followed him down a road depressingly familiar. My worst fears were confirmed when he turned into the driveway of the same cheesy motel he had taken me to the first time. I pulled around back in anticipation, and sure enough they pulled in and parked, crossing the lot with their arms wrapped around each other. As he opened the door to Unit 49 they kissed again. It was disgusting. I was stunned. This had to be the other Mrs. Fletcher . . . or one of the many Mrs. Fletchers! Proof that he was cheating! Still the lowlife, still playing around, still a liar.

So what, Andrea! What does this prove? That he's untrue to you? What did you expect from a man who cheats on his wife!

I forgot the shopping spree and headed home, pain and anger twisting like a knife. The next time I saw that bastard would be the last! I couldn't go through hell over him again. I didn't need him. I knew what I had to do.

But I wasn't ready for that; I was afraid to put an end to our affair, to chase him out of my life again. And so it went on. I couldn't trust him, but I couldn't live without him. Only a fool would mistake this charade for love, and I stared at that fool every morning in the mirror with growing revulsion. But this time it wasn't only the woman in the mirror telling me what a fool I was. The other Mrs. Fletcher now ridiculed me from the dark corners of my mind.

Mentally I was a basket case, incapable of making the smallest decision. Having to choose the right shade of panty hose was enough to bring me to tears, after which I usually ended up staying home, unless, of course, I was meeting Richard.

And I forgot things. Everything.

"Ma, I'm out of underwear!" Brian, frustrated, stood at my bedroom door at 6:30 one morning.

"Brian, I thought you were doing your own laundry these days," I answered sleepily from the cozy comfort of my bed. I had decided to take the day off work. I'd call in sick or something later . . .

"Mo-ommm, I do my own laundry all the time, but yesterday you said not to worry, that you'd take care of it for me. Now what am I going to wear?" He slammed his fist against the wall as he turned away, and I imagined my chin under that hand. Poor kid, I thought, he should have told me he had nothing left to wear. My eyes closed again, and Richard smiled seductively until I dropped back off to sleep . . .

Several times I went into the grocery store but left after aimlessly walking up and down the aisles. There were too many people around, and it was so noisy that I couldn't remember what we needed. Eggs, we must need eggs. It was a standing joke between Stuart and Brian that I had bought more ketchup and sugar in the space of a month than we'd use in three years! We ate a lot of scrambled eggs.

I thought things couldn't possibly get any worse. But they did. I lost my job.

Mr. Murphy called me into his office one Friday morning, at the end of a particularly bad week.

"Andrea, is everything okay?"

"Yes, Bob, sure, I'm fine," I fumbled, trying to focus my thoughts. I hadn't slept the night before, after a run-in with Stuart, but something told me I wanted to be on the ball during this conversation. "Why?"

"At home?"

"Sure. What's the problem, Bob?"

"You know how I hate to pry, but, well, I've been watching you lately, and become increasingly concerned. The quality of your work has deteriorated over the past few months, you've been making mistakes the other gals have been covering up. "Quite frankly, your work has become unacceptable."

Don't hold back, Bob, just give it to me straight, I thought bitterly.

"There's going to be a major reorganization here and the upshot is that your job is being eliminated. Joyce will be working full time, and we'll have no need of a part-time secretary any longer. I had hoped you'd have that course finished and we could move you over to paralegal. Bill Grover waited as long as he could for you, but he hired someone the other day to fill that slot . . . he starts next week. You've been a valued employee, and I hate to lose you, but, quite frankly, Andrea, I think you have to get your personal life in order. If you think I can be of help . . . ?"

I was numb with shock, and couldn't answer him. He shrugged his shoulders, and gave up.

"You can work until the end of next week, if you like, and we'll arrange for four weeks salary, until you get yourself organized. Andrea . . ." he added, no doubt at the sight of tears rolling down my cheeks, "we've been friends for a long time. I wish you'd let me help."

Awkwardly heaving myself out of the leather womb that passed for a client chair in his office, I stumbled to the door, fumbling in my skirt pocket for a tissue. "No, Bob, there's nothing you can do . . . but thanks." I closed the door gently behind me. I had to get myself under control before the whole office found out what had happened, but at the sight of a few pale, stricken faces, I ran to the ladies' room, crying hysterically.

Oh my Lord, I thought, when I was able to, I've been fired! I couldn't believe it, and Stuart would be horrified. What was I going to tell Stuart? He'd be angry and disappointed, and I was in for a lecture on responsibility. I left work early, planning to go back on Saturday to collect my things.

Stuart was wonderful. He was disappointed, of course, but he didn't lecture. Instead, he put his arms around me and let me cry for a while, and I was surprised at the comfort I found there.

"Don't worry about it, sweetheart. You can get yourself a better job tomorrow, if you want to. But this might be a good time to take a break, get over whatever it is that's preying on your mind. You might consider therapy—"

He got no further. "So you think I'm crazy? I need a shrink? Thanks for the vote of confidence, Stuart." I pulled away from him and went into the kitchen for a cup of tea, opted for a glass of wine instead, and went out to the back deck to sit alone in the dark and brood.

Twenty-five

Spring slipped by unnoticed, and before we knew it Kelley's first year at college was over. She had her summer job again at TasteeTreet, but without Phil she hated it. She spent all her free time with him, or yakking on the phone with one or another of her girlfriends.

The long youth hockey season was finished at last, and Brian found other pursuits to occupy his time, like long hours in front of the TV set playing video games. He seemed very popular with the girls, if the phone calls he ducked were any indication.

"Mom, just tell her I'm studying, I can't be disturbed, I'm asleep, anything, please!" he begged when they called. He was interested in another sweet young thing, but those phone calls were made from the privacy of his bedroom.

Stuart's work seemed to be taking him to places he had not traveled before. He mentioned trips to New Orleans, and Topeka, several visits to Chicago. There was nothing significant in this; his company audited many other companies. As a vice-president, he normally wasn't involved in the actual bookwork, but he met with the executives of these firms, cementing relationships, soliciting new business. Besides being Janice's home, Chicago is a major business center, and there was no reason his visits there should stand out in my mind.

He might have told me that he met Jan in Chicago on one of his trips. He knew both Janice and Mike, and it wouldn't surprise me if he got in touch with them. If I knew, the knowledge fell into the back of my mind, and was immediately lost.

If he was lonesome or unhappy I didn't notice. Perhaps time hung heavy for him; for me the season flew by. Spring blossomed into summer with no significant improvement or change in our lives. I washed, ironed, gardened, cleaned house and waited, the days of my life measured by my meetings with Richard, the time between a wasteland of hot, muggy days.

Richard and I lay quietly, wrapped around each other, savoring the afterglow of sexual fulfillment. After all these months we had established a pattern. We had a place of our own; an old Victorian hotel on the ocean road about five miles out of the city, and it had begun to feel like home. Country decor, dainty wallpaper, nicely framed prints on the walls, lacy curtains, nice view, nice hotel! Not at all the seedy rundown joint of sneaky lovers, shown in the movies and engraved on my mind invariably bathed in the red glow of a flashing neon sign glimpsed through a dirty window. Here we had clean white towels, the bleached clean smell of freshly laundered sheets, the lovely view.

Looking back, I hate that whole period of time, preferring to recapture the innocent spontaneity and total abandon of our first encounter in the woods. Now we made arrangements and took precautions. By no stretch of the imagination could our carefully planned assignations at nice hotels be considered impulsive. These meetings were premeditated and dishonest.

But when I was with Richard I forgot all that, exulting at my good luck in finding him again, saving the guilt for later, when I was alone.

On this particular day in July he had conjured up a fictitious lunch with a business associate, scheduled to go on late into the afternoon, and would not return to his office. I wasn't working, of course, and my time was my own until dinner. Seldom did we have so much time together, and we reveled in it.

On the way over I had stopped at a little shop in the village, happily choosing a romantic picnic for two. French rolls, a slice of pate au poivre, a tiny Boursin cheese, a bunch of grapes; perfect complements to the chilled bottle of champagne he had picked up, which we drank in heavy plastic tumblers from the bathroom.

Passion spent for the moment, we were lazily feeding each other grapes, and talking, for a change, about ourselves and our lives.

"What are you like, now that you're all grown up?" I asked. He laughed, but I was serious, hoping to get to know the person he had become.

He stared off into the distance, marshalling his thoughts, and I watched his eyes turn from warm brown to dark opaque glass. A well-remembered change, creating the illusion that we had been together like this all of our lives.

"I guess I'm a romantic, a dreamer. I reach too high, set impossible goals for myself, then fall short and settle for less. I've done that in my career, and in my personal life, too. Take you, for instance. You were so special, a dream come true . . ."

I permitted myself a tiny smile into his shoulder.

" . . . I almost had you, but you turned out to be an elusive dream, an unfulfilled fantasy. In the end you let me down, and I've had to learn to live without you."

My smile faded. The past, with all its heartache, had slammed into the present.

"I let you down? What the hell are you

talking about? I planned my entire life around you!"

"Ah, but how could I know that? You were impossible to read. I wanted you, but you didn't appear to feel the same for me. You refused any intimacy with me," he continued. "At first I thought it was cute, and I loved you, so I curbed my needs, but eventually I had to accept your refusal as rejection. You had none of the passion or the unquenchable desire that I felt for you. Your feelings for me were very immature."

A sinking sensation began in the pit of my stomach, but I couldn't let this pass. I had to fight back. "You wanted sex so badly it was impossible to know if you loved me. The things you wanted to do felt wrong to me, and I didn't know if you loved me, or just wanted to get laid. I needed to trust you, to know that you would always be there for me. I never felt that about you, Richard."

This all happened twenty-five years ago, back in the dark ages, but the pain was back, fresh and stabbing. He had it all wrong. I had loved him with all my heart, but he had made a fool of me.

While I talked the sick feeling had

hardened to anger, and sarcastically, I added, "I guess commitment and fidelity was asking too much of the man who professed to love me. Or have you forgotten that you screwed anything that moved? Oh God, Richard, you broke my heart, and now you lay here, accusing *me* of letting *you* down?" Unable to continue, my anger dissolved into tears.

He reached for me, slowly gathering me into the shelter of his arms, relieving the pain, while his eyes, expressive as always, registered surprise and hurt, and the dawning understanding of my love for him.

"Andrea, I swear to you, I had no idea . . . you've carried this pain all your life. We might have had a future together, but my behavior—I tried to make you jealous, to force some kind of response out of you. I loved you so much . . . my God, we were young."

Brokenhearted tears filled me and overflowed. We had stood on opposite sides of a wall, unable to scale it, to cross the barrier, to trust each other. He was right—we had been young, and unrealistic.

He stroked my hair, holding me close

to him, trying to close the floodgates that had been opened. He didn't use words, but made soft, soothing sounds to calm the storm of my broken heart. Gradually an overwhelming weight, anguish carried for a lifetime, lifted and disappeared, and I absolved him for the hurt he inflicted years ago.

Did I say to myself, Andrea, he's still doing it? Did I give the present a second's thought? Not me. I was busy sorting out the past, and for the moment I was content, held securely against his chest, the sound of his heartbeat comforting in my ear, while the hand that cupped my breast gently rubbed the nipple lying against his palm. He went on . . .

"Dear, sweet love, at last we have the opportunity to straighten out our lives. I've wanted you all of my life, but never expected anything to come of my wishes. But here we are, fulfilling that dream. Think of it, we have the rest of our lives for each other."

I understood the words, but his meaning was unclear. The rest of our lives? To spend together, or to sneak around, meeting on the sly, lying and cheating?

One of many, or was he finally talking about commitment?

"Richard, I have to know what you mean. What we have now isn't a life. It's a dream, a fantasy, with no commitment, no future. Is this all you want? Or are we going to love each other openly and honestly? Have you ever considered leaving your wife, and spending the rest of your life with me?"

A faint shadow crossed his face—doubt, maybe, or fear, gone in an instant. It troubled me, but I shoved it aside, trying also to ignore the growing stimulation as his hands stroked my body sensually.

"I'm still confused, Rich. You're talking about want, and desire, but you never mention love. Is this relationship only about sex, or do you love me?"

"Andrea, of course I love you, and I will always love you. But a great part of that love is physical—my body needs to be fulfilled by you. Is that wrong? I love you, and I want you, too." The tone of his voice changed, became more playful, sexy. "And now I've got you!"

And so he did, God help me. He smothered me in his arms, sweeping my questions and fears away with the touch of his hand, his tender kisses in every secret place on my body, and the promise of yet another incredible adventure in lovemaking. He awakened the animal inside me, obscuring my need for answers, and in the immediate need for fulfillment, I was ready to make love again. But those questions returned to haunt me on the drive home, as the cloud of lighthearted satisfaction grew torn and ragged at the edges.

The look I had surprised on his face told me more clearly than words that he wasn't going to rock his boat. He had no need to change his life, with a rich wife, a thriving business, and more women than he could count. He didn't care about commitment. He wanted a sexual romp.

I felt that I was thinking clearly for the first time in many months, and I let my thoughts wander.

More than twenty-five years ago our future had been jeopardized by his infidelity, and slowly I was realizing that life was repeating itself. He was infinitely charming, but insubstantial and shallow. Unlike Stuart, whose honesty and stability had given me a sense of permanence that I never found with Richard.

With one I had romance, but no security; with the other safety, but no fantasy. And just when my life had settled into a rut of boredom and routine, along came Richard, fresh and exciting and new. Meeting him again mixed the past with the present, he had become an extension of Stuart, like bookends, each contributing something I needed, each supporting me in his own way. But I couldn't keep them both, and the day was coming when I would be forced to choose. I couldn't continue to live in a dream world. If Richard didn't want me, and I couldn't find some spark to light up my life with Stuart, I would be better off with neither of them.

Richard was a dreamer, expecting the best of everything to come his way. But I understood dreamers, and like me, he never worked hard enough at the things he wanted, leaving his path to chance, considering his life a compromise. Some concession, I thought with a snort, saddled with a rich wife he said he didn't want but wouldn't leave.

He was also an opportunist, with an

eye on the prize, and when the time was right, he went for it. Maybe his wife did trap him into marriage by getting pregnant, but it was more likely that he made that story up to play on my sympathy. I easily saw him baiting the trap with sex to catch himself a rich wife, someone who would set him up in business, his dream.

Me? Just a loose end in his life, an unattainable dream made desirable by my elusiveness, and drifting back into his life at the wrong time. But now that the gap on his shelf of trophies had been filled, I might find myself shoved to the back of his closet, gathering dust. No doubt about it, he had everything he wanted, and I would have to look out for myself.

But what about Stuart, and the marriage I had shoved aside while scheming to get myself into bed with Richard? In many ways I was dissatisfied with Stuart, but we had built a life together, a family unit that I wasn't quite ready to toss away. Though Stuart didn't provide the storybook romance that I had found with Richard, he was the solid foundation of my life.

I was on a treadmill, but I had to come to some kind of conclusion. Soon. If I continued to go around in circles, I would be very surprised if I ended up with Stuart, Richard, or my sanity.

As often happens, events followed some predestined course, and that decision was taken out of my hands.

Twenty-six

I let myself into the empty house, wondering absently where Brian was. His books had been dropped just inside the door in the front hall, as always, so he had been home, but he was supposed to leave a note on the kitchen counter if he went out. Ah well, I guess we were all breaking rules these days. The mantel clock chimed the hour; by six o'clock his stomach should have been crying out for food. When I looked into the den the light on the answering machine was blinking, and I pressed the button for messages. There were three calls, the first two of no consequence after I heard the third.

"Mom, Dad and I are at Aunt Lorraine's. You'd better call here when you get home. It's 5:30. Where are you?"

I immediately called Lorraine's, but heard only the endless ringing of her telephone at the other end.

I hesitated to call Mom, afraid to scare her if there had been an accident of some kind at Lorraine's, but by 7:00 I was frantic, and finally called her. But there was no one there either, and thoroughly frustrated by now, I called Lorraine's again. This time, thank God, Brian answered.

"What's going on? How come no one called me? I'm going nuts!"

He said Stuart, Lorraine and Mom were at the hospital, where my Dad had been taken after an apparent heart attack. He was in an intensive care unit, and Brian supposed everything was going to be okay.

"We were just sitting around the waiting room, so Dad brought me back here, in case you called."

Thank you, Stuart, thank you.

"Which hospital?"

"The General, you know, near Grandma and Grandpa's house."

"Okay, I'm leaving now, and I'll get to the hospital as quickly as I can. Tell Dad that if he calls you. Just stay where you are. Are you babysitting Steve and Maureen? Well, put them to bed, or whatever, I'll see you in a while."

I exceeded every speed limit and an hour and forty minutes—an eternity—later, I raced across the hospital lobby and took the elevator to the fourth floor, where emergency heart patients were kept for observation. My mother saw me and came into the corridor to talk.

"Thank God you're here. They did some tests on him late this afternoon. He's sedated, because of the pain. He never had a heart attack before, but the doctor says he's in pretty good shape for a man of seventy-two. With medication and, um . . . uh, maybe a bypass, his chances of recovery are good."

Chin quivering, her eyes dark hollows in her pale, tired face, I watched the tears spilling over down her cheeks, as she willed me to tell her he would be all right. Smothering my own fears, I wrapped my arms around her. "He said my sauce was too spicy, Andrea, and all the time . . ."

"He'll be fine, Mom, of course he'll be just fine."

Looking through the small window in

the door I could make out the lump in the bed that was my Dad, attached to tubes and wires which were in turn hooked up to bottles and monitors, little red and green lights blipping across their screens. The lights were dim, adding to the nightmare quality of the scene inside the room. A nurse checking information on the monitors stood on one side of the bed, and Stuart sat on the other.

Mom and I went into the room and I went to stand next to him, looking at Dad motionless on the neat white bed.

"Sweetheart, he's okay," Stuart whispered, reaching out to touch my arm.

I grabbed his hand, holding on as though my life depended on it, and began to cry. For Dad? Oh yes, at first, but then for so much more. Once the tears began, I cried for myself, for forgiveness. For the mess I was making of my life. For Stuart.

He stood and put his arm around my shoulders, prompting me to start sobbing out loud. The nurse raised a disapproving face, her demeanor strongly suggesting that we leave the room, which we did, while Mom resumed her seat next to the bed.

We walked down the hall to the solarium at the end, fortunately empty, and I collapsed onto the first ugly green vinyl couch I came to. Stuart sat next to me, and I cried into his shoulder for a while. He seemed to understand that I needed to cry it out, because he said nothing, sitting with his arms around me. It was good to have him here to lean on. He was where he belonged, and everything would be all right.

After several minutes, he said "Hon, your father is going to be okay. He has had an angina attack, very painful, but the easiest of the heart problems to solve. There's some blockage, he may need a bypass, but they won't make that decision until tomorrow. Meantime, Dr. Wei, the heart surgeon, thinks we can take it easy, go home and get some rest."

"Sure, easy for him to say. His father isn't lying in there."

"But he's comfortable, and stable, and by the way, Doctor. Wei is a woman."

A woman would perform an operation on Dad! I could just imagine his reaction. "Does he know?"

My mother came into the room. "Lorraine's here! We've been looking for you." Lorraine had brought food, and she followed Mom into the gloomy solarium. Surprisingly, we were all hungry, and the four of us, including Mom, quickly emptied each little white box from the Chinese restaurant.

We hung around for a couple of hours, wandering in and out of his room to stare at Dad, the machinery, willing him to be well. Around midnight a nurse suggested that they wheel a cot into the room next to Dad, so Mom could lie down, since she wanted to stay for the night, and the rest of us should leave. Lorraine invited us to stay with her, but Mother overrode her. "There's no sense in crowding in with your sister when our house is empty. You can sleep in our twin beds, or in your old room," she suggested.

It made sense. Lorraine's house was small, and she would keep Brian with her overnight, since he was probably asleep already, and we drove away in silence to Mom and Dad's for the night.

The bed in my room was a double, handed down when the folks got their twin beds, and if we were to sleep in it together Stuart and I would be very close indeed. Though we usually slept in my room when we stayed here, I expected Stuart to go into my parents' room. But, after brushing my teeth, I was surprised and pleased, to see that he had settled into my bed. I needed comfort, and I wanted him with me tonight.

I slid into my accustomed spot next to him, and his arms encircled me, enclosing and protecting, and I snuggled close in relief and satisfaction. Stuart would take care of me. He was calling a truce, dispelling the cloud of dishonesty and suspicion. With no thought to my part in creating this nightmare, I took simple pleasure in his presence, and breathed a deep sigh of relief.

But I was not to be let off the hook that easily. Sensing my need, Stuart saw his advantage, and struck. With lips pressed close to my ear, he said, "Andrea, sweetheart, we have to talk. We can't go on like this."

The lovely swell of well-being shrivelled and died. How stupid of me to think our problems were over. As usual, I expected Stuart to make it better, but simply having him in his accustomed place, assuming his role of protector, did not change the situation. He wanted to break through the wall of silence, and he deserved to know what it was all about. But he had no idea why it had grown, didn't know there were outside factors involved.

More than anything I wanted to open my heart, to repair the breach between us. But how could I find the words to tell him about my dissatisfaction, my unfaithfulness, while held tightly in his loving arms? Which magic words would explain, and soften the blow, of my affair with Richard? In despair, I realized that there were none. Tied in with my wish to purge myself was the image of Dad lying in a hospital bed. It was the kind of trade I would have made with God as a child. "Dear God, I'll be really, really good if you make my daddy better."

I didn't think my need to unburden myself, though good for my soul, was an excuse to finally and permanently break Stuart's heart.

"Oh Stuart, this isn't a very good time to talk, with Dad . . ."

"Andrea, you're avoiding the issue; we have to get this into the open. We used to talk about everything, to discuss our problems . . . please, talk to me."

"There's really nothing to talk about. I have to sort this out for myself."

"Sweetheart, I love you so much, and I'm so ashamed of the things I said. I know I hurt you, but you haven't been yourself for a long time, and I was angry and afraid that something, or someone, had come between us. I guess I made a bad situation worse. Can you forgive me for the things I said?"

Valentine's Day! He was asking my forgiveness for the things he said in anger on Valentine's Day. He was apologizing for what he thought was a false accusation, but shameless bitch that I was, I had spent this very afternoon proving him right. Though an eternity had passed, I had been making love with Richard today, only a few hours ago, while my father was on his way to the hospital, while Stuart was rushing to his side because I wasn't home when Lorraine called.

"Of course I forgive you, Stuart." Incredible! Was this what they called chutzpah! "But you've done nothing wrong. There's something inside me that isn't satisfied. I don't know what I want or who I am anymore. A mid-life crisis, I guess. I'm searching for some kind of utopia that probably doesn't exist. I have you, the children, our lovely home, but it doesn't seem to be enough. I feel restless, and I don't know what to do about it. It's not your fault, Stuart—it's me. It'll run it's course, I'm sure, and everything will go back to normal."

He was quiet for so long I thought he was satisfied, had perhaps fallen asleep. But in the silence of the dark night, when he finally spoke, his voice had a hard edge, and his words shook me to the core.

"I'd like to believe you're restless, or bored, but I can't go along with that. I still think you're hiding something from me, and it's driven a wedge between us. If that's normal, I don't want it any more. Andrea, you should know that I'm making it my business to learn what it's all about. When I know for sure, we'll talk again."

His voice broke, and he rolled over as though he were going to sleep, but his body was rigid, and his ragged breathing told me he was crying.

Huddled on my side of the narrow bed, thoroughly miserable, I sifted through what he had said, wondering what he guessed, and what he knew, feeling as dirty as a whore.

I didn't like lying to Stuart, but he'd die if I told him the truth. He trusted me, loved me, and I had blatantly betrayed him. He didn't know about Richard, or he would never have told me he loved me, but I was surprised at his intuition, and stunned at the depth of emotion he kept hidden. Never in all our years together had I seen him passionate about anything, and suddenly he was a boiling cauldron. It shocked me to see him shaken when he had always been as solid as a foundation under my house of cards.

But I wanted more than comfort and safety. I needed passion, romance, and Stuart couldn't provide it. I had come back full circle, notwithstanding my thoughts today in the car, and I wasn't ready to make any changes. I didn't want to give up the excitement I had found with Richard. Now this is really good, Andrea, lying here filled with flaming desire and lust for another man, while my husband, who loved me, lay weeping next to me. Stuart finally fell asleep, and I spent the long night in agony, wondering how long it would be before we all went right around the bend.

The next morning, after a cup of coffee which we drank in total silence, Stuart and I went to the hospital to see Dad. He was awake, had good color and was feeling quite happy.

"Don't worry about me. If anything else happens, I'm in the right place. They'll do a bypass, probably a double bypass, sometime in the next week or so. I trust Dr. Wei; she's done dozens of these operations, and I know she'll look out for me. Don't give me that look, Andrea, I know what you're thinking! But I'm a modern kind of guy! There's room for change in all of us, and I have reconsidered my position on women in the professions since I met her."

Laughing, I kissed Dad goodbye, and promised Mom that I'd be back to stay with her over the weekend to give her some moral support, and to satisfy myself that Dad was going to be okay.

Stuart, of course, had his own car, and telling my mother that he to get to work, left the hospital without saying goodbye to me and drove back to Boston. I stopped at Lorraine's long enough to collect my son, refusing her invitation to stay for lunch, and drove back to the city. Brian provided occasional breaks in the brooding silence as I mulled over the miserable unresolved soap opera of my life.

On Friday Dr. Wei performed her magic, and Mom and I were allowed to look at Dad, back in ICU, after the four hour surgery. The diminutive surgeon had performed a double bypass to ensure that his heart received an adequate supply of fresh blood and hopefully prevent the pain of angina from recurring. He lay in the center of an incredible room, with windows in every wall so he could be monitored from all sides. He was surrounded by instruments that might have been born in the imagination of Stephen King—huge, ugly machines, frighteningly awesome, yet performing tasks I took for granted. Basically these machines took over the vital functions of

Dad's cardiovascular system, giving his own system time to mend, become adjusted to its new circuitry. This room full of equipment was required to replace one little human heart. He looked pathetically small in the huge white space.

"He looks dreadful, his skin is green."

"But he's going to be fine, Mom. He'll be home soon."

"What would I do if I lost him?"

"Dr. Wei says that the shape his heart's in now, Mom, he'll outlast us all."

"He's always been there to take care of me," she went on, not hearing me at all. "All these years together he's been the strong one. For forty-eight years I've depended on him . . . I couldn't live without him . . ." She broke off, tears spilling over, as she looked at the inert shape on the narrow bed. I was thinking of how I relied on Stuart, and wondered if I'd be saying those words in another twenty-five years.

". . . such a mess . . . I think he knew . . . and still he loved me . . ."

"C'mon, Mom, time to leave. Let's go shopping or something."

I led her down the corridor and out of the hospital. First some food, then home for a while. She needed a rest. She was distraught and tired, and I let her sit quietly while I drove and pondered what she was talking about. What did she mean by "I think he knew"? Knew what? Who? Dad, I presumed, but what could she be referring to? She had made a mess of something or other, and I decided, knowing those two, that it had to be something trivial.

My parents were so lucky. Falling in love with the right person is an uncertain game at best, yet the first time out they had found a love to last forever. I envied them the certainty of their love for each other, especially in light of all the questions I had about mine.

But still something niggled at the back of my mind. Other times, other comments she had made, half-uttered remarks I had picked up here and there, that sounded like nonsense at the time . . .

"Mom," I asked, "Dad was your first serious boyfriend, your first love, right?"

She answered defensively, her vehemence taking me by surprise. "Of course he was—haven't I always told you that.

And he's been there for me all these years, not like some men I could name . . . !"

I'd asked for it! I was in for a lecture on men who were unreliable, like the jerk Dad's sister Lucy had married, a story I'd heard many times.

"Mom, here's the Italian bakery, why don't we get something special for dessert?" It worked, and by the time we got inside she was happily making a mental list of the food she had to buy.

I stayed with her for a few days, driving her over to visit with Dad much of the time, happy to see him apparently recovering so well. He couldn't communicate with us yet, but mother was permitted to visit the intensive care unit for a few minutes, where she was allowed to touch his hand. They were going to move him out of there in another couple of days, and the joy on her face was a pleasure to see.

"He must be getting better, right? He will come home soon–I'm sure of it now."

Lorraine and I spent an afternoon shopping at the huge mall, recently completed, just outside of town. It wasn't near the water, but set back in the empty fields a couple of miles from our old neighborhood. It was impressive, and my sister and I thought it ironic that it had been built on the south side of the river. A plum for our side! Now the nabobs on the other side had to cross over the bridge to shop at the finest stores in town.

"Well," said Lorraine, "maybe this will nudge the town to pave the streets over here! River Road is nothing but holes now—it's like driving on Swiss cheese!"

"I don't use it any more. I damaged the oil pan on my car last year, and now I take the long way around to get to Mom and Dad's house. It's a shame, really. It could be so pretty along here, if it was cleaned up a little."

Passing the Churnys' house, next door to Mom's, Lorraine remembered that Janice was in town.

"I almost forgot! I saw her at the drug store this morning. She's here for a week or so, and she wants to get in touch with you. I told her you were here, with Mom."

"That's terrific! I haven't seen her

since last summer. I'll call her as soon as I get in."

I walked into my mother's house, thinking of how my life had changed since the last time I saw Janice, and was surprised to see her with Mom in the kitchen having a cup of tea.

"Lori just this second told me you were here," I said, rushing in to hug her, a gesture she half-heartedly returned. She looked pale, and more than a little tired, with dark circles under her eyes.

"Is Mike here?"

"No, just me and the kids. Mike's in California for three weeks, so it seemed a great time to visit. I was going to call you, but I came by instead. I tried to get you at your place last night."

"I've been here for a few days . . . I'm sure Mom told you about Dad's bypass operation." I gave her a huge smile. "It's been so long since we were home together," I said, "I can't even remember when."

"Your mother told me about the operation, and Stuart told me you were here when I called last night. Andy, I talked to him for quite a while last night."

Her last words seemed filled with hidden meaning, and she stared at me intently as she spoke. It dawned on me that her mood was less exuberant than mine, that she had something on her mind. I had known her a lifetime, and the signals hadn't changed. There was some kind of message in her words, and I decided it would be wise to get her out of the kitchen, to someplace where Mom wouldn't be part of the conversation.

"I want to get out of these clothes. Come up to my room, we can chat while I get changed."

She followed me up the stairs to my bedroom, and we sat cross-legged, facing each other on my bed, a pose that came naturally even though it had been many, many years since the last time we'd been in my room together, and it wasn't long before I found out what was on her mind.

"Andrea, what the hell have you been doing? Stuart is beside himself with worry over you, and you haven't told me anything, so I couldn't cover for you when he started pumping me for information, asking questions about the reunion. I didn't know what to say and now I think I've gone and made things worse."

Couldn't cover for me! A phrase from the years when we hid things from everyone but each other, and lied if we thought it necessary to protect each other. But what had she found it necessary to hide?

"What on earth are you talking about? What information was he looking for? Did you give away some deep, dark . . . Oh, Jan . . . the reunion? You told him about Richard, didn't you."

"When we had dinner together in Chicago, he asked about . . ." My expression of surprise stopped her. "Andrea, you didn't know? What is going on between you two?"

"Just get down to Stuart's questions, Janice. I'll explain after."

"Well, about a month, maybe five or six weeks ago now—I lose track of time—he called and said he was in Chicago on business. I asked him to come over to visit, but he was too busy with meetings that trip, maybe next time.

"We talked for a few minutes, and then he asked if I had heard from you recently. I said not in months—in fact, you haven't even answered my last letter!—and then he asked if I knew you had been hit by a car. I said of course, that was ages ago, last summer, and had anything gone wrong since then. He said no, and asked if I had seen you since the accident, and I said of course, at the reunion, and then he said he had to run, but he suggested we get together for dinner the next time he came into town.

"So two weeks ago . . ." She rolled to a complete stop, apparently halted by the expression on my face. "Jeez, we went out together for dinner two weeks ago, you know, with Mike . . . he didn't tell you?"

"No, but that's no big deal—he's away a lot. Maybe he did mention it, but just get on with it, Janice, what the hell happened at dinner?"

"Nothing really, he brought up your accident again, and said you'd been acting kind of moody—which isn't like you at all—and he thought it started around the time of your accident. He asked me if I had noticed anything strange about you last time we were together, like maybe at the reunion, and he wondered if you might have told me about something that was bothering you. Well, of course

I said no, I hadn't seen anything strange in your behavior last summer, but then we hadn't spent that much time together, and I had no idea what he was talking about, but he didn't seem inclined to elaborate, so pretty soon the subject was dropped entirely.

"But since then I've been kind of worried about you, and I was anxious to see you on this visit home. When I called you last night and told him I was here in Oakville, I must have triggered something in his memory, because he asked when I had visited last, and I told him it was last summer, for the reunion. Then he said he was sorry he had missed it, and asked if I had a good time, and if you did too, and of course I said certainly, with all the friends you had.

"Meet any old flames?" he asked. Teasing, you know, and I said no, I went with Mike right through school, and then he asked if you did—have any old boyfriends, I mean—and I said, of course, Richard Osborne. He said, Oh yes—he'd heard of him—but had never met him, and was he at the reunion too? I said certainly, and what a handsome devil he was, you made such a good-looking couple, he should have been there to keep an eye on you. And we laughed, and he asked me what he looked like, and I described him, and he asked me where he lived, and I told him somewhere around Boston, I didn't know where exactly, and why did he want to know, and he said no particular reason, and then he told me you were here with your mom . . . and oh my God, Andy, I just know there's something wrong and I've gone and made it worse."

Janice hadn't changed a bit. As always, when she was upset her speech picked up speed, words spilling over each other in their haste to be spoken until finally, the story told, she took a deep breath and stared at me, looking miserable.

Trying to talk calmly around the nausea building in my chest, I took a deep breath and plunged into an impromptu fairy tale.

"Jan, of course you did nothing wrong. I have seen Richard a couple of times since last summer, met him for lunch in the city. No big deal, just old friends, you know, we both live in the area, just keeping in touch since the reunion. I didn't bother to tell Stuart, since he doesn't know Richard anyway, but I guess it's possible that he saw me downtown and wondered who I was with."

If Stuart had seen me with Richard, I was dead meat. But that was impossible, since I was quite sure I'd only met Richard when Stuart was away on business. Still, it seemed to me that he was checking up on me, or surely he would have said something about meeting Jan and Mike in Chicago?

"Andrea Corelli, I have known you for a long time and I know when you're lying. You are now. Come on. Tell all."

"Really, there's nothing to tell, Jan. Stuart has this strange idea that I might be interested in someone else—we've been married a long time, and I guess we're in a little slump just now. We'll get over it, I'm sure. I don't know what's wrong—I'm bored or something—menopause . . . who knows?

"He thinks something's wrong with me, and it bothers him, so he's looking for an explanation. You know Stuart, he never leaves anything to chance. Everything has a logical, mathematical progression, with no allowance for anything emotional and unreasonable."

I heard the sarcasm in my voice, and of course Janice picked up on it.

"I know you aren't telling me the whole truth. Are you sure you and Stuart are okay?"

"Oh yeah, just too much of the same old thing, I guess. How about you and Mike? You've been married a long time too. Don't you ever get bored?"

"Bored? That might be a nice change for us. I don't see enough of him to get bored."

She looked at me directly then, and again I was struck by how tired and drawn she looked.

"He travels a lot, too, but he goes away for weeks at a time . . . No, it's worse than that." She had decided to confide in me.

"I never told you, but things haven't been good for us for a long time. Sometimes I think it was a mistake to marry him after going together all those years. We were too accustomed to each other, like friends, and there were no surprises left by the time we got married. Even sex—God, we started having sex right after puberty!"

I laughed, remembering that they had gone together from the eighth grade.

"It turns out that Mike likes things off-balance all the time, says life is more exciting that way. One of the things he likes is other women. I guess I'm used to it now.

"I'm not sure if he has something going on the side now, but he's been going out to California frequently, staying out there for weeks on some engineering project or other. Can't imagine he hasn't hooked up with someone out there. I don't think he misses me while he's gone, and he doesn't need me when he comes home. After all this time, I don't miss him either. But he always comes back, and he takes good care of us, so I'm not complaining." She looked away.

"Jan, my God, I didn't know—you never said things were so rotten. But how can you be so calm about it? That's not a life. Don't you want more than that? Don't you feel gypped?"

"I suppose so, but this is okay for now. I used to think I might want to get away, find someone better, but then the kids started coming, and . . . well, you can get used to just about anything, I guess. Maybe if someone better comes along . . . but not right now. I don't like to rock boats. I've got the kids, they're great, and I don't think I could stand the upheaval."

"But if Mike is fooling around, how can you stay with him? How can you trust him?"

"Well, I don't, really, but I'm used to it. He's always had other women, ever since we got married. I used to think it was the kind of job he had, you know, on the road a lot, away from home, but other husbands aren't like that. It's just the way he is, I guess, and I'm used to it now."

She sat with her shoulders slumped forward, head hanging down, totally defeated.

"I was so jealous when you met Stuart. Bet he's never run around on you! Must be nice to have someone who likes to come home to you at night . . . who's still nuts about you after all this time. What could be boring about that?"

"Like you said, you get used to anything. Variety is the spice of life, as they say." I was so flip, so amusing! "But Jan, you have to do something, you can't live like this."

Suddenly she was defensive. "But I do, and I probably won't ever do anything about it. Imagine the kids finding out about their father, everybody laughing at me behind my back. My mother would laugh the hardest—she didn't like Mike, you know, she thought he treated me like dirt. I couldn't stand it . . ."

She squared her shoulders and sat up straight, a smile on her lips that didn't reach her haunted, unhappy eyes. "Now, what do you think of the new mall here in town? I was over there yesterday . . ."

Twenty-seven

She left an hour later, with a promise to come and visit me before she went back to Chicago. I followed her out the door, yelling to Mom that I'd be back in a few minutes. I jumped into my car and headed for the river, to the spot where I used to go years ago after a fight with my mother.

My favorite rock was still there, and after kicking off my sandals, I dangled my feet in the cool, murky water, watching the ripples spread away from me, listening to the waves lap the shore, staring absently at the lovely brick homes across the river.

Lovely on the outside, but inside? Were those people happy? I used to think that simply because their houses were solid, and pretty, their lives must be perfect, and for the first time in my life I wondered about them. That woman, stretched out in the shade on her chaise longue, watching a couple of children frolic in a little backyard pool—was she looking forward to her husband's return home? Did she have a husband? A first or second marriage? Did he beat her up? Did he love her?

So many women had so little . . . . wonderful women like Janice. I was shocked, and upset, over what she had told me today. She had never said a word about her miserable marriage. I suppose if we saw more of each other I might have guessed, or she might have told me about it, but intimacy was difficult for people living a thousand miles apart, even best friends. What bothered me most was that she simply accepted it as her lot. Janice was an intelligent woman, but she was totally lacking in self-esteem. She was victimized by a man who professed to love her, a handsome bully, a sleazebag who chased other women, who couldn't be trusted.

It came to me, what I didn't like about Mike. He really was very attractive, and women swarmed like flies to honey . . .

and to trash. The man was garbage. Those bedroom eyes, always a hand somewhere on whichever woman he was talking to, a warm sexy smile that made women feel so special. I'd seen him at the reunion, the nucleus of a gang of females, flattering and flirting . . . he never treated Jan that way. In fact, he usually made tasteless jokes at her expense. He'd start telling a story on himself, but somehow you'd realize at the punch line that Janice had come up short once again, and the laughter turned against her. Often, I remembered, she would sit beside him, an embarrassed smile plastered to her face throughout an entire evening, while Mike entertained a roomful of people with his tales of her shortcomings. Who knew how he behaved when they were alone!

And all along knowing that he had other women . . . Oh God, Janice, you deserve so much more.

But who was I to talk! No doubt about it, Mike was a worm, a man who didn't deserve what he had, but I was behaving in the same slimy fashion. Didn't Stuart deserve better? *Let the one without sin cast the first stone* . . . the Bible verse flashed through my mind.

I watched the water swirl around my rock and thought about Dad, hoped he was okay, wondered how my mother was holding up without him, thought about Kelley, and Brian. Water is calming, peaceful. Sitting here reminded me of the old days, when mother and I used to fight about Richard, and I'd run down to the river to think. I was now a grown woman, perched on the same damned rock, my life a shambles over the same damned man.

Mother had never liked Richard, had been set against him from the first. I thought it was because he came from the other side of the river. She never shut up about how rich he was! But she was happy with Stuart, who had grown up with virtually the same background as Richards. Stuart wasn't from Oakville, so maybe that made a difference. Was it something about Richard that bothered her?

Would my life be different if my mother had not been so dead set against Richard? Knowing what I knew now about him? Was it written on his face back then?

I fell ass over teakettle in love with Richard when romance and thrills were spectacularly missing from my life, and proved to myself that I could have him if I wanted him. But like a shiny new toy, the lustre was fading fast. Richard was very much like Mike, a two-timing playboy who had never grown up. And I had been behaving like a child.

I had reached the point of no return. There was no going back from here. I would either stay with Stuart, sending Richard back to the past where he belonged, or I would leave Stuart. Something bleak and cold hit me in the gut.

I couldn't imagine life without Stuart. A bit dull, maybe, but solid, and honest, and all mine! Maybe there were no thrills, but the comforting glow I felt when he came home to me was love, a love that had grown steadily over the years! He was always there when I needed him, and I wanted what I had before, the security, the absolute surety that Stuart loved me. But I had broken the bond of trust, the strongest tie in a marriage. Would I ever see love for me in Stuart's eyes again? Oh God, I hoped so, because at long last I realized that I loved him as I had never loved Richard, as I could never love anyone else.

Impatiently wiping tears from my face, I tried to think clearly. Stuart had probably already figured out that I'd been seeing Richard since the reunion, but if there was a chance for us, I would have to tell him everything. Somehow his knowing already made it easier to imagine telling him, I wouldn't shock him with the news. Janice might never know it, but she had helped me by talking to Stuart. I had a starting point, and with luck things could be straightened out.

I resolved to tell him about Richard as soon as I returned home the following day. The whole truth, trusting in his love for me, hoping he would see how much I loved him, and I prayed that Stuart's love was strong enough to forgive me.

The affair with Richard was over, a love affair that stretched back more than thirty years into the past. My future was with Stuart, if he would have me. I had to talk to Richard, but I couldn't face him, afraid that he might charm me until I forgot what had to be said. Dear John, I thought, and decided to write him a letter.

I slipped wet feet into my sandals and left the river much happier than I had been in months, the burden of guilt and dishonesty much lighter. With or without Stuart, I reflected, optimistically planning on having him around, it was time to rebuild my life.

"Are you okay, Andrea?" asked my mother when I sat down in her kitchen, after whistling my way up the path and giving her a bear hug at the door.

"I'm just fine and dandy, Mom," I answered, and really felt that my troubles were over. I slept soundly that night, without a dream or a nightmare. Beyond a doubt this was the right thing to do, no matter what the consequences were.

The next morning I made a pot of strong coffee and sat down to write my letter. It was more difficult than I thought, trying to find the words to explain that I loved him, but an affair wasn't enough, that we had families, and responsibilities, and we had to remember them. And I couldn't resist adding that he would probably find someone else to replace me, but in spite of my remark, tears started as I sealed the letter. For most of my life I had dreamed of this man, a dream that came magically to life for a short time, and I felt my heart wrench as I finally and absolutely put him away.

The next day, Tuesday, I called Janice to tell her I was on my way home. She was staying in Oakville for the rest of the week, but promised to come and visit me on Friday.

"We'll have a long weekend together, since I'm not going back to Chicago until next Tuesday," she said.

That was fine with me; it gave me some time alone with Stuart. I was filled with anticipation, happy to get home, anxious to see my husband for the first time in many months. He would understand, he would forgive, we would make up in the age-old way, and life would merrily roll along, happy and carefree.

Richard was behind me forever. He

might be momentarily hurt by my letter, but I was sure he would be relieved that it was over.

As usual, I was sadly mistaken on all counts.

When I got home there was a note on the kitchen counter, from Stuart.

"Grand Rapids—back Thursday. We have to talk."

That was it. Short, cold, to the point. No signature, or his usual "Love, S." It scared me, it was so empty. But of course he would have been upset after talking to Janice. I certainly had my work cut out, but things would work out.

I busied myself cleaning house, did the laundry, and baked a couple of blueberry pies, his favorite. I told myself everything would be just fine, but I didn't sleep well, and Wednesday morning I woke up with a headache. Coffee didn't help much, and as the day wore on I grew more nervous, I could tell by the nausea that churned. Later that afternoon, I went over to see Ellen.

" . . . acting like a typical bored housewife, looking for a few cheap thrills. I'm so ashamed."

Ellen poured me another cup of coffee, just what I needed, my main source of energy and nourishment these days.

"You're being too hard on yourself."

"Hard? Ellen, look at what I've done. Lying and cheating—my God, what was I thinking? Stuart has always been honest, loving and caring for me. I've only thought of myself, like life owed me something, and Stuart was responsible for providing it. When he couldn't measure up I blamed him for my unhappiness, and just buried myself in my dreams.

"And then sneaking around and having an affair, I didn't care if I was hurting him . . . I've been searching for fireworks, Ellen, but they shone in his eyes every time he looked at me, and I didn't even know until they burned out! Everything I needed was right here! What am I going to do?"

"Andrea, calm down. Right now you're scared. Stuart knows and you have to face up to what you've done. But look, if this had never happened do you really think you would have suddenly out of the blue begun to appreciate Stuart? I don't think so. Meeting Richard again was just what you needed. You got some questions answered and now he's out of your system. You can use this experience to your advantage."

Of course I was crying, and she put her arm around my shoulder, trying to give me some comfort.

"Just think how lucky you are. You know positively that Stuart is the right man for you. How many people can say that? You two have a really good life together."

"After *this?*" I sobbed.

She ignored my look of disbelief. "Didn't you say you trusted Stuart to love you, no matter what? And that he trusted you to love him, no matter what?" I didn't remember ever saying anything like that, but maybe in the dim, distant past, it had been true. "Well, my friend," she continued, "I think your 'no matter what' just happened! And you love him even more than you did before.

"Stuart's coming home tomorrow night, right? He's been wanting you to talk to him for months. So start communicating! You love him, and you'll find the words. It may be tough going, because he's hurt, but he loves you too, and he wants it to work out. It may take time, but in the end I'm sure everything will work out!"

Twenty-eight

"Ode to Joy" chimed through the house.

About a year ago, Brian had conned me into buying one of those digital doorbells that played the first few measures of a bunch of different songs, thirty-two, I think, including classical, pop, and Christmas carols. I hated the damned thing, and couldn't wait for it to run out of whatever made it tick, so it could be replaced.

Beethoven chimed again. "Brian, get off your duff and answer the door!" I yelled.

Stuart was coming home tonight from Iowa, in time for dinner, and I was preparing wienerschnitzel, his favorite meal. When the bell rang I was coated in flour up to the elbows.

"Mom, it's some guy for you!"

If someone was selling door-to-door religion at this time of the night I would explode! Grabbing a handful of paper towel to clean my messy hands, I pounded loudly across the tiled floor of the front hall and whipped open the door in my most forbidding manner.

My heart stopped beating. Richard stood there, his eyes filled with pain and unshed tears, my letter crumpled in his hand.

Oh no! Sickness clutched at my insides. I'd have to talk to him, but where? I couldn't ask him in with Brian here, and Stuart would be home in half an hour. What to do? Mutely, he pointed to the driveway, and I followed him out to his car on shaking legs. We sat for a few minutes listening to the silence while a fine coat of misty rain covered the windshield. His first words made me jump.

"Andrea, how could you do this to me?"

I swallowed the rising wave of nausea that threatened to choke me and attempted an answer.

"There was nothing else to do. This

thing had to end. One of us had to do it."

"But I love you. We love each other."

"Once upon a time, maybe, that was true, but our time is past. It's too late for us. Rich, I've been dreaming, but I'm finally waking up. I've jeopardized my marriage, and though it's kind of late in the day, it is valuable to me, and I want it to work. I've been wrestling with guilt for a long time now, and I can't deal with it any more.

"You and I have different views on fidelity. Your marriage seems to be a business arrangement, so maybe you don't have the same commitment. Maybe that's a stupid thing to say . . . I don't know, and I don't care any more. I can't go on like this, unfaithful to Stuart, unfair to you, disgusted with myself. I'm constantly on the edge of tears, worried about how much Stuart knows, praying he won't find out, feeling like a prostitute with you. Oh, Richard, we should never have stirred up something that ended a long time ago!"

"But it isn't over, Andrea—we have today, we have our love."

"We had yesterday, and we're trying to

relive it today. We have memories, not a future."

Quiet settled around us once again, except for the gentle spatter of rain on the windshield, and I stole a glance at him. He looked miserable, and I wanted to reach out to him, but forcibly restrained myself. Touch him and you're dead, dearie! Back at square one, in way over your head. But I sensed that I was the one in control, and I felt like an adult dealing with an unhappy child.

"But you love me, I know you do!" he insisted.

"Yes, Richard, I love you, but it's a fairy tale kind of love. Once upon a time you and I loved each other, and that love ended abruptly, unsatisfactorily, for both of us. We never had the chance to put it away, and it lived on in memory. Twenty-five long years later, when we're 'trapped' in everyday living, we meet again and that memory is fanned into a burning hot romance. But it isn't real, it's a trip into dreamland. We've tried to change the end of an old story, adding a few thrills, taking pleasure today, while we can. But what about tomorrow, Rich? Tell me about tomorrow."

He didn't answer, but stared straight ahead at my garage door.

"Stuart is my life, and I can't afford to throw it all away over this fantasy you and I have created." A look of hurt cross his face. "If that bothers you, I'm sorry.

"Tell me something, Rich—you're supposedly stuck in an unhappy marriage, but not once have you ever suggested that we start again, try to make a life of our own, just you and me."

"Well—"

"And how about the other women in your life, Richard?" I continued. "Don't insult me by denying it," I hurled at his startled face, "I saw you with one of your Mrs. Fletchers one day. Your life is just dandy, and you aren't going to disrupt it for me."

I leaned against the door, my heart in my throat, waiting for his answer. I was angry, but in a way I was challenging him to profess his love, to throw caution to the winds . . . if he showed the least initiative, the smallest sign that he wanted me, I might, even now, give in. My face was set in an expression that probably looked hard as nails, hiding the big, soft, empty place inside me as I waited for him to beg me to leave Stuart and spend the rest of my life with him.

It was hard to stay aloof, and I was considering just throwing myself into his arms, when I observed that he had the presence of mind to stay on his side of the car, and had made no attempt whatsoever to bridge the small gap between us, a span that grew much larger as I thought about it. We were as far apart as it was possible to be in this tiny space. Body language, I thought, speaks volumes . . .

With neither a yes or a no, he started talking about luck, and timing. Not commitment, not that he wanted me, or that he loved me too much to see it all come to an end. Nothing.

"If only we had followed our hearts so many years ago . . ." he began.

Shithead! I tuned him out. His non-answer had confirmed my decision, and now I just wanted him to leave. He didn't see any tomorrows for us, either. At least he was being realistic, or I had finally caught on. Richard took what he wanted as long as it lasted, while I was the romantic, seeing things as I wished them to be. And Stuart was . . . I had been watching for Stuart, who was already late. This thing with Richard was over, and nothing I was about to hear would change it, and despite his presence here tonight, I firmly believed Richard wanted it to be over too.

"Richard, I asked you a question," cutting him off brusquely, "and I think I deserve an answer. Do you want me to leave Stuart for you? Will you leave your wife for me?"

His silence, the evasiveness in his eyes, confirmed what I knew to be true. Neither of us believed in a future together, what we had was based on the past. We had completed the circle, it was over. Now I wanted only for him to go, and quickly.

"This is the wisest course," he conceded, very graciously, I thought. "I had come to the same conclusion myself."

Oh sure! I bet he was just about to sit down and write me a letter when he got mine in the mail! My anger flared, but I held it in check. He was trying to save face, as the Japanese say. No doubt he had much more to say in the way of ending our relationship, but at that moment Stuart's car turned into the driveway.

"Oh God! Oh no!" I was horrified! As I stared, wide-eyed, the action switched to slow motion, and I watched as Stuart slowly rolled to a stop next to Richard's car, slowly turned off wipers and lights, slowly turned his head and looked inside at Richard, studying him for what seemed an eternity. Slowly he got out of his car, making absolutely no sound as he slowly slammed the car door, and walked up the path, disappearing into the house, letting the screen door slowly close behind him.

I began to pray. If you have any compassion, Lord, let Stuart understand me, or let me die now! But I was appealing to a God who exacted vengeance, and my plea fell on deaf ears. Of all the times in my life when I've wished things were different, or that I might be transported somewhere else, be swallowed up in a crater, this definitely topped the list. I wished desperately that Richard had not come. But it didn't make any difference now. He was here, and I had to face Stuart.

"You'd better go, unless you want to witness the end of my life. I don't know how I'll explain this to Stuart. Please

Richard, please don't ever call me again."

Under other circumstances I might have had more to say, maybe that I would always love him, just hold him one more time, something to remember him by . . . but not today! My mind was filled with Stuart waiting for me in the house.

I crawled out of the car and watched him drive away quickly. Squaring my shoulders, I walked jauntily up the path to the front door, faking a gaiety I did not feel, frantically trying in that short space of time to come up with something plausible to tell Stuart. I failed miserably, but I painted a smile on my face, and entered the lion's den.

"That was your lover!"

"Stuart!"

"Kind of nervy, don't you think? I thought there was someone, I prayed there wasn't, but now I've seen him, haven't I? That's the same guy that Janice described to me, the old high school sweetheart!"

There was no way out of this now. If

we cleared the air, get this into the past . . . but no, he wasn't going to give me a chance.

"Andrea, I loved you, I trusted you, I've spent a lifetime with you and I didn't know you at all. I thought since your dad got sick, well, things seemed a shade better, and I hoped there was some chance for us, but now I see I was wrong."

"Stuart, no, you're mistaken. There was something going on, but it was over ages ago. I wanted to tell you, I was waiting for the right time, I wanted—"

"You wanted? I don't give a damn what you want, any more, ever again, do you hear me? I've put up with this nonsense long enough, waiting and hoping, like a damned fool!

"Now here's what I want, Andrea, and you'd better do as I say. I want you to leave, now. If your boyfriend is still here, he can drive you wherever you want to go. But just go."

He turned away from me, his face a hard mask of fury, and stomped up the stairs to our bedroom, slamming the door.

I was dumbfounded, too stunned to

cry. Here I was finally getting my head together, and in just a few minutes everything fell apart! Stuart wouldn't listen, didn't let me explain, and if he thought I was going to crawl up those stairs and beg him to listen to me, to forgive me . . . Not on a bet!

I was angry, and it felt good. I wouldn't stick around cringing in shame. Not me. I had tried, I had broken up with Richard, I had done my best, and this was how I was repaid! I wouldn't stay in this damned place another night if he begged me! He wouldn't listen to me, but now I didn't care! I'd show him!

In a black cloud of righteous anger I grabbed a few things from the bathroom, deciding I'd come back some other time for clothes. On my way to the garage for my car I passed through the family room and saw Brian, forgotten, scrunched up on the couch, and my anger dissolved at the sight of his tears. I hugged and kissed him as though I'd never see him again.

"Mom, what's happening? What's wrong?"

"Nothing, really. Dad and I had a little argument, that's all. I'll be staying with

Aunt Lorraine for a few days, so call me there if you need me. Be good. I love you."

In tears, I started the car and left my home. I hate him, I thought . . . hate both of them . . . slowly realizing that the one I hated most was me. I had screwed up badly, and I was about to pay for my sins. My marriage to Stuart was over just when I thought it had a new beginning.

Lorraine was home. Lorraine was kind. For two days she asked no questions, just let me mope around and wallow in misery. When I cried she was there, armed with tissue, sitting beside me in sympathetic silence until I cried myself out.

Lorraine's house was near the hospital where Dad was recuperating, and I visited him a couple of times. We didn't talk much, but he smiled weakly, and seemed happy to have me there. I didn't tell him about Stuart and me—it was too much for him to take in all at once, and I cried whenever I thought about it. Dad needed happy uplifting news, not the dismal scoop that his daughter's marriage had fallen apart. I met Mother there one morning, surprising her, but I didn't tell her, either. She had her worries about Dad, and she'd find out soon enough.

Brian phoned Saturday morning.

"The house is real quiet, Mom. Dad doesn't talk much, and I think he's going away again. We're out of cereal. When are you coming home?"

"Soon, honey, I'll be home soon. Dad and I need a little time apart, to think things over. But don't worry, I love you, Brian. Call me when he's gone, I'll come and stay with you. Things will work out okay—you'll see. Get Dad to buy you some cereal."

I burst into serious tears when he hung up, and Lorraine came into the room with a box full of tissues, two cups of coffee, and a face that said she was going to get to the bottom of this. Now.

"It all started last summer, when I saw my old boyfriend again," I began. "Do you remember Richard Osborne? I went to school with him, and we went out together for a long time—yeah, the good-looking one, you used to think he was so much fun!—he was at the reunion. I hadn't seen him in all that time, and he was just as handsome as ever, and . . . oh, I'm not sure I know why, but he kind of swept me off my feet, and for a while I kind of forgot about Stuart, the kids, and the fact that I'm a middle-aged housewife, and pretended I was eighteen again.

"Oh, Lori, he made me feel so good about myself. You can't imagine how exhilarating it's been to have someone interested in me, just for me. Not because I'm Mom with the groceries, or Susie homemaker with the shirts ironed, but a person, to laugh and talk with, and listen to . . . someone to make love to . . ."

She gulped, taking this in. "Yes," I said defensively, "we made love, and he's great in bed! I know it's shocking, but please don't be judgmental, Lorraine. He made me feel special, something Stuart doesn't know how to do. I'm not trying to excuse my actions, but in a twisted way I'm glad it happened. My life had become such a bore, I felt like an old, old woman, and this affair, even though it was wrong, made me feel good about myself again."

"I noticed that," said Lorraine. "Ever since Christmas, you've looked pleased with yourself. Kind of distracted sometimes, but there's a glow about you, and your eyes shine, like a young girl in love."

"Richard reminded me of how good it feels to be in love. I don't think I was in love with him, just with being in love, one more time—that breathless excitement that flips around in your stomach, the thrilling anticipation that something good is about to happen to you . . . I can't describe it, but I've never felt that with Stuart. Of course, when I met Stuart I was trying to be so-o-o mature and grown up . . ." I paused, annoyed, while she laughed, then I joined her.

"Anyway, I missed out on all the fun. Being in love should be fun, but after all this I realize that I really do love Stuart. It's a quiet, steady kind of love, like a light that's always on, giving off a warm glow. Richard is bright and shiny, a brilliant flash that doesn't last. I began to value Stuart more, to understand how good he is for me, how much I count on him, and how much I love him. I don't think I can explain to you, much less to

Stuart, but the qualities I thought were boring are the things I love best about him, and it's taken me all this time to realize . . ." Tears stopped me, but somehow I managed to tell Lorraine the rest of the story—ending with Stuart throwing me out of our house."

"Oh Andrea, Stuart loves you! I'm sure he'll forgive . . ." A look of worry crossed her face. "But he's such a stick in the mud, I can't imagine him ever forgetting about this," she said.

I was about to object to what she said, but I shut my mouth, fully aware that I felt the same way.

Stuart would never be able to forgive me.

Since her school was nearby, later that day I went to spend a couple of hours with Kelley. I thought she should know something about the situation at home.

"I'm staying with Lorraine for a few days, so Dad and I can cool off a little." I hoped.

"I just knew something was wrong. I knew it when I was home for spring break!" she said to me.

"Well, we are going to work it out, honey. Try not to worry too much."

The words sounded good, and I hoped she didn't notice my lack of confidence. Work it out. How? Stuart wouldn't change his mind, and in my shame I had to admit he would be absolutely right not to. I had behaved abominably, and he had every right to be angry. I couldn't imagine us ever working it out.

"Really, sweetie, it'll be all right—you'll see."

I remembered to call Janice on Friday morning, letting her know that I was back in Oakville for a few days.

"Is it your dad?"

"Not really—he's doing really well. No, it's just . . . oh, I'll tell you when I see you."

We made a date to have lunch together on Sunday, and Sunday at noon found us sitting on the rocks at the Point, giggling like teenagers. I had brought a cooler filled with sandwiches and fruit, Jan had a sixpack and some wine coolers in an insulated bag.

"I can't tell you how good it is to be

here with you, Jan," I said, or tried to, around a mouthful of capicolla, provolone, and escarole between thick slabs of crusty Italian bread. When my mother made sandwiches, she didn't fool around.

"Brings back the good old days, doesn't it?" said Jan.

"Were they really that good?"

"They were for me. I was on top of the world. I had Mike, and the future lay ahead, bright and shiny and unwrapped. Today, I don't want Mike any more, and there is no future—just one sad, tarnished day after another." She stared out over the river, her beer forgotten in her lap.

"Jan, you have to do something. You can't just go on, day after day, living like a zombie until you die. This is the only go-around, hon, and you've got to make the most of it. I can't stand seeing you defeated and broken by that cheating . . ."

"Andy, I don't want to spoil our picnic. Let's talk about you. And Stuart. Boy, were you lucky."

"Hah! Depends on which day it is. Things are not great at the moment, and

I have no one to blame but me. Remember Richard Osborne?"

"Wasn't he at the reunion last year?"

"He certainly was, and that was the beginning of the mess I'm in. In a nutshell, Jan, . . ."

I told her a condensed version, just the highlights, a quick overview of how my stupidity and selfishness had landed me back in Oakville, alone, wondering about my future.

"Stuart will come around, Andy—he's nuts about you. You'll see. It's funny," she went on, "I would never have told you about my life if I hadn't felt there was something wrong with yours. I'm glad you told me about you and Richard. I feel like I'm trading secrets, but now I can tell you. I've left Mike! He doesn't know about it yet, won't find out until he gets home sometime next week. I don't know how he's going to deal with our leaving, but I can take anything now that I'm away from him. I thought my folks wouldn't understand, but they have been so supportive. Mom even said she was glad I'd left him, there was something about him she never liked . . ."

We finished our lunch leaning shoulder to shoulder on a rock in the midafternoon sun, two middle-aged women with very hazy futures, swigging down the last of the wine coolers, each cautiously optimistic in her own way.

"We'll open a bookstore," I suggested, and we laughed uproariously. "At the new mall. Two gay old divorcees, running a bookshop together. What fun!"

Jan's life could only improve, and though mine had reached previously unknown depths, I simply couldn't imagine that it wouldn't somehow get better.

Twenty-nine

The next day, five long days since Stuart had asked me to leave, and ten days since his operation, I went to visit my Dad for what turned out to be the last time.

He looked good, and he wanted to talk.

"Our wills . . . we made them years ago," he said, so low I could barely hear him.

"Good, Dad, that's great," I answered, patting his arm and rolling my eyes at the nurse in the room. "You'll have lots of time to change them when you get out of here."

"The house, Andrea . . . she loves the place, but it's too big for her, alone . . ."

He rested, and I took the opportunity

to get a few words in, trying for a tongue-in-cheek attitude.

"Dad, what is this, post-partum depression? The doctor says you're doing really well, you should be home in a week or so. Mom is anxious for you to come home—she's cooking up a storm, and cleaning that place to beat the band! You two can go back to being the lovebirds you've always been."

"Lovebirds . . ." I got a weak smile. "That reminds me . . . I don't like . . . Stuart comes alone to visit at night, you come alone in the day. Doesn't look like lovebirds to me."

Stuart came to visit my dad, on his own. They had always gotten along well together, but it pleased me to know that Stuart genuinely cared for Dad, that it wasn't a marital duty to be nice to my parents. The way things were between us right now, I thought in that way I had of underrating Stuart, I hadn't expected him to visit my dad in the hospital. There was so much about Stuart that I didn't know.

"Aw, Dad, it's nothing, just a little spat—don't worry. It'll blow over soon."

"Andrea, don't say it's nothing. Stuart

tells me things between you are not good, and he doesn't know how to make it better. Do you remember, years ago, bella, I told you to cherish that man, that he loved you. Did you understand me?"

"I guess you meant he would make me happy," I answered, not really remembering.

"No, not that . . . no one can *make* you happy but a man like Stuart, he gives you space to blossom and grow, so you can make yourself happy. This is love. I thought you understood."

"Dad, all these years I wanted the kind of love you and Mom have. When you look into each other's eyes the rest of the world doesn't exist! But I wanted excitement, and didn't think I had it with Stuart!"

He interrupted me. "I see you have not grown up, Andrea. Stuart is your strength, you depend on him. But you expect him to make every day a holiday, giving nothing in return, like a selfish child.

"You have to give love away, or it goes bad. Your mother and I are lovebirds because we give to each other, we don't take . . ." His breathing seemed labored, his face worked with the effort to communicate. "I was lucky . . . she had so much love to give. She must never know that I knew . . . Promise me, Andrea."

"Sure, Dad, I promise, but what is it, what do you know?" He was tired, and worn out from talking, but I had to find out what he meant. "Does this have to do with Mom?"

"We had a good life. What came before . . . not important . . ."

This was going to drive me crazy! They had a secret, they wouldn't tell me what it was, and I had just promised not to talk about it! I'd be in big trouble if another nurse came in—I was only supposed to be with him for ten minutes, but I had to get to the bottom of this.

I leaned over his bed, my face inches from his.

"Dad, tell me what this secret is."

But he didn't answer, just pressed my hand weakly and drifted back to sleep. Tomorrow, I thought, I'll come back tomorrow. I bent to kiss his forehead, and heard him whisper her name.

Walking down the long echoing corridors I tried to make sense of our strange conversation. *What came before,* he had said. I'd have to get it from Dad, because Mother would never give away a secret!

His reference to giving, not taking, love, was very clear, though, and I swore I'd give to Stuart for the rest of my life . . . if only he'd let me.

Dad died during the night. The heart attack that had brought him to the hospital had damaged the lower chamber of his heart beyond repair, and even though the bypass had been successful, the muscle was too weak to continue its vital work.

I didn't bother to go home. Lorraine lent me something decent to wear, and late the following afternoon we collected Mom and drove together to the funeral parlor. Holding hands, perhaps to share our apprehension, the three of us approached the casket together. I swore I'd support Mom, but in the end, it was she who provided strength for my sister and me.

Kneeling to say a prayer, I smiled when I saw the tie he was wearing. I had given it to him years before, telling him his taste was stuffy and dull and that he should wear brighter colors. The bright pattern blurred as my eyes filled with tears . . .

He was gone. I looked at his beloved face, calm and serene, and was flooded with memories of the man who had been my father.

The young man whose warmth and love made my days joyful, when at two or three years old I waited for him to come home from work to be taken on his lap squirming with pleasure when he listened to me babble about my day. I loved the sound of laughter rumbling deep in his chest, his eyes bright with wonder at whatever magical new thing I had discovered in our short time apart.

I remembered Sundays when his work-roughened hand held mine tightly as we took our weekly promenade, alone together, visiting friends and relatives in the neighborhood, without Mom to scold and lecture. I remembered braving a ferocious thunder storm in galoshes and hooded slickers, trembling when thunder roared and being held on his shoulder to be first to see the pot of gold at the end of the rainbow, sloshing through the puddles on the way back home. I remembered "Paper Doll," a song he taught me himself, and his proud expression when I sang it at the age of four . . . *A doll that other fellas cannot steal* . . . Dad, there will never be a fella to replace you . . .

He was the man I tried to please with good grades, whose opinion I valued more than any other, whether I was modeling a new dress, baking my first cake, or ironing a shirt without a crease. His approval was my goal, his slow smile adequate reward.

When Mother shrieked that I looked like a "scarlet woman" with all that make-up on my fifteen-year-old face, and I stomped up the stairs and screamed back at her that I would never take it off, his slight frown sent me scurrying to the bathroom to wash some of the offensive war-paint from my face.

The man whose quiet wisdom helped me through so many crises, real or imagined, in my life, the man I turned to for love and comfort . . . until the day I met someone just like him, the only other man who gave me his unquestioning love and support. My Stuart.

The next three days whirled by in a hazy blur of flowers, incense, coffee, and tired feet. We stood in line, my mother, Lorraine, and I, with George and Stuart flanking us, for hours on end, greeting and hugging the family, and their many friends. Smiling without recognition when we heard the words ". . . these are my daughters, Andrea and Lorraine. This is . . . he and your dad used to . . ." So many friends, each with a favorite memory to share with us, stories that spanned the decades.

Someone I knew once said that heaven, or hell, is the way you are remembered on earth. If she was right, my dad was already knocking at the pearly gates!

My mother sat, walked, talked and ate like a zombie, her face blank, her eyes empty. For the first time in my life, I realized how small in stature she was. And alone, without Dad by her side.

I stayed with her at night, stood with her during the long days, giving what I could, but I was running on empty myself. I was filled with grief for Dad, and like her, my support was missing.

I don't know who told Stuart about Dad—Lorraine, I guess, or George, her husband. I would have called, but he was there before the thought was complete, and he stayed with us most of the time. Between them the two men were indispensable, making the necessary arrangements with the hospital, the funeral director, even the church. Stuart kept Kelley and Brian with him, giving me more time to spend with my mother.

We talked to each other a few times, quite civilly, I thought, though he made me uncomfortable when he looked searchingly into my eyes. What was he looking for? I longed for his arms around me, comforting me, sharing my sorrow. God knows I needed his support, but after what I had done, I didn't deserve his comfort, and he didn't offer it.

During the long hours at the funeral parlor he stared at me from across the room, his face a mask of anger, cold and unyielding, closed away from me. He showed no sign of pain or hurt—no emotion of any kind. There was no hint of vulnerability, of anything to which I might appeal in an effort to heal the breach between us. Well, what did I expect, I asked myself. I didn't deserve his love. He didn't offer it.

There were hundreds of people at the funeral, and that made Mother very proud.

"Your father would be pleased to see so many old friends," she said, forgetting for the moment that nothing would ever please him again. Everything was going smoothly, and she seemed fine until she broke down at the cemetery, collapsing quietly in a little heap beside the grave. Stuart came to the rescue, picking her up and carrying her to the limo to lie down on the back seat. I walked beside them, silently, and sat in the car with her, since the service was almost over. Watching over her gave me something to do, and provided a barrier against my own grief.

We went back to Mother's for lunch, to eat and drink and share our grief. And like every Italian funeral I've ever attended, the party went on well into the night.

It was eleven o'clock at night before the last guests had gone, and close to midnight by the time Lorraine and I had all the dishes washed and the last ash-trays emptied.

"Good heavens," said Lorraine, clean-ing out the last one, "how did all these people live to be seventy-five or eighty years old? They smoke like chimneys!"

She left, and I was heading up the stairs to my bedroom when mother's wid-owed sister, my aunt Sofia, decided to kick me out. "I will stay for a few days," she said. "Your mother and I have lots to talk about. I can help her now," she said, "better than you." Which was prob-ably true. She had experience at this business of losing husbands.

"Go home to your man, and get some rest," she advised. I went back to Lor-raine's.

It was after midnight when I got there, and my spirits sank even lower when I saw Stuart's car in the driveway. He'd been so remote during the last few days, I couldn't imagine what he wanted here.

Maybe he wanted to talk about a di-vorce? Oh no, I thought, I can't face that, not now, and went around the back of the house to the kitchen door, plan-ning to creep down the hall to the spare bedroom in an effort to avoid a showdown. It was hours later before I remembered that he had expected me to be at my mother's.

I opened the door quietly, standing just inside the back porch to get my bearings in the dark. Barely breathing, I crossed the kitchen and stood in the doorway, waiting for an opportunity to slip down the hall unseen. They say you never hear anything good about yourself when you eavesdrop, but my jaw dropped in shock.

Stuart had come to talk to Lorraine, and he sat in the living room, pouring his heart out, telling her things I had never known. I couldn't help but overhear. As his voice droned low and miserable in the other room, I froze on the spot at his words.

"I love your sister, Lorraine, and I want her to know that I don't care about what happened. I was angry, I said things I shouldn't have, but, oh God, I miss her. Through this sad business with your dad, I wanted to reach out to her, to protect her, she seemed so fragile . . . but she avoided me, and refused to meet my eyes . . . those big, sad eyes of hers reminded me of when I first met her. She was trying so hard to behave like a sophisticated woman of the world, but her beautiful dark eyes were filled with sadness. Somehow I knew she had been badly hurt.

"I fell in love with her the moment I laid eyes on her. She seemed so delicate, and needed someone to take care of her, and I considered myself just the guy for the job. So, just like one of those swash-buckling pirates in the old movies, I set out to capture her. I had a romantic vision of myself in those days. I was making pretty good money by then, and I took her places she had never been—fancy restaurants, concerts at Symphony Hall . . . she loves music, you know."

I couldn't see Lorraine, and I wondered if she wanted to add a few words here and there. If so, she didn't have a chance, as Stuart rambled on.

"I need her, I'm not complete without her. But though we've been together almost twenty-five years, and I'm perfectly content, there's an elusive spark missing between us . . ."

That elusive thing, I thought, listening from my hideout behind the kitchen door. He had noticed, and missed it too. What could it be? Imagination? The giving to each other that Dad had talked about? Whatever it was, I just knew it was the difference between marriages like theirs that worked, and those that didn't. I was mulling this tidbit over when his next words blew me away.

"Andrea's looking for something, and it hurts me that I can't give it to her. She has an image of me as a fatherly sort of man—the kind you bring your troubles to but not the kind of virile lover that dreams are made of. When I married her, she needed someone like that, but there's always been a fantasy lover in the back of her mind. I think he came to life last year, and I can't compete with a dream come true. You know, I never gave it a thought till now, but I guess our life *is* humdrum and predictable, and I let it happen. It's all my fault, Lorraine. I'd forgotten how she loves surprises, and flowers, and concerts . . . she's such a romantic. God, I haven't given her so much as a candy bar or a kiss on the back of her neck in years!"

Oh no, Stuart, I thought, you're wrong,

it's all my fault . . . He was quiet for a while, thinking, no doubt, of the despised other guy, and I collapsed against the kitchen cabinets, finally giving way to tears. I was distraught, and afraid I'd attract their attention if I stayed in the kitchen bawling my eyes out, so I left the house as quietly as possible, sniffling and sobbing as I walked the quiet streets of my sister's neighborhood.

I couldn't believe what I'd heard! Stuart thought me fragile, delicate, someone to be nurtured and cared for. He had to be thinking about someone else—I wasn't like that at all! I'd always seen myself as a strong, self-sufficient woman. But he didn't have my imagination, he had only my behavior to judge by. And if he saw only one side of me, was there perhaps more to Stuart than I knew? What did I see of him, and what might be hidden from me?

The Stuart I knew was solid and dependable; he was the anchor in my life. I trusted him and counted on him, and in all these years he had never let me down. Tall, dark and handsome? No. But when I first looked into those steady gray eyes and held his warm strong hands, I knew I could safely put myself into his care.

All these years I'd thought of him as kind of dull, and compared to Richard, he probably was. I was always on the lookout for something different and exciting to do, and filled my mind with fantasies and dreams. Stuart enabled me to indulge those dreams, because I knew that whatever happened, he would be there. God gave me Stuart to take care of details, to bridge the gap from earth to heaven, reality to dream, paving the road along which I traveled. As my dad said, he gave me room to grow.

Though I had spent much of my life wishing for someone more exciting than Stuart, in fact he filled all criteria for the perfect husband. So what was missing? Risk? Danger? Did I really long for the immature uncertainty of breaking up and making up again, the highs and lows of a roller coaster relationship?

I didn't really want that, and it was high time for me to grow up and hold on to what I had with both hands. What I wanted was Stuart, and Stuart wanted me, with all my quirks and shortcomings. Maybe it wasn't too late for us to find the magic that seemed to be lacking. We both wanted the same thing, and if we worked at it together, we were going to make it happen.

My spirits had lifted appreciably in the course of my walk, and now I turned to go back to Lorraine's, practically bouncing down the street. If I was lucky he would still be there.

Something my father said to me, long ago, crossed my mind: Knights don't all ride shiny white horses. Some stand quietly in the shadows, armed only with steadiness and love.

More than half an hour had passed when I returned to find Lorraine's house silent, and Stuart's car gone from the driveway. The living room was in darkness and only a night light glowed in the kitchen. I ran down the hall and unceremoniously threw open my sister's bedroom door. George was sound asleep, but I scared Lorraine right out of her nightgown. She had been reading, apparently, and she began to scold me while

I picked up the book that flew to the floor when I had burst in.

"Andrea! Good Lord, where have you been? I called Mom and she said you were over *here*. Stuart was—!"

"I know Stuart was here. I came in while he was talking to you. Where did he go?"

"He wanted to wait for you, but it was late and we had no idea where you were. He left just a little while ago. He was tired, and so depressed. Lord, Andrea, if I thought George loved me half as much as Stuart loves you . . . He wants you to call him in the morning. I think there's a good chance for you to work it out."

"You're damned right it's going to work out, but I'm not waiting until tomorrow to call him—I'm going home now!" I smothered her in a bear hug, grateful for her understanding heart. "Thanks for everything, Lor—I'll be in touch!"

I drove home much too fast, along highways blessedly deserted at this time of night. Would he be willing to take the chance, to start again? Suppose he had decided we had nothing worth saving, that my unforgivable behavior was more than he could live with. What would I do then? I tried to put those negative thoughts out of my mind, concentrating instead on how much I loved him, praying he remembered that he loved me too. He couldn't turn me away.

It was two in the morning when I drove through the dark and quiet streets of our neighborhood. I passed one darkened house after another, but when I turned into our street, our house, the third one from the corner, stood out like a beacon in the night. You could always tell when Stuart was home, there were lights on in every room in the house! He never turned lights off when he left a room, a bad habit I constantly nagged about, but tonight I couldn't be happier. The bright lights sent out a warm glow of welcome and lit up my soul. I was so glad to be home.

I stopped the car in front of the house and sat for a second, pondering, but no course of action suggested itself to me. I couldn't plan what I wanted to say, so I gave up and ran across the front lawn, anxious to find Stuart, praying that he'd listen and not shut me out, and that the words would come when I needed them.

I threw open the unlocked front door and collided with him in the entrance hall. He was standing right behind the door, about to open it.

"Thought I heard a car out here," he said, cool as ever. "I was just coming to investigate."

He blocked the doorway, but he didn't step back, although I was smack up against his chest. We stared at each other in stunned shock for a moment. Then a secret little smile started in his eyes and spread over his face as he looked down at me, with all the magnetic force of those wonderful gray eyes, eyes that grew velvety as they softened with love. His smile grew wider, and my soul soared with joy. He put his arms around me, and gently pulled me to him. I continued to stare up at him, while tears, my stock in trade, filled my eyes and obscured my vision. The rigid stiffness of my body softened slowly, melting to fit against his, and I dropped my head on his shoulder.

"Stuart, oh Stuart . . ."

Tenderly he raised my chin, forcing

me to look at him, his eyes capturing and holding mine.

"Stuart," I whispered, "I don't know where to start. Can you ever . . . ?"

He said nothing, his eyes held mine in his steady gaze, and he shut me up with a tender kiss trembling with love and hope. Then, crushing me in a fierce hug, he kicked the door shut behind me, picked me up and carried me up the stairs to our bedroom.

"Welcome home, sweetheart," he whispered.

Thirty

"Bourque takes the puck, passes it up to Neely, Neely, off the boards to Adam Oates! Oates through center ice—shoots! HE SCORES! Adam Oates scores! His third goal of the series! Oates scores in the last second of play! Right over the head of the sprawling goalie! The Bruins win three straight in this seven game series against the Canadiens! Ohhh, there's rejoicing in Beantown tonight, folks . . ."

The third of May, spring for the rest of the world, maybe, but the height of hockey season for diehard fans like us! A few friends had come over to watch the game, and the win had contributed to the atmosphere of celebration.

We were watching the Stanley Cup

semifinals, and the Bruins were leading their great archrival, the Montreal Canadiens. Derek Sanderson was shouting over the din behind him in Boston Garden, but he could barely be heard above the whooping and hollering in our family room. The noise was deafening, but the only way to get the full flavor of the series.

"Three straight, Dad. Whoopee!!!" Brian, so excited he could barely contain himself, scooted into the kitchen to get a glass of milk, and heard the weak electronic warble that passes for a ringing telephone these days. A moment later he was back, looking concerned. "It's Kelley, and she doesn't sound very good," he said to me. "She wants you."

Stuart turned down the volume as I left the room, and I went into the kitchen to get the phone that Brian had left dangling from the wire on the wall.

"Hi, honey. What's up?"

"Mom, oh God, Mom, I don't know what to do!"

Gulping sobs, sniffles, and a loud childish wail followed this disturbing opener.

"What's wrong? Exams too tough for you?"

This was the week before finals, and I knew she had been working straight out, hoping to stuff a few more valuable tidbits into her head. Stress ran high on campus at this time of the year, and any little thing was liable to set off a crying jag.

"Is the food that bad?" I asked, hoping to coax a tiny giggle through her tears. Nothing.

"Have you had a fight with Phil?"

"Ohh, no . . ." she sniffled. "Nothing like that, nothing that simple. I don't think I can talk about this on the phone."

That didn't make sense. Since she had no roommate this semester, her phone was as private as mine.

"I don't know how to . . ." She dissolved into more tears.

"Do you want me to come down?"

UMass was more than two hours away; it was after eight o'clock in the evening, and she knew that whatever was wrong had better be earth shattering for me to drive down there at night.

"Could you?" In the tiniest voice.

"I'll be there as soon as I can."

I reported to Stuart, now standing at

my elbow. "Maybe the stress of studying, who knows?"

"Do you want me to go with you?" he asked.

"Nah, we've got company, and we can't just send them home. She wouldn't tell me what's wrong, but how bad could it be? You stay here and socialize—I'll be fine. It's so late, though, I'll stay with her overnight. There's another bunk in her room. I'll call you later to let you know what it's all about."

I could tell by the grin on his face that this suited him very nicely, but to be fair, Stuart hadn't heard her crying. He happily returned to the TV, engrossed in the post-game wrap-up before I was out of the driveway. I hit the road, carrying a bag with nightie and toothbrush. I flew along the Turnpike, laughing at Mom to the rescue, faster than a speeding bullet, leaping over tall buildings, rushing to the aid of the fair damsel in distress!

I had plenty of time to think, alone in the car for two hours. It must be stress, I thought, she gets so wound up over exams.

Stress . . . a word I understood very well, having spent the past nine months getting over it. Not to mention the guilt . . . but I'd always be haunted by guilt over what I had done to Stuart. He had been terrific, far more wonderful than I deserved.

"Sweetheart," he'd said when I tried to explain my obsession with Richard. "I don't need a graphic description of what you did and where you went. To be honest, I don't ever want to hear about that stuff. Let's put that behind us, forever. I want you to go back, way back, to where things started going bad between us. If we don't clear that up we'll never get through this."

That was easy, though difficult to put into words that wouldn't hurt. "Stuart, when I married you I had fantasies that Richard would come and rescue me—you know, the knight on the white horse stuff—I didn't appreciate you right from the start. How can I possibly make up for all the years I deceived you?"

"You didn't deceive me" he replied. "I knew there was someone lurking in there, but as long as he was only in your dreams he wasn't a threat. That changed when you met him again, and you lied to me for the first time. You aren't very good, you know."

"How did you—?"

"When you came home from your reunion, I asked you if there were any old boyfriends I had to worry about, and you said no. You blushed, couldn't meet my eyes, and I knew you were lying to me."

"But how did you know about Richard? I never told you about him!"

"Your dad did, before we were married."

"Dad! How dare he—"

"Don't go getting all upset, Leo didn't give away any of your secrets. He was afraid you were on the rebound, and tried to . . . to warn me, I guess. He liked me, you know," he added with a smirk.

"He thought you were perfect for me ten minutes after he met you," I added, tapping his bare chest playfully. "But enough about you, you conceited man."

"He asked me to take good care of you, that you had been badly hurt, and he worried that there might be lasting effects. And he said the strangest thing, I remember. All the women in this family have secrets, he said. Your sister, or your mother, obviously, but he didn't elaborate."

"It had to be my mother," I said immediately, remembering my conversation with Dad in the hospital, "but he didn't explain then, either. I wonder what it could be?"

I was lying naked next to Stuart at the time we had that particular chat, a condition that invariably led from one thing to another these days, and we soon forgot about Mom.

Stuart let me know in countless ways that I was special to him, that the past was behind us, the only thing that mattered to him was that we were together. At first I questioned his sanity, but soon found myself responding to him in positive ways, and after a few months, by Christmas in fact, we had become the mushiest of lovebirds.

"Couldn't be closer if you were joined at the hip," said Ellen, with some envy, I thought, in her voice. "Maybe I should try your method!"

"Not amusing, El, but maybe you should

give Kevin another look. There's good stuff in these guys of ours!"

When Stuart suggested that I get my ass in gear and finish up the second half of the paralegal course, I signed up enthusiastically, and the week after diplomas were handed out, I met Leona Hansbury at the hairdresser.

"Don't you work for Bob Murphy?" she asked, by way of a greeting.

"Not any more. It's a long story, Leona, but I am looking for work now as a paralegal. I just graduated," I added proudly.

As a result of that meeting, I'd been working for two weeks in my new capacity with Leona, and I loved it. Truth to tell, I love every second of my life these days. Forty-eight years old, and this was like starting over!

Life, I love ya! I quoted, with a huge grin out the car window at the guy passing me on the left. Bet he's wondering about my sanity, I thought, and laughed out loud. "Diamonds on the soles of her shoes," I warbled lustily, joining Paul Simon on the cassette.

I mulled over what Kelley was so upset about, but if it wasn't exams or a fight with Phil, I was at a loss. I'll have her sorted out in no time, I decided confidently.

Not in my wildest dreams would I have guessed at the mess my daughter was in.

As I walked into Kelley's dishevelled dorm room I had time to observe a very unhappy Phil slumped on the old beatup couch before she threw herself into my arms, sobbing hysterically.

I looked at Phil over her shoulder for some hint of the problem, but he wouldn't meet my eyes. As I looked at his downcast head and listened to her wailing, it hit me like a punch in the stomach, and her garbled words, when she blurted out the news, were anticlimactic.

"I'm going to have a baby, Mom. I'm pregnant."

Standing in the center of this tiny overcrowded room, holding my own baby tightly in my arms, I tried to remain calm.

There would be no satisfaction in saying "I told you so," so I left her standing there and went to sit beside Phil. Actually, I sat as far away from him on the "loveseat" as possible.

"How far along?"

"I saw the people here at the clinic yesterday. About two months, they think."

We discussed various solutions. They'd had almost a month to consider the situation, and they had made some tentative plans. First and foremost they wanted to keep the baby. For Kelley there could be no alternative, believing, as I did, that a fetus is a life begun, a treasure to be nurtured and protected. Abortion was unacceptable to her. In a strange way, I felt proud of Phil, who either felt the same way or was willing to honor her feelings.

"I'm going to finish out the term, and we want to get married right after finals. Not a big affair, just our families, if that's okay with you."

"My parents have that in-law apartment they added on when my grandmother lived with us," added Phil, "and I think we could live there quite well on my salary."

Kelley looked wretched. Her face was swollen from crying, her skin very pale. Eventually I convinced Phil to go home. He no longer lived on campus, and had a job to go to in the morning. There wasn't anything he could do here, and they both needed some sleep.

Slowly we got ready for bed, each busy with our own thoughts. It was half past two in the morning when I remembered that I hadn't called Stuart. The situation certainly warranted a phone call, but it was far too late now, and surely he would have called if he'd been worried. I'd give him one more night of illusion before I broke his heart with the news.

Sleep was out of the question, and I spent what was left of the night listening to Kelley crying into her pillow.

Morning finally came, and I slipped out of my bunk, studying her tear-stained face in the grey light that filtered through the window. She looked vulnerable and child-like in sleep, and I decided not to wake her. I wrote her a short note, lightly brushed her cheek with my finger as I adjusted the blanket over her shoulders, and left for home.

But I didn't want to go back to an empty house. Not yet. I needed to talk to someone, and I thought of my mother. Just as Kelley had turned to her mother, I ran home to mine. I left the campus in the bright golden sunshine of a New England May morning, and drove through the green, rolling hills of central

Massachusetts, oblivious to the songs of birds, or the beauty of flowers, back to the home of my childhood.

After much talk and indecision, Mother had decided to keep their house after Dad died. It was really too big a place for one person, and she realized that, but she didn't want to leave all her memories behind.

She would wait a few months, she said. She invited her older widowed sister, my aunt Sofia, to stay as long as she wanted. The aunt had been living alone in an apartment in a town across the state, and apparently was quite lonesome. In no time Mother convinced her to give up the apartment and come and live with her, accomplishing several things at once. Her sister was happy, they were company for each other, Mother had someone to care for, and she could live in this house until it was, as she said, her time to go.

The two of them made a great pair, yakking and arguing in a mixture of English and Italian, cooking and cleaning together, sharing memories of their husbands. They had a lot in common, and though each was quite strong willed, the house was big enough for two women.

At last my mother and I were friends. It had taken me a long time to forgive her for the miseries of my youth, real or imagined, but I guess we all grow up sometime.

When I arrived, I saw Mother on her knees in the garden doing something to the tulips. Sitting down in the grass beside her, I broke the news to her as gently as I knew how.

"Kelley's pregnant, Mom. She's quitting school." I expected her to become hysterical, but she looked at me with a calm and steady gaze.

"That's a shock," she said, "but it's not really surprising."

"What?"

"I was always afraid this would happen," she continued, "but I expected it to happen to you."

I thought this a strange remark, and said so.

"You see, I was so sure I would have to pay for my sin, and the worst punishment I could imagine would be if the same thing happened to you. But now Kelley is the one who will pay! This is all my fault!" She put down her trowel and leaned close to me. Andrea, after all this time I have something to tell you, a confession. No one else in the world has ever heard this, including your father. It's a secret I've carried with me for almost fifty years, and I realize now that I don't want to take it to my grave. I need to share it, and I want you to be the one to know about it . . . perhaps I should have told you long ago."

We sat side by side, amid the tulips, while my mother told her story.

"It was 1945, almost the end of the War and I was very much in love. He lived here in Oakville. His father was the manager down at the mill, and he was the handsomest boy around. We started dating during the war, and in March of 1945 we were engaged, and planned to get married a year later. We expected the war to be over by then, but he was called up to serve in Germany and France; he was going right into the middle of it all. I was beside myself with worry.

"He went for three months basic training to a camp in North Carolina, and came home for a week before he was to be shipped out.

"We spent every minute together. The war was almost over we knew that. He'd be back in a few months and we would get married in June. But we were so much in love, we wanted to stay together just for one night before he went away. A couple of nights before he was to leave I told my mother we were going to the movies, but I lied. I said I would sleep for the night with my friend, Maria, but instead we went to a hotel room, alone, and . . . pretended we were married."

She stopped here and looked at me, obviously expecting my reaction to be shock. "*Oh boy, Mom, the things I could tell you* . . .

"It was a bad thing, I know, but if you understood how we loved each other, how real was the possibility that he would be killed before I saw him again. The world was a different place; there are no rules in time of war. *Dio mio,* I paid dearly for that night. It was very wrong, and the good Lord punished me severely."

"You got pregnant?"

She nodded, and I did some fast figuring, but no matter how you stretched things, I was not her punishment. I was not that baby. I was born in 1948, three years later. There were no children before me; I was the firstborn, or so I had always been led to believe.

"So there you were, pregnant. What happened?"

"I was so frightened . . . I couldn't tell anyone about it. My father would have sent me from his house, and I had no money to run away, to care for a baby alone . . ." She began crying softly, a trickle of tears rolling down her face. No tearing sobs or wrenching hurt, only these quiet tears.

"What did you do, Mom? Did you have the baby?"

"No, I . . . he . . . died when . . ."

"You lost the baby?"

"Yes, yes, I lost him. I had a miscarriage. I lifted, carried things too heavy . . . I worked too hard, on purpose . . ."

I realized that all her pain and tears had been cried out long ago. These gentle tears were memories of the pain and anguish she had suffered.

"But why? You were going to get married . . . Didn't you tell him?"

"When I found out I was pregnant, I wrote him and let him know, asking him to arrange leave so we could be married sooner. I made arrangements to go away for a weekend to New York so we could be married by a Justice of the Peace, and I waited for his answer.

"It was a month or more before he wrote back . . . a long letter. He wasn't ready for marriage, or fatherhood. Since we had been together only one night, he refused to believe it was his baby. He never wanted to see me again."

All this was delivered in a flat voice devoid of emotion, as though she were reading from a very dull history book.

"I was almost three months gone when it happened. I wasn't being careful. I feel that I . . . killed my baby, my son."

She stared off into space, into another time, but eventually she picked up the thread again.

"My body healed well. But my mind, my mood was black, depressed. My mother thought I was lonesome with my young man gone so far away, and she talked to me all the time about the wonderful life I would have when he came home, living in the manager's house at the mill, or in a house of our own across the river . . . her daughter would be one of the rich women in town. She was so proud. I was too ashamed to tell her we would never see him again.

"When your father and I were married, I lied to him, letting him think he was the first. I never told him the truth, and he died without knowing my shame. I did not deserve such a good man, but I came to love him, Andrea, and I was grateful for all the days we had together."

Now I knew what my father had been talking about in the hospital. He knew, but he loved her too much to give her secret away. He had pretended all those years, and I wasn't about to break her heart by telling her that he had always known. She continued to cry softly, and I searched for words of consolation. She would never find forgiveness for losing her baby, but at least she had found a good man who loved her, and hadn't been stuck with that lousy bastard for the rest of her life. Whoever he was, she was better off without him.

In an attempt to lighten the mood, I said, in my best soap opera voice-over imitation, "And as the sun sets in the golden west, we say goodbye to the happy

Corelli family . . ." She smiled a little, and I laughed. "You were lucky, Mom, your sad story had a happy ending. At least you never had to see that jerk again!"

Her face fell. "Oh, but I did. I told you I was punished for my sin all my life, and in a way I made you pay, too."

I would be the first to agree! She certainly had played the heavy when it came to sex and morals! But at last I understood and could forgive her She must have been sick with worry that the same thing might happen to me.

"He came home after the war with a French bride, and settled right here in town, in the mill manager's house with his father. Of course he had a good job at the mill, when other, more deserving men, did not. Soon he was a big wheel there. When his father died, and left him some money, he and his wife bought a big house across the river.

"But Oakville then was a small town, and I saw them everywhere. His son . . . they had two children, two boys . . ." She frowned in concentration, then said, "The older boy was a friend of yours, I think. You went to school together."

"No kidding! Who was that, Mom?"

She stared off into space, and at first I thought she didn't remember, but the set of her jaw told me that she knew perfectly well, but didn't want to tell me. After a minute she said, very quietly, "Osborne. His name was Richard Osborne."

She waited until I had composed myself, then stood, gave me her hand, and led me into her house.

"You will stay to eat?" she said, still holding my arm.

I had eaten nothing since dinner the previous night, and I was starving. Bubbling away in the pot was stracciatella soup, that mixture of cheese and eggs that turned threadlike when added to the simmering broth, my personal favorite since childhood. We had the soup, followed by sliced hot Italian ham and crispy rolls.

I wondered if my mother would want to continue our conversation, but she said nothing in front of her sister. The only reference came as I was leaving, when she hugged me and said, "I was lucky, Andrea, and so are you. We both have good men, thank the stars in heaven above."

The weather was still as nice as it had been in the morning, and I had a pleasant drive ahead of me, through the rolling hills, green with spring, to the rugged coastline where I now made my home. I was glad to be alone, with time to think.

Richard's father! I would never get over the shock as long as I lived! She had been in love with Richard's father! Of all the people in the world . . . his father would have been mine! We might have been brother and sister. A strange and uncomfortable thought.

Then the bastard deserted her! Dad wasn't her first love, as she had always led me to believe. No wonder she always made light of puppy love!

That reminded me of Kelley, and I felt that sinking feeling in the pit of my stomach. Kelley and her problems were very real.

The speedometer needle passed seventy miles an hour, and I closed in on the car ahead of me for the third time. I hit the brakes, slowed down, and decided I had to get off the road for a while. I wasn't paying attention.

I pulled off the Turnpike to grab some

coffee at a diner, but at the exit I saw a sign for a state park. My goal was clear. At a roadside stand I bought a can of soda and a bag of popcorn and pointed the Toyota in the direction of this oasis. Not my personal park, but a place to sit under the trees, soothed and mesmerized as always by the sparkling water . . .

I wandered along a path that led through the trees down to the water, a large pond or a small lake, and found myself a comfortable spot on the mossy bank.

My thoughts tumbled over each other, pell mell. I remembered Richard . . . the Richard of my youth.

All the time we went out, my mother had been fighting a battle of her own. Suddenly I had a flash image of Mom and Richard's father at our wedding . . . if we had married. It would have been a nightmare for her. I had met him, of course, years before, and had found him a cold, remote man. Maybe he knew who I was, which would explain his apparent aversion to me, and I wondered if he had kept track of Mother as the years passed. It was hard to picture him in a warm moment, never mind making passionate love to my mother. Far easier to imagine was his cold-hearted refusal to acknowledge his child and his abandonment of the mother—my mother, who had paid for her fall from grace for the rest of her life. "Holy temples," she had called girls' bodies and hers had been defiled.

What a hard time she had given us!

Too bad she had never seen a shrink; I might have been spared hours of grief! On the other hand, she had probably saved me from a whole lifetime of grief with an unfaithful husband.

I sipped my drink, and ate my popcorn, thinking about Mom and Dad, and his overwhelming love for her. Dad knew all along about Osborne and Mom. They were of a generation when things were kept hidden, but people love to gossip and spread rumors. He had kept her secret safe, and they had both been quite happy into the bargain. A wise man, my Dad.

I watched the glints of light bouncing off the water in the late afternoon sun. This was my favorite time of day, with the sky growing rosy in the west with the sunset imminent. Time to get home to Stuart, I thought, gulping the last of my warm soda, finally at peace with myself.

Without a doubt, Stuart and I had found a lasting love, and had been given a second chance to share it. He was the right man for me, and it had taken me only twenty-five years to learn the truth.

Epilogue

Happy birthday, dear Zachary,
Happy birthday to you!

It was the 12th of December, and we had gathered in Phil and Kelley's apartment to celebrate young Zach's second birthday.

"Gamma," he crowed, as he crawled onto my lap. I fed him a chunk of the chocolate cake Kelley had cut, and watched her contented smile as she served a piece to Phil.

"Wow, real cake, made from scratch! Just like Mom used to bake!" He was teasing her, and she clearly loved it.

With a broad smile, she answered, "It is the cake that my mom used to bake, and she baked it this time too!" We all joined in the laughter that followed.

They are really happy together, I thought. Kelley was determined to become a pharmacist, and had returned to school in September to continue her studies as an evening student at a school in the city. Most evenings she had to leave before Phil came home, and although in bygone days I had sworn I'd never be a free babysitter for my children, now I was happy to eat those words and take my turn watching Zachary two evenings a week, sharing the duty with Phil's parents. Stuart laughed at me, but I argued that I hadn't been a grandmother when I issued that ultimatum. What did I know! Grandchildren were definitely made for love, and Stuart and I were enjoying ours immensely. Zach was chubby, with rosy cheeks and an abundance of dark hair, a bundle of energy with a hundred-watt smile, long dark lashes and his grandpa's beautiful gray eyes.

"Some girl will get herself in trouble one day," I whispered, bending close to his ear, while his damply curling hair tickled my nose, "falling for these eyes." He turned them up at me, dark and smoky, seen through a veil of lashes, and

I couldn't resist giving him a big kiss. "There goes Grandma, molesting the baby again," said Stuart, reaching for my hand, a warm, loving smile on his face. "By the way," he announced to the table at large, "you haven't forgotten that Mom and I are off to Bermuda over the Christmas vacation?"

Two tickets to Bermuda, an early Christmas gift from Stuart, and a total surprise, had come tucked into a bouquet of carnations delivered by the florist almost a month ago. Mmmm, yes, flowers for me. Stuart was a quick study!

"How can we forget," said Brian, sitting across the table from us, "when you bring it up every chance you get!"

"You may remember we were going to go a few years ago," Stuart said, looking directly at me, "but your old mom went and got run over by a car, so we put it off for a while."

My eyes filled with tears of love, and gratitude, as he glossed over the terrible mess I had made of our lives.

At first I wasn't too happy that he had chosen to book the trip over Christmas, but apparently he had talked to the kids beforehand, and they were prepared to celebrate the holiday after we returned.

"Suits me very well," said Kelley. "I can buy all my gifts the day after Christmas, at the sales, and save pots of money!"

"Lord, what a cheapskate! You must take after your father!" I threw up my hands in mock horror.

There would be no open house at the Walsh home this year. We were breaking with tradition in many ways. "Time for a break," said Stuart. "Next year we'll have a 'Caribbean Christmas' theme, and we'll have costumes, the works!" he added, laughing. "I think you'll look terrific in a sarong, my dear."

"Wrong island, you silly man. But thanks."

He was apt to behave with less restraint these days, and I was pleased to have had something to do with that.

We had survived my affair with Richard, and had fallen in love again, but better, I thought. We shared a closeness missing during the earlier years of our marriage, when I was looking for some impossible dream. We had revived many separate interests that appealed to each of us as individuals—Stuart could be found on a golf course on Saturday mornings with anyone else but me, and I went shopping more often with my sister.

We went to both musical revues and symphony concerts, trying to appreciate each other's interest. We ate dinner out more often, something he loved to do, though I still couldn't convince him to try Indian food, and we gave small dinner parties, the kind of entertaining I enjoyed most. Frequently we cooked together, although Stuart still professed an innate inability to run the dishwasher. And we loved to curl up together on the couch in front of the fireplace, discussing our workdays, now that I was a career woman.

We had a good laugh one day last winter when Kelley, informed that we were going skiing for a weekend, asked if Brian was going too or were we going "on a date!"

"A date, of course," I replied.

Here we were, married almost thirty years now, behaving like newlyweds beginning our journey together. With luck we might have thirty more wonderful years.

We still had differences of opinion, but we talked things over. I didn't sulk; he didn't brood. It was an interesting mathematical contradiction that though each of us gave sixty percent to our marriage, each got one hundred percent in return!

Stuart had taken Zach from my lap and tossed him into the air, ignoring his mother's loud protests.

"Dad, you'll drop him. You're giving me a heart attack! He'll throw up all over you!"

Zachary loved this game, but every time he reached the top of the toss a look of fear crossed his face.

Don't you worry, Zachary, I assured him silently, *Grandpa will always be there to catch you. He's a man you can trust.*